A *Wall Street Journal* Bestselling Book

A *Publishers Weekly* Best Book of 1998

Best Anthology of the Year: *Legends*
—*Rocky Mountain News*

#3 on "Science Fiction and Fantasy: Top 10 of 1998" List
—Amazon.com

"Microcosmic glimpses of broadly imagined worlds and larger-than-life characters distinguish this hefty volume of heavyweight fantasy. . . . There's enough color, vitality, and bravura displays of mythmaking in this rich sampler to sate faithful fans and nurture new readers on the stuff of legends still being created."
—*Publishers Weekly* (starred review)

"All the writing is of the highest caliber; and each of the tales is compelling. To top it off, artists such as Michael Whelan, Keith Parkinson, and Erik Wilson have contributed illustrations that become icing on the cake. *Legends* makes for a fine road map to the worlds of masters of the genre and serves as a perfect milestone for future fantasy anthologists. Silverberg has put together an anthology of which he and his fellow writers can be justly proud."
—*Des Moines Daily Register*

"Superb Baedeker to the fantasy worlds of the field's finest writers."
—*Dallas Morning News*

"A collection of short novels by legends in the field writing about imaginary worlds and characters that made them famous. Taken on their own, Silverberg's haunting story of what an older Lord Valentine finds in a long-forgotten tomb of a cursed city, or King's story of a younger Gunslinger meeting murderous harridans in the world of the Dark Tower, would be worth the price of the book."
—*Sentinel* (Orlando, Florida)

"An appetizer plate of good-quality fiction . . . This would be a good primer for anyone intereested in the works of any of the authors included."
—*San Diego Union-Tribune*

"They are full-fleshed, full-blown entries in each of the series of stories. Full of the action, setting, and character that have made each of these writers, as the title boldly states, modern legends in their genre. There isn't a misfire in the bunch, a rarity in anthologies, and very much a rarity in the fantasy field. This is a collection of grace, style, and substance.

"So if you are a follower of any of these series, you need this book. And if you've never tried modern fantasy, this is a wonderful place to be introduced to its masters."
—*The Statesman Journal* (Salem, Oregon)

"This is an excellent way to visit old friends, or get clued in on some multivolumed epics."
—*The Denver Post*

"A collection of short novels by some of the biggest names in fantasy, all set in their best-known secondary worlds. There are delights aplenty in this huge volume."
—*Edmonton Journal*

"*Legends* more than lives up to its name. Its purpose is to bring us those writers who have created modern-day legends with such skill that they became what they created, and it does its job. To put it bluntly, everyone involved with this book did one hell of a job."
—*Queen's College Quad*

"A fascinating assortment of short novels by fantasy's powerhouse authors, set in the most-loved world each created. Each tale stands alone, which is an added bonus for those readers who may not have read every series represented. Every tale in *Legends* is original, high-quality, and adds gloriously to the world in which it is set. Some are amusing and charming, others tragic, but all reflect the nobility of the human spirit."
—*The Herald* (Rock Hills, South Carolina)

Legends

VOLUME I

SHORT NOVELS BY THE MASTERS OF MODERN FANTASY

edited by

ROBERT SILVERBERG

TOR®

A TOM DOHERTY ASSOCIATES BOOK
NEW YORK

This is a work of fiction. All the characters and events portrayed in this book are either products of the authors' imagination or are used fictitiously.

LEGENDS: VOLUME I

Copyright © 1998 by Agberg, Ltd.

A Tor Book
Published by Tom Doherty Associates, LLC
175 Fifth Avenue
New York, NY 10010

www.tor.com

Tor® is a registered trademark of Tom Doherty Associates, LLC.

ISBN: 0-812-56663-7
Library of Congress Card Catalog Number: 98-23593

First edition: October 1998
First mass market edition: September 1999

Printed in the United States of America

0 9 8 7 6 5 4 3 2 1

FOR MARTY AND RALPH
who certainly know why

CONTENTS

INTRODUCTION

❦

Here is a book of visions and miracles—the first volume in a set of three containing eleven rich, robust new stories by the best-known and most accomplished modern creators of fantasy fiction, each one set in the special universe of the imagination that made that writer famous throughout the world.

Fantasy is the oldest branch of imaginative literature—as old as the human imagination itself. It is not difficult to believe that the same artistic impulse that produced the extraordinary cave paintings of Altamira and Chauvet, fifteen and twenty and even thirty thousand years ago, also probably produced astounding tales of gods and demons, of talismans and spells, of dragons and werewolves, of wondrous lands beyond the horizon—tales that fur-clad shamans recited to fascinated audiences around the campfires of Ice Age Europe. So too, in torrid Africa, in the China of prehistory, in ancient India, in the Americas: everywhere, in fact, on and on back through time for thousands or even hundreds of thousands of years. I like to think that the storytelling impulse is universal—that there have been storytellers as long as there have been beings in this world that could be spoken of as "human"—and that those storytellers have in particular devoted their skills and energies and talents, throughout our long evolutionary path, to the creation of extraordinary marvels and wonders.

We will never know, of course, what tales the Cro-Magnon storytellers told their spellbound audiences on those frosty nights in ancient France. But surely there were strong components of the fantastic in them. The evidence of the oldest stories that *have* survived argues in favor of that. If fantasy can be defined as literature that depicts the world beyond that of mundane reality, and mankind's struggle to assert dominance over that world, then the most ancient story that *has* come down to us—the Sumerian tale of the hero Gilgamesh, which dates from about 2500 B.C.—is fantasy, for its theme is Gilgamesh's quest for eternal life.

Homer's *Odyssey,* abounding as it does in shapeshifters and wizards and sorceresses, in Cyclopses and many-headed man-eating creatures, is rich with fantastic elements too, as are any number of other Greek and Roman tales. As we come closer to our own times we meet the dread monster Grendel of the Anglo-Saxon *Beowulf*, the Midgard serpent and the dragon Fafnir and the apocalyptic Fenris-wolf of the Norse sagas, the hapless immortality-craving Dr. Faustus of German legend, the myriad enchanters of *The Thousand and One Nights*, the far-larger-than-life heroes of the Welsh *Mabinogion* and the Persian *Shah-Nameh*, and an infinity of other strange and wonderful creations.

Nor did the impulse toward the creation of the fantastic disappear as the modern era, the era of microscopes and telescopes, of steam engines and railway systems, of telegraphs and phonographs and electric light, came into being. Our fascination with the unseen and the unseeable did not end simply because so many things previously thought impossible now had become realities. What is more fantastic, after all, than having the sound of an entire symphony orchestra rise up out of a flat disk of plastic? Or to speak into a device that one holds in one's hand, and be heard and understood ten thousand miles away? But the same century that gave us the inventions of Thomas Alva Edison and Alexander Graham Bell gave us Lewis Carroll's two incomparable tales of Alice's adventures in other realities, H. Rider Haggard's innumerable novels of lost civilizations, and Mary Wollstonecraft Shelley's *Frankenstein*.

Nor did the twentieth century—the century of air travel and atomic energy, of television and computers, of open-heart surgery and sex-change operations—see us losing our taste for tales of the extraordinary. A host of machine-age fantasists—James Branch Cabell and A. Merritt and Lord Dunsany, E. R. Eddison and Mervyn Peake and L. Frank Baum, H. P. Lovecraft and Robert E. Howard and J. R. R. Tolkien, to name a few of the best-known ones—kept the world well supplied with wondrous tales of the fantastic.

One change of tone did occur in the twentieth century, though, with the rise to popularity of science fiction—the branch of fantasy that applies immense ingenuity to the task of making the impossible, or at least the implausible, seem altogether probable. As science fiction—which was given its essential nature well over a hundred years ago by Jules Verne and H. G. Wells, and developed in modern times by such writers as Robert A. Heinlein, Isaac Asimov, and Aldous Huxley—came to exert its immense appeal on the atomic-age reading public, ''pure'' fantasy fiction (that is, fantasy that makes no attempt at empirical explanation of its wonders) came to be thought of as something largely reserved for children, like myths and fairy tales.

The older kind of fantasy never disappeared, of course. But in the United States, at least, it went into eclipse for nearly fifty years. Science fiction, meanwhile, manifested itself to the reading public in the form of magazines with names like *Amazing Stories* and *Astounding Science Fiction* and readerships composed largely of boys and earnest young men with an interest in gadgets and scientific disputation. The only American magazine dealing in the material we define as fantasy fiction was *Weird Tales,* founded in 1923, but that magazine published not only fantasy but a great many other kinds of genre fiction that might not be thought of as fantasy today—tales of pure terror, for example, with no speculative content.

The separation between fantasy and science fiction is not always easy to locate, but some distinctions are fairly clear-cut, if not entirely rigid. Stories that deal with androids and robots, spaceships, alien beings, time machines, viruses from outer space, galactic empires, and the like usually can be described as science fiction. These are all matters that are *conceptually possible* within the framework of scientific law as we currently understand it. (Although such things as time machines and faster-than-light vehicles certainly stretch that framework to its limits, and perhaps beyond them.) Fantasy, meanwhile, uses as its material that which is *generally believed to be impossible or nonexistent* in our culture: wizards and warlocks, elves and goblins, werewolves and vampires, unicorns and enchanted princesses, efficacious incantations and spells.

Fantasy fiction per se did not have a real magazine of its own until 1939, when John W. Campbell, Jr., the foremost science-fiction editor of his time, brought *Unknown* (later called *Unknown Worlds*) into being in order to allow his writers greater imaginative latitude than his definitions of science fiction would permit. Many of the same writers who had turned Campbell's *Astounding Science Fiction* into the most notable magazine of its type yet published—Robert A. Heinlein, L. Sprague de Camp, Theodore Sturgeon, Lester del Rey, Jack Williamson—also became mainstays of *Unknown,* and the general structural approach was similar: postulate a far-out idea and develop all its consequences to a logical conclusion. The stories about being nasty to water gnomes or selling your soul to the devil wound up in *Unknown;* those about traveling in time or voyaging to distant planets were published in *Astounding.*

But *Unknown,* though it was cherished with great

fondness by its readers and writers, never attained much of a public following, and when wartime paper shortages forced Campbell to choose between his two magazines in 1943, *Unknown* was swiftly killed, never to reappear. Postwar attempts by nostalgic ex-contributors to *Unknown* to recapture its special flavor were largely unsuccessful; H. L. Gold's *Beyond* lasted ten issues, Lester del Rey's *Fantasy Fiction* managed only four. Only *The Magazine of Fantasy,* edited by Anthony Boucher and J. Francis McComas, succeeded in establishing itself as a permanent entity, and even that magazine found it wisest to change its name to *Fantasy and Science Fiction* with its second issue. When science fiction became a fixture of paperback publishing in the 1950s, fantasy once again lagged behind: few fantasy novels were paperbacked, and most of them—Jack Vance's *The Dying Earth* and the early reprints of H. P. Lovecraft and Robert E. Howard are good examples—quickly vanished from view and became collector's items.

It all began to change in the late 1960s, when the sudden availability of paperback editions of J. R. R. Tolkien's *Lord of the Rings* trilogy (previously kept from paperback by an unwilling hardcover publisher) aroused a hunger for fantasy fiction in millions of readers that has, so far, been insatiable. Tolkien's books were such an emphatic commercial success that publishers rushed to find writers who could produce imitative trilogies, and the world was flooded with huge Hobbitesque novels, many of which sold in extraordinary quantities themselves. Robert Howard's *Conan* novels, once admired only by a small band of ardent cultists, began to win vast new readers about the same time. And a few years later Ballantine Books, Tolkien's paperback publisher, brought out an extraordinary series of books in its Adult Fantasy series, edited by Lin Carter, which made all the elegant classic masterpieces of such fantasists as E. R. Eddison, James Branch Cabell, Lord Dunsany, and Mervyn Peake available to modern readers. And, ever since, fantasy has been a dominant factor in modern publishing. What was a neglected stepsibling of science fiction fifty years ago is, today, an immensely popular genre.

In the wake of the great success of the Tolkien trilogy, newer writers have come along with their own deeply imagined worlds of fantasy, and have captured large and enthusiastic audiences themselves. In the late 1960s, Ursula K. Le Guin began her searching and sensitive Earthsea series, and Anne McCaffrey co-opted the ancient fantastic theme of the dragon for her Pern novels, which live on the borderline between fantasy and science fiction. Stephen King, some years later, won a readership of astounding magnitude by plumbing the archetypical fears of humanity and transforming them into powerful novels that occupied fantasy's darker terrain. Terry Pratchett, on the other hand, has magnificently demonstrated the comic power of satiric fantasy. Such writers as Orson Scott Card and Raymond E. Feist have won huge followings for their Alvin Maker and Riftwar books. More recently, Robert Jordan's mammoth Wheel of Time series, George R. R. Martin's Song of Ice and Fire books, and Terry Goodkind's Sword of Truth tales have taken their place in the pantheon of modern fantasy, as has Tad Williams' Memory, Sorrow and Thorn series.

And here is the whole bunch of them, brought together in one huge three-volume collection in which fantasy enthusiasts can revel for weeks. A new Earthsea story, a new tale of Pern, a new Dark Tower adventure, a new segment in Pratchett's playful Discworld series, and all the rest that you'll find herein—there has never been a book like this before. Gathering such an elite collection of first-magnitude stars into a single volume has not been an easy task. My gratitude herewith for the special assistance of Martin H. Greenberg, Ralph Vicinanza, Stephen King, John Helfers, and Virginia Kidd, who in one way or another made my editorial task immensely less difficult than it otherwise would have been. And, too, although it goes without saying that I'm grateful to my wife, Karen, for her inestimable help in every phase of this intricate project, I think I'll say it anyway—not just because she's a terrific person, but because she came up with what unquestionably was the smartest idea of the whole enterprise.

—Robert Silverberg
December, 1997

THE DARK TOWER

~oɯɯ෧~

Stephen King

These novels, using thematic elements from Robert Browning's poem "Childe Roland to the Dark Tower Came," tell the saga of Roland, last of the gunslingers, who embarks on a quest to find the Dark Tower for reasons that the author has yet to reveal. Along the way, Roland encounters the remains of what was once a thriving society, feudal in nature but technologically quite advanced, that now has fallen into decay and ruin. King combines elements of fantasy with science fiction into a surreal blend of past and future.

The first book, *The Gunslinger,* introduces Roland, who is chasing the Dark Man, an enigmatic sorcerer figure, across a vast desert. Through flashbacks, the reader learns that Roland was a member of a noble family in the Dark Tower world, and that that world may or may not have been destroyed with help from the Dark Man. Along the way, Roland encounters strange inhabitants of this unnamed world, including Jake, a young boy who, even though he is killed by the end of the first book, will figure prominently in later volumes. Roland does catch up with the Dark Man, and learns that he must seek out the Dark Tower to find the answers to the questions of why he must embark on this quest and what is contained in the Tower.

The next book, *The Drawing of the Three,* shows Roland recruiting three people from present-day Earth to join him on his way to the Dark Tower. They are Eddie, a junkie "mule" working for the Mafia; Suzannah, a paraplegic with multiple personalities; and Jake, whose arrival is startling to Roland, who sacrificed Jake in his own world during his pursuit of the Dark Man. Roland saves Jake's life on Earth, but the resulting schism nearly drives him insane. Roland must also help the other two battle their own demons, Eddie's being his heroin addiction and guilt over not being able to save his brother's life, and Suzannah's the war between her different personalities, one a kind and gentle woman, the other a racist psychopath. Each of the three deals with his problems with the help of the others, and together the quartet set out on the journey to the Tower.

The third book, *The Waste Lands,* chronicles the first leg of that journey, examining the background of the three Earth-born characters in detail. The book reaches its climax when Jake is kidnapped by a cult thriving in the ruins of a crumbling city, led by a man known only as Flagg (a character who has appeared in several of King's other novels as the embodiment of pure evil). Roland rescues him, and the group escapes the city on a monorail system whose artificial-intelligence program has achieved sentience at the cost of its sanity. The monorail challenges them to a riddle contest, with their lives as the prize if they can stump the machine, who claims to know every riddle ever created.

Wizard and Glass, the fourth volume in the series, finds Roland, Jake, Eddie, and Suzannah continuing their journey toward the Dark Tower, moving through a deserted part of Mid-World that is eerily reminiscent of twentieth-century Earth. During their travels they encounter a *thinny,* a dangerous weakening of the barrier between different times and places. Roland recognizes it and realizes that his world is breaking down faster than he had thought. The *thinny* prompts him to recall the first time he encountered it, many years before on a trip out West with his friends Cuthbert and Alain, when Roland had just earned his gunslinger status. It is this story—of the three boys uncovering a plot against the ruling government and of Roland's first love, a girl named Susan Delgado—that is the central focus of the book. While the three manage to destroy the conspirators, Susan is killed during the fight by the townspeople of Hambry. The story gives Jake, Eddie, and Suzannah new insight into Roland's background and why he may sacrifice them to attain his ultimate goal of saving his world. The book ends with the foursome moving onward once more toward the Tower.

THE LITTLE SISTERS
OF ELURIA

༄

Stephen King

*[Author's Note: The Dark Tower books begin with
Roland of Gilead, the last gunslinger in an exhausted world that has "moved on," pursuing a
magician in a black robe. Roland has been chasing
Walter for a very long time. In the first book of the
cycle, he finally catches up. This story, however,
takes place while Roland is still casting about for
Walter's trail. A knowledge of the books is therefore not necessary for you to understand—and
hopefully enjoy—the story which follows. S. K.]*

I. Full Earth. The Empty Town. The Bells. The Dead Boy. The Overturned Wagon. The Green Folk.

On a day in Full Earth so hot that it seemed to suck the breath from his chest before his body could use it, Roland of Gilead came to the gates of a village in the Desatoya Mountains. He was traveling alone by then, and would soon be traveling afoot, as well. This whole last week he had been hoping for a horse doctor, but guessed such a fellow would do him no good now, even if this town had one. His mount, a two-year-old roan, was pretty well done for.

The town gates, still decorated with flowers from some festival or other, stood open and welcoming, but the silence beyond them was all wrong. The gunslinger heard no clip-clop of horses, no rumble of wagon wheels, no merchants' huckstering cries from the marketplace. The only sounds were the low hum of crickets (some sort of bug, at any rate; they were a bit more tuneful than crickets, at that), a queer wooden knocking sound, and the faint, dreamy tinkle of small bells.

Also, the flowers twined through the wrought-iron staves of the ornamental gate were long dead.

Between his knees, Topsy gave two great, hollow sneezes—*K'chow! K'chow!*—and staggered sideways. Roland dismounted, partly out of respect for the horse, partly out of respect for himself—he didn't want to break a leg under Topsy if Topsy chose this moment to give up and canter into the clearing at the end of his path.

The gunslinger stood in his dusty boots and faded jeans under the beating sun, stroking the roan's matted neck, pausing every now and then to yank his fingers through the tangles of Topsy's mane, and stopping once to shoo off the tiny flies clustering at the corners of Topsy's eyes. Let them lay their eggs and hatch their maggots there after Topsy was dead, but not before.

Roland thus honored his horse as best he could, listening to those distant, dreamy bells and the strange wooden tocking sound as he did. After a while he ceased his absent grooming and looked thoughtfully at the open gate.

The cross above its center was a bit unusual, but otherwise the gate was a typical example of its type, a western commonplace which was not useful but traditional—all the little towns he had come to in the last tenmonth seemed to have one such where you came in (grand) and one more such where you went out (not so grand). None had been built to exclude visitors, certainly not this one. It stood between two walls of pink adobe that ran into the scree for a distance of about twenty feet on either side of the road and then simply stopped. Close the gate, lock it with many locks, and all that meant was a short walk around one bit of adobe wall or the other.

Beyond the gate, Roland could see what looked in most respects like a perfectly ordinary High Street—an inn, two saloons (one of which was called The Bustling Pig; the sign over the other was too faded to read), a mercantile, a smithy, a Gathering Hall. There was also a small but rather lovely wooden building with a modest bell tower on top, a sturdy fieldstone foundation on the bottom, and a gold-painted cross on its double doors. The cross, like the one over the gate, marked this as a worshipping place for those who held to the Jesus-man. This wasn't a common religion in Mid-World, but far from unknown; that same thing could have been said about most forms of worship in those days, including the worship of Baal, Asmodeus, and a hundred others. Faith, like everything else in the world these days, had moved on. As far as Roland was concerned, God o' the Cross was just another religion which taught that love and murder were inextricably bound together—that in the end, God always drank blood.

Meanwhile, there was the singing hum of insects

that sounded *almost* like crickets. The dreamlike tinkle of the bells. And that queer wooden thumping, like a fist on a door. Or on a coffintop.

Something here's a long way from right, the gunslinger thought. *'Ware, Roland; this place has a reddish odor.*

He led Topsy through the gate with its adornments of dead flowers and down the High Street. On the porch of the mercantile, where the old men should have congregated to discuss crops, politics, and the follies of the younger generation, there stood only a line of empty rockers. Lying beneath one, as if dropped from a careless (and long-departed) hand, was a charred corncob pipe. The hitching rack in front of the Bustling Pig stood empty; the windows of the saloon itself were dark. One of the batwing doors had been yanked off and stood propped against the side of the building; the other hung ajar, its faded green slats splattered with maroon stuff that might have been paint but probably wasn't.

The shopfront of the livery stable stood intact, like the face of a ruined woman who has access to good cosmetics, but the double barn behind it was a charred skeleton. That fire must have happened on a rainy day, the gunslinger thought, or the whole damned town would have gone up in flames; a jolly spin and raree-show for anyone around to see it.

To his right now, halfway up to where the street

opened into the town square, was the church. There were grassy borders on both sides, one separating the church from the town's Gathering Hall, the other from the little house set aside for the preacher and his family (if this was one of the Jesus-sects which allowed its shamans to have wives and families, that was; some of them, clearly administered by lunatics, demanded at least the appearance of celibacy). There were flowers in these grassy strips, and while they looked parched, most were still alive. So whatever had happened here to empty the place out had not happened long ago. A week, perhaps. Two at the outside, given the heat.

Topsy sneezed again—*K'chow!*—and lowered his head wearily.

The gunslinger saw the source of the tinkling. Above the cross on the church doors, a cord had been strung in a long, shallow arc. Hung from it were perhaps two dozen tiny silver bells. There was hardly any breeze today, but enough so these smalls were never quite still . . . and if a real wind should rise, Roland thought, the sound made by the tintinnabulation of the bells would probably be a good deal less pleasant; more like the strident parlay of gossips' tongues.

"Hello!" Roland called, looking across the street at what a large false-fronted sign proclaimed to be the Good Beds Hotel. "Hello, the town!"

No answer but the bells, the tunesome insects, and that odd wooden clunking. No answer, no movement . . . but there were folk here. Folk or *something*. He was being watched. The tiny hairs on the nape of his neck had stiffened.

Roland stepped onward, leading Topsy toward the center of town, puffing up the unlaid High Street dust with each step. Forty paces farther along, he stopped in front of a low building marked with a single curt word: LAW. The Sheriff's office (if they had such this far from the Inners) looked remarkably similar to the church—wooden boards stained a rather forbidding shade of dark brown above a stone foundation.

The bells behind him rustled and whispered.

He left the roan standing in the middle of the street and mounted the steps to the LAW office. He was very aware of the bells, of the sun beating against his neck, and of the sweat trickling down his sides. The door was shut but unlocked. He opened it, then winced back, half-raising a hand as the heat trapped inside rushed out in a soundless gasp. If all the closed buildings were this hot inside, he mused, the livery barns would soon not be the only burned-out hulks. And with no rain to stop the flames (and certainly no volunteer fire department, not any more), the town would not be long for the face of the earth.

He stepped inside, trying to sip at the stifling air rather than taking deep breaths. He immediately heard the low drone of flies.

There was a single cell, commodious and empty, its barred door standing open. Filthy skin-shoes, one of the pair coming unsewn, lay beneath a bunk sodden with the same dried maroon stuff that had marked the Bustling Pig. Here was where the flies were, crawling over the stain, feeding from it.

On the desk was a ledger. Roland turned it toward him and read what was embossed upon its red cover:

REGISTRY OF MISDEEDS & REDRESS
IN THE YEARS OF OUR LORD
ELURIA

So now he knew the name of the town, at least—Eluria. Pretty, yet somehow ominous, as well. But any name would have seemed ominous, Roland supposed, given these circumstances. He turned to leave, and saw a closed door secured by a wooden bolt.

He went to it, stood before it for a moment, then drew one of the big revolvers he carried low on his hips. He stood a moment longer, head down, thinking (Cuthbert, his old friend, liked to say that the wheels inside Roland's head ground slow but exceedingly fine), and then retracted the bolt. He opened the door and immediately stood back, leveling his gun, expecting a body (Eluria's Sheriff, mayhap) to come tumbling into the room with his throat cut and his eyes gouged out, victim of a MISDEED in need of REDRESS—

Nothing.

Well, half a dozen stained jumpers which longer-term prisoners were probably required to wear, two bows, a quiver of arrows, an old, dusty motor, a rifle that had probably last been fired a hundred years ago, and a mop . . . but in the gunslinger's mind, all that came down to nothing. Just a storage closet.

He went back to the desk, opened the register, and leafed through it. Even the pages were warm, as if the book had been baked. In a way, he supposed it had been. If the High Street layout had been different, he might have expected a large number of religious offenses to be recorded, but he wasn't surprised to find none here—if the Jesus-man church had coexisted with a couple of saloons, the churchfolk must have been fairly reasonable.

What Roland found was the usual petty offenses, and a few not so petty—a murder, a horse-thieving, the Distressal of a Lady (which probably meant rape). The murderer had been removed to a place called Lexingworth to be hanged. Roland had never heard of it. One note toward the end read *Green folk sent hence.* It meant nothing to Roland. The most recent entry was this:

> *12/Fe/99. Chas. Freeborn,*
> *cattle-theef to be tryed.*

Roland wasn't familiar with the notation *12/Fe/ 99,* but as this was a long stretch from February, he supposed *Fe* might stand for Full Earth. In any case, the ink looked about as fresh as the blood on the bunk in the cell, and the gunslinger had a good idea that Chas. Freeborn, cattle-theef, had reached the clearing at the end of his path.

He went out into the heat and the lacy sound of bells. Topsy looked at Roland dully, then lowered his head again, as if there were something in the dust of the High Street which could be cropped. As if he would ever want to crop again, for that matter.

The gunslinger gathered up the reins, slapped the dust off them against the faded no-color of his jeans, and continued on up the street. The wooden knocking sound grew steadily louder as he walked (he had not holstered his gun when leaving LAW, nor cared to holster it now), and as he neared the town square, which must have housed the Eluria market in more normal times, Roland at last saw movement.

On the far side of the square was a long watering

trough, made of ironwood from the look (what some called "seequoiah" out here), apparently fed in happier times from a rusty steel pipe which now jutted waterless above the trough's south end. Lolling over one side of this municipal oasis, about halfway down its length, was a leg clad in faded gray pants and terminating in a well-chewed cowboy boot.

The chewer was a large dog, perhaps two shades grayer than the corduroy pants. Under other circumstances, Roland supposed the mutt would have had the boot off long since, but perhaps the foot and lower calf inside it had swelled. In any case, the dog was well on its way to simply chewing the obstacle away. It would seize the boot and shake it back and forth. Every now and then the boot's heel would collide with the wooden side of the trough, producing another hollow knock. The gunslinger hadn't been so wrong to think of coffintops after all, it seemed.

Why doesn't it just back off a few steps, jump into the trough, and have at him? Roland wondered. *No water coming out of the pipe, so it can't be afraid of drowning.*

Topsy uttered another of his hollow, tired sneezes, and when the dog lurched around in response, Roland understood why it was doing things the hard way. One of its front legs had been badly broken and crookedly mended. Walking would be a chore for it, jumping out of the question. On its chest was a patch of dirty white fur. Growing out of this patch was black fur in a roughly cruciform shape. A Jesus-dog, mayhap, hoping for a spot of afternoon communion.

There was nothing very religious about the snarl which began to wind out of its chest, however, or the roll of its rheumy eyes. It lifted its upper lip in a trembling sneer, revealing a goodish set of teeth.

"Light out," Roland said. "While you can."

The dog backed up until its hindquarters were pressed against the chewed boot. It regarded the oncoming man fearfully, but clearly meant to stand its ground. The revolver in Roland's hand held no significance for it. The gunslinger wasn't surprised—he guessed the dog had never seen one, had no idea it was anything other than a club of some kind, which could only be thrown once.

"Hie on with you, now," Roland said, but still the dog wouldn't move.

He should have shot it—it was no good to itself, and a dog that had acquired a taste for human flesh could be no good to anyone else—but he somehow didn't like to. Killing the only thing still living in this town (other than the singing bugs, that was) seemed like an invitation to bad luck.

He fired into the dust near the dog's good fore-paw, the sound crashing into the hot day and temporarily silencing the insects. The dog *could* run, it seemed, although at a lurching trot that hurt Roland's eyes . . . and his heart, a little, too. It stopped at the far side of the square, by an overturned flatbed wagon (there looked to be more dried blood splashed on the freighter's side), and glanced back. It uttered a forlorn howl that raised the hairs on the nape of Roland's neck even further. Then it turned, skirted the wrecked wagon, and limped down a lane which opened between two of the stalls. This way toward Eluria's back gate, Roland guessed.

Still leading his dying horse, the gunslinger crossed the square to the ironwood trough and looked in.

The owner of the chewed boot wasn't a man but a boy who had just been beginning to get his man's growth—and that would have been quite a large growth, indeed, Roland judged, even setting aside the bloating effects which had resulted from being immersed for some unknown length of time in nine inches of water simmering under a summer sun.

The boy's eyes, now just milky balls, stared blindly up at the gunslinger like the eyes of a statue. His hair appeared to be the white of old age, although that was the effect of the water; he had likely been a towhead. His clothes were those of a cowboy, although he couldn't have been much

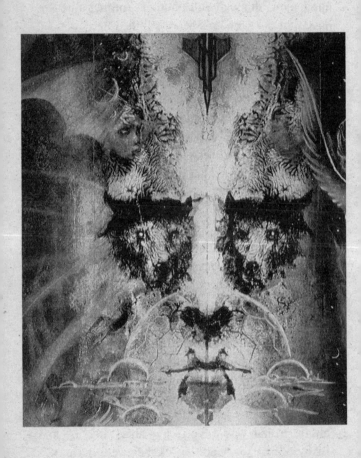

more than fourteen or sixteen. Around his neck, gleaming blearily in water that was slowly turning into a skin stew under the summer sun, was a gold medallion.

Roland reached into the water, not liking to but feeling a certain obligation. He wrapped his fingers around the medallion and pulled. The chain parted, and he lifted the thing, dripping, into the air.

He rather expected a Jesus-man *sigul*—what was called the crucifix or the rood—but a small rectangle hung from the chain, instead. The object looked like pure gold. Engraved into it was this legend:

James
Loved of family, Loved of GOD

Roland, who had been almost too revolted to reach into the polluted water (as a younger man, he could never have brought himself to that), was now glad he'd done it. He might never run into any of those who had loved this boy, but he knew enough of *ka* to think it might be so. In any case, it was the right thing. So was giving the kid a decent burial . . . assuming, that was, he could get the body out of the trough without having it break apart inside the clothes.

Roland was considering this, trying to balance what might be his duty in this circumstance against his growing desire to get out of this town, when Topsy finally fell dead.

The roan went over with a creak of gear and a last whuffling groan as it hit the ground. Roland turned and saw eight people in the street, walking toward him in a line, like beaters who hope to flush out birds or drive small game. Their skin was waxy green. Folk wearing such skin would likely glow in the dark like ghosts. It was hard to tell their sex, and what could it matter—to them or anyone else? They were slow mutants, walking with the hunched deliberation of corpses reanimated by some arcane magic.

The dust had muffled their feet like carpet. With the dog banished, they might well have gotten within attacking distance if Topsy hadn't done Roland the favor of dying at such an opportune moment. No guns that Roland could see; they were armed with clubs. These were chair legs and table legs, for the most part, but Roland saw one that looked made rather than seized—it had a bristle of rusty nails sticking out of it, and he suspected it had once been the property of a saloon bouncer, possibly the one who kept school in the Bustling Pig.

Roland raised his pistol, aiming at the fellow in the center of the line. Now he could hear the shuffle of their feet, and the wet snuffle of their breathing. As if they all had bad chest colds.

Came out of the mines, most likely, Roland thought. *There are radium mines somewhere about. That would account for the skin. I wonder that the sun doesn't kill them.*

Then, as he watched, the one on the end—a creature with a face like melted candle wax—*did* die . . . or collapsed, at any rate. He (Roland was quite sure it was a male) went to his knees with a low, gobbling cry, groping for the hand of the thing walking next to it—something with a lumpy bald head and red sores sizzling on its neck. This creature took no notice of its fallen companion, but kept its dim eyes on Roland, lurching along in rough step with its remaining companions.

"Stop where you are!" Roland said. " 'Ware me, if you'd live to see day's end! 'Ware me very well!"

He spoke mostly to the one in the center, who wore ancient red suspenders over rags of shirt, and a filthy bowler hat. This gent had only one good eye, and it peered at the gunslinger with a greed as horrible as it was unmistakable. The one beside Bowler Hat (Roland believed this one might be a woman, with the dangling vestiges of breasts beneath the vest it wore) threw the chair leg it held.

The arc was true, but the missile fell ten yards short.

Roland thumbed back the trigger of his revolver and fired again. This time the dirt displaced by the slug kicked up on the tattered remains of Bowler Hat's shoe instead of on a lame dog's paw.

The green folk didn't run as the dog had, but they stopped, staring at him with their dull greed. Had the missing folk of Eluria finished up in these creatures' stomachs? Roland couldn't believe it . . . although he knew perfectly well that such as these held no scruple against cannibalism. (And perhaps it wasn't cannibalism, not really; how could such things as these be considered human, whatever they might once have been?) They were too slow, too stupid. If they had dared come back into town after the Sheriff had run them out, they would have been burned or stoned to death.

Without thinking about what he was doing, wanting only to free his other hand to draw his second gun if the apparitions didn't see reason, Roland stuffed the medallion that he had taken from the dead boy into the pocket of his jeans, pushing the broken fine-link chain in after.

They stood staring at him, their strangely twisted shadows drawn out behind them. What next? Tell them to go back where they'd come from? Roland didn't know if they'd do it, and in any case had decided he liked them best where he could see them. And at least there was no question now about staying to bury the boy named James; that conundrum had been solved.

"Stand steady," he said in the low speech, beginning to retreat. "First fellow that moves—"

Before he could finish, one of them—a thick-chested troll with a pouty toad's mouth and what looked like gills on the sides of his wattled neck—lunged forward, gibbering in a high-pitched and peculiarly flabby voice. It might have been a species of laughter. He was waving what looked like a piano leg.

Roland fired. Mr. Toad's chest caved in like a bad piece of roofing. He ran backward several steps, trying to catch his balance and clawing at his chest with the hand not holding the piano leg. His feet, clad in dirty red velvet slippers with curled-up toes, tangled in each other and he fell over, making a queer and somehow lonely gargling sound. He let go of his club, rolled over on one side, tried to rise, and then fell back into the dust. The brutal sun glared into his open eyes, and as Roland watched, white tendrils of steam began to rise from his skin, which was rapidly losing its green undertint. There was also a hissing sound, like a gob of spit on top of a hot stove.

Saves explaining, at least, Roland thought, and

swept his eyes over the others. "All right; he was the first one to move. Who wants to be the second?"

None did, it seemed. They only stood there, watching him, not coming at him . . . but not retreating, either. He thought (as he had about the crucifix-dog) that he should kill them as they stood there, just draw his other gun and mow them down. It would be the work of seconds only, and child's play to his gifted hands, even if some ran. But he couldn't. Not just cold, like that. He wasn't that kind of killer . . . at least, not yet.

Very slowly, he began to step backward, first bending his course around the watering trough, then putting it between him and them. When Bowler Hat took a step forward, Roland didn't give the others in the line a chance to copy him; he put a bullet into the dust of High Street an inch in advance of the Bowler Hat's foot.

"That's your last warning," he said, still using the low speech. He had no idea if they understood it, didn't really care. He guessed they caught this tune's music well enough. "Next bullet I fire eats up someone's heart. The way it works is, you stay and I go. You get this one chance. Follow me, and you all die. It's too hot to play games and I've lost my—"

"Booh!" cried a rough, liquidy voice from behind him. There was unmistakable glee in it. Roland saw a shadow grow from the shadow of the overturned freight wagon, which he had now almost reached, and had just time to understand that another of the green folk had been hiding beneath it.

As he began to turn, a club crashed down on Roland's shoulder, numbing his right arm all the way to the wrist. He held on to the gun and fired once, but the bullet went into one of the wagon wheels, smashing a wooden spoke and turning the wheel on its hub with a high screeing sound. Behind him, he heard the green folk in the street uttering hoarse, yapping cries as they charged forward.

The thing which had been hiding beneath the overturned wagon was a monster with two heads growing out of his neck, one with the vestigial, slack face of a corpse. The other, although just as green, was more lively. Broad lips spread in a cheerful grin as he raised his club to strike again.

Roland drew with his left hand—the one that wasn't numbed and distant. He had time to put one bullet through the bushwhacker's grin, flinging him backward in a spray of blood and teeth, the bludgeon flying out of his relaxing fingers. Then the others were on him, clubbing and drubbing.

The gunslinger was able to slip the first couple

of blows, and there was one moment when he thought he might be able to spin around to the rear of the overturned wagon, spin and turn and go to work with his guns. Surely he would be able to do that. Surely his quest for the Dark Tower wasn't supposed to end on the sun-blasted street of a little far western town called Eluria, at the hands of half a dozen green-skinned slow mutants. Surely *ka* could not be so cruel.

But Bowler Hat caught him with a vicious side-hand blow, and Roland crashed into the wagon's slowly spinning rear wheel instead of skirting around it. As he went to his hands and knees, still scrambling and trying to turn, trying to evade the blows which rained down on him, he saw there were now many more than half a dozen. Coming up the street toward the town square were at least thirty green men and women. This wasn't a clan but a damned *tribe* of them. And in broad, hot daylight! Slow mutants were, in his experience, creatures that loved the dark, almost like toadstools with brains, and he had never seen any such as these before. They—

The one in the red vest was female. Her bare breasts swinging beneath the dirty red vest were the last things he saw clearly as they gathered around and above him, bashing away with their clubs. The one with the nails studded in it came down on his lower right calf, sinking its stupid rusty fangs in deep. He tried again to raise one of the big guns (his vision was fading, now, but that wouldn't help them if he got to shooting; he had always been the most hellishly talented of them, Jamie DeCurry had once proclaimed that Roland could shoot blind-folded, because he had eyes in his fingers), and it was kicked out of his hand and into the dust. Al-though he could still feel the smooth sandalwood grip of the other, he thought it was nevertheless already gone.

He could smell them—the rich, rotted smell of decaying meat. Or was that only his hands, as he raised them in a feeble and useless effort to protect his head? His hands, which had been in the polluted water where flecks and strips of the dead boy's skin floated?

The clubs slamming down on him, slamming down all over him, as if the green folk wanted not just to beat him to death but to tenderize him as they did so. And as he went down into the darkness of what he most certainly believed would be his death, he heard the bugs singing, the dog he had spared barking, and the bells hung on the church door ringing. These sounds merged together into strangely sweet music. Then that was gone, too; the darkness ate it all.

II. Rising. Hanging Suspended. White Beauty. Two Others. The Medallion.

The gunslinger's return to the world wasn't like coming back to consciousness after a blow, which he'd done several times before, and it wasn't like waking from sleep, either. It was like rising.

I'm dead, he thought at some point during this process . . . when the power to think had been at least partially restored to him. *Dead and rising into whatever afterlife there is. That's what it must be. The singing I hear is the singing of dead souls.*

Total blackness gave way to the dark gray of rainclouds, then to the lighter gray of fog. This brightened to the uniform clarity of a heavy mist moments before the sun breaks through. And through it all was that sense of *rising,* as if he had been caught in some mild but powerful updraft.

As the sense of rising began to diminish and the brightness behind his eyelids grew, Roland at last began to believe he was still alive. It was the singing that convinced him. Not dead souls, not the heavenly host of angels sometimes described by the Jesus-man preachers, but only those bugs. A little like crickets, but sweeter-voiced. The ones he had heard in Eluria.

On this thought, he opened his eyes.

His belief that he was still alive was severely tried, for Roland found himself hanging suspended in a world of white beauty—his first bewildered thought was that he was in the sky, floating within a fair-weather cloud. All around him was the reedy singing of the bugs. Now he could hear the tinkling of bells, too.

He tried to turn his head and swayed in some sort of harness. He could hear it creaking. The soft singing of the bugs, like crickets in the grass at the end of day back home in Gilead, hesitated and broke rhythm. When it did, what felt like a tree of pain grew up Roland's back. He had no idea what its burning branches might be, but the trunk was surely his spine. A far deadlier pain sank into one of his lower legs—in his confusion, the gunslinger could not tell which one. *That's where the club with the nails in it got me,* he thought. And more pain in his head. His skull felt like a badly cracked egg. He cried out, and could hardly believe that the harsh crow's caw he heard came from his own throat. He thought he could also hear, very faintly, the barking of the cross-dog, but surely that was his imagination.

Am I dying? Have I awakened once more at the very end?

A hand stroked his brow. He could feel it but not see it—fingers trailing across his skin, pausing

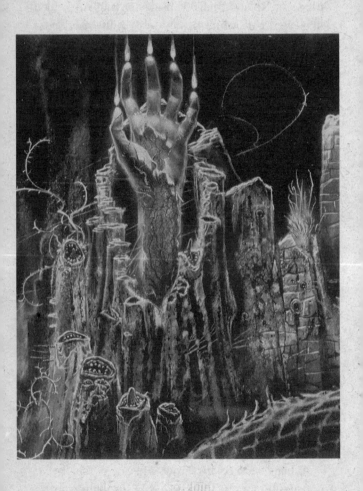

here and there to massage a knot or a line. Delicious, like a drink of cool water on a hot day. He began to close his eyes, and then a horrible idea came to him: suppose that hand were green, its owner wearing a tattered red vest over her hanging dugs?

What if it is? What could you do?

"Hush, man," a young woman's voice said . . . or perhaps it was the voice of a girl. Certainly the first person Roland thought of was Susan, the girl from Mejis, she who had spoken to him as *thee*.

"Where . . . where . . ."

"Hush, stir not. 'Tis far too soon."

The pain in his back was subsiding now, but the image of the pain as a tree remained, for his very skin seemed to be moving like leaves in a light breeze. How could that be?

He let the question go—let all questions go—and concentrated on the small, cool hand stroking his brow.

"Hush, pretty man, God's love be upon ye. Yet it's sore hurt ye are. Be still. Heal."

The dog had hushed its barking (if it had ever been there in the first place), and Roland became aware of that low creaking sound again. It reminded him of horse tethers, or something

(hangropes)

he didn't like to think of. Now he believed he

could feel pressure beneath his thighs, his buttocks, and perhaps . . . yes . . . his shoulders.

I'm not in a bed at all. I think I'm above a bed. Can that be?

He supposed he could be in a sling. He seemed to remember once, as a boy, that some fellow had been suspended that way in the horse doctor's room behind the Great Hall. A stablehand who had been burned too badly by kerosene to be laid in a bed. The man had died, but not soon enough; for two nights, his shrieks had filled the sweet summer air of the Gathering Fields.

Am I burned, then, nothing but a cinder with legs, hanging in a sling?

The fingers touched the center of his brow, rubbing away the frown forming there. And it was as if the voice which went with the hand had read his thoughts, picking them up with the tips of her clever, soothing fingers.

"Ye'll be fine if God wills, sai," the voice which went with the hand said. "But time belongs to God, not to you."

No, he would have said, if he had been able. *Time belongs to the Tower.*

Then he slipped down again, descending as smoothly as he had risen, going away from the hand and the dreamlike sounds of the singing insects and chiming bells. There was an interval that might have been sleep, or perhaps unconsciousness, but he never went all the way back down.

At one point he thought he heard the girl's voice, although he couldn't be sure, because this time it was raised in fury, or fear, or both. "No!" she cried. "Ye can't have it off him and ye know it! Go your course and stop talking of it, do!"

When he rose back to consciousness the second time, he was no stronger in body, but a little more himself in mind. What he saw when he opened his eyes wasn't the inside of a cloud, but at first that same phrase—*white beauty*—recurred to him. It was in some ways the most beautiful place Roland had ever been in his life . . . partially because he still *had* a life, of course, but mostly because it was so fey and peaceful.

It was a huge room, high and long. When Roland at last turned his head—cautiously, so cautiously— to take its measure as well as he could, he thought it must run at least two hundred yards from end to end. It was built narrow, but its height gave the place a feeling of tremendous airiness.

There were no walls or ceilings such as those he was familiar with, although it was a little like being in a vast tent. Above him, the sun struck and diffused its light across billowy panels of thin white silk, turning them into the bright swags that he had first mistaken for clouds. Beneath this silk canopy, the room was as gray as twilight. The walls, also silk, rippled like sails in a faint breeze. Hanging from each wall panel was a curved rope bearing small bells. These lay against the fabric and rang in low and charming unison, like wind chimes, when the walls rippled.

An aisle ran down the center of the long room; on either side of it were scores of beds, each made up with clean white sheets and headed with crisp white pillows. There were perhaps forty on the far side of the aisle, all empty, and another forty on Roland's side. There were two other occupied beds here, one next to Roland on his right. This fellow—

It's the boy. The one who was in the trough.

The idea ran goose bumps up Roland's arms and gave him a nasty, superstitious start. He peered more closely at the sleeping boy.

Can't be. You're just dazed, that's all; it can't be.

Yet closer scrutiny refused to dispel the idea. It certainly *seemed* to be the boy from the trough, probably ill (why else would he be in a place like this?) but far from dead; Roland could see the slow rise and fall of his chest, and the occasional twitch of the fingers that dangled over the side of the bed.

You didn't get a good enough look at him to be sure of anything, and after a few days in that trough, his own mother couldn't have said for sure who it was.

But Roland, who'd had a mother, knew better than that. He also knew that he'd seen the gold medallion around the boy's neck. Just before the attack of the green folk, he had taken it from this lad's corpse and put it in his pocket. Now some-one—the proprietors of this place, most likely, them who had sorcerously restored the lad named James to his interrupted life—had taken it back from Roland and put it around the boy's neck again.

Had the girl with the wonderfully cool hand done that? Did she in consequence think Roland a ghoul who would steal from the dead? He didn't like to think so. In fact, the notion made him more uncomfortable than the idea that the young cow-boy's bloated body had been somehow returned to its normal size and then reanimated.

Farther down the aisle on this side, perhaps a dozen empty beds away from the boy and Roland Deschain, the gunslinger saw a third inmate of this queer infirmary. This fellow looked at least four times the age of the lad, twice the age of the gun-slinger. He had a long beard, more gray than black, that hung to his upper chest in two straggly forks. The face above it was sun-darkened, heavily lined, and pouched beneath the eyes. Running from his left cheek and across the bridge of his nose was a thick dark mark which Roland took to be a scar. The bearded man was either asleep or unconscious—Roland could hear him snoring—and was suspended three feet above his bed, held up by a complex series of white belts that glimmered in the dim air. These crisscrossed each other, making a series of figure eights all the way around the man's body. He looked like a bug in some exotic spider's web. He wore a gauzy white bed-dress. One of the belts ran beneath his buttocks, elevating his crotch in a way that seemed to offer the bulge of his privates to the gray and dreaming air. Farther down his body, Roland could see the dark shadow-shapes of his legs. They appeared to be twisted like ancient dead trees. Roland didn't like to think in how many places they must have been broken to look like that. And yet they appeared to be *moving*. How could they be, if the bearded man was unconscious? It was a trick of the light, perhaps, or of the shadows . . . perhaps the gauzy singlet the man was wearing was stirring in a light breeze, or . . .

Roland looked away, up at the billowy silk panels high above, trying to control the accelerating beat of his heart. What he saw hadn't been caused by the wind, or a shadow, or anything else. The man's legs were somehow moving without moving . . . as Roland had seemed to feel his own back moving without moving. He didn't know what could cause such a phenomenon, and didn't want to know, at least not yet.

"I'm not ready," he whispered. His lips felt very dry. He closed his eyes again, wanting to sleep, wanting not to think about what the bearded man's twisted legs might indicate about his own condition. But—

But you'd better get ready.

That was the voice that always seemed to come when he tried to slack off, to scamp a job or take the easy way around an obstacle. It was the voice of Cort, his old teacher. The man whose stick they had all feared, as boys. They hadn't feared his stick as much as his mouth, however. His jeers when they were weak, his contempt when they complained or tried whining about their lot.

Are you a gunslinger, Roland? If you are, you better get ready.

Roland opened his eyes again and turned his head to the left again. As he did, he felt something shift against his chest.

Moving very slowly, he raised his right hand out of the sling that held it. The pain in his back stirred and muttered. He stopped moving until he decided the pain was going to get no worse (if he was careful, at least), then lifted the hand the rest of the way to his chest. It encountered finely woven cloth.

Cotton. He lowered his chin to his breastbone and saw that he was wearing a bed-dress like the one draped on the body of the bearded man.

Roland reached beneath the neck of the gown and felt a fine chain. A little farther down, his fingers encountered a rectangular metal shape. He thought he knew what it was, but had to be sure. He pulled it out, still moving with great care, trying not to engage any of the muscles in his back. A gold medallion. He dared the pain, lifting it until he could read what was engraved upon it:

James
Loved of family, Loved of GOD

He tucked it into the top of the bed-dress again and looked back at the sleeping boy in the next bed—*in* it, not suspended over it. The sheet was only pulled up to the boy's rib cage, and the medallion lay on the pristine white breast of his bed-dress. The same medallion Roland now wore. Except . . .

Roland thought he understood, and understanding was a relief.

He looked back at the bearded man, and saw an exceedingly strange thing: the thick black line of scar across the bearded man's cheek and nose was gone. Where it had been was the pinkish red mark of a healing wound . . . a cut, or perhaps a slash.

I imagined it.

No, gunslinger, Cort's voice returned. *Such as you was not made to imagine. As you well know.*

The little bit of movement had tired him out again . . . or perhaps it was the thinking which had really tired him out. The singing bugs and chiming bells combined and made something too much like a lullaby to resist. This time when Roland closed his eyes, he slept.

III. Five Sisters. Jenna. The Doctors of Eluria. The Medallion. A Promise of Silence.

When Roland awoke again, he was at first sure that he was still sleeping. Dreaming. Having a nightmare.

Once, at the time he had met and fallen in love with Susan Delgado, he had known a witch named Rhea—the first real witch of Mid-World he had ever met. It was she who had caused Susan's death, although Roland had played his own part. Now, opening his eyes and seeing Rhea not just once but five times over, he thought: *This is what comes of remembering those old times. By conjuring Susan, I've conjured Rhea of the Coos, as well. Rhea and her sisters.*

The five were dressed in billowing habits as white as the walls and the panels of the ceiling. Their antique crones' faces were framed in wimples just as white, their skin as gray and runneled as droughted earth by comparison. Hanging like phylacteries from the bands of silk imprisoning their hair (if they indeed had hair) were lines of tiny bells which chimed as they moved or spoke. Upon the snowy breasts of their habits was embroidered a blood red rose . . . the *sigul* of the Dark Tower. Seeing this, Roland thought: *I am not dreaming. These harridans are real.*

"He wakes!" one of them cried in a gruesomely coquettish voice.

"Oooo!"

"Ooooh!"

"Ah!"

They fluttered like birds. The one in the center stepped forward, and as she did, their faces seemed to shimmer like the silk walls of the ward. They weren't old after all, he saw—middle-aged, perhaps, but not old.

Yes. They are *old. They changed.*

The one who now took charge was taller than the others, and with a broad, slightly bulging brow. She bent toward Roland, and the bells that fringed her forehead tinkled. The sound made him feel sick, somehow, and weaker than he had felt a moment before. Her hazel eyes were intent. Greedy, mayhap. She touched his cheek for a moment, and a numbness seemed to spread there. Then she glanced down, and a look which could have been disquiet cramped her face. She took her hand back.

"Ye wake, pretty man. So ye do. 'Tis well."

"Who are you? Where am I?"

"We are the Little Sisters of Eluria," she said. "I am Sister Mary. Here is Sister Louise, and Sister Michela, and Sister Coquina—"

"And Sister Tamra," said the last. "A lovely lass of one-and-twenty." She giggled. Her face shimmered, and for a moment she was again as old as the world. Hooked of nose, gray of skin. Roland thought once more of Rhea.

They moved closer, encircling the complication of harness in which he lay suspended, and when Roland shrank back, the pain roared up his back and injured leg again. He groaned. The straps holding him creaked.

"Ooooo!"

"It hurts!"

"Hurts him!"

"Hurts so fierce!"

They pressed even closer, as if his pain fascinated them. And now he could smell them, a dry and earthy smell. The one named Sister Michela reached out—

"Go away! Leave him! Have I not told ye before?"

They jumped back from this voice, startled. Sister Mary looked particularly annoyed. But she stepped back, with one final glare (Roland would have sworn it) at the medallion lying on his chest. He had tucked it back under the bed-dress at his last waking, but it was out again now.

A sixth sister appeared, pushing rudely in between Mary and Tamra. This one perhaps *was* only one-and-twenty, with flushed cheeks, smooth skin, and dark eyes. Her white habit billowed like a dream. The red rose over her breast stood out like a curse.

"Go! Leave him!"

"Oooo, my *dear*!" cried Sister Louise in a voice both laughing and angry. "Here's Jenna, the baby, and has she fallen in love with him?"

"She has!" laughed Tamra. "Baby's heart is his for the purchase!"

"Oh, so it *is*!" agreed Sister Coquina.

Mary turned to the newcomer, lips pursed into a tight line. "Ye have no business here, saucy girl."

"I do if I say I do," Sister Jenna replied. She seemed more in charge of herself now. A curl of black hair had escaped her wimple and lay across her forehead in a comma. "Now go. He's not up to your jokes and laughter."

"Order us not," Sister Mary said, "for we never joke. So you know, Sister Jenna."

The girl's face softened a little, and Roland saw she was afraid. It made him afraid for her. For himself, as well. "Go," she repeated. " 'Tis not the time. Are there not others to tend?"

Sister Mary seemed to consider. The others watched her. At last she nodded, and smiled down at Roland. Again her face seemed to shimmer, like something seen through a heat-haze. What he saw (or thought he saw) beneath was horrible and watchful. "Bide well, pretty man," she said to Roland. "Bide with us a bit, and we'll heal ye."

What choice have I? Roland thought.

The others laughed, birdlike titters which rose into the dimness like ribbons. Sister Michela actually blew him a kiss.

"Come, ladies!" Sister Mary cried. "We'll leave Jenna with him a bit in memory of her mother, who we loved well!" And with that, she lead the others away, five white birds flying off down the center aisle, their skirts nodding this way and that.

"Thank you," Roland said, looking up at the owner of the cool hand . . . for he knew it was she who had soothed him.

She took up his fingers as if to prove this, and caressed them. "They mean ye no harm," she said . . .

yet Roland saw she believed not a word of it, nor did he. He was in trouble here, very bad trouble.

"What is this place?"

"Our place," she said simply. "The home of the Little Sisters of Eluria. Our convent, if'ee like."

"This is no convent," Roland said, looking past her at the empty beds. "It's an infirmary. Isn't it?"

"A hospital," she said, still stroking his fingers. "We serve the doctors . . . and they serve us." He was fascinated by the black curl lying on the cream of her brow—would have stroked it, if he had dared reach up. Just to tell its texture. He found it beautiful because it was the only dark thing in all this white. The white had lost its charm for him. "We are hospitalers . . . or were, before the world moved on."

"Are you for the Jesus-man?"

She looked surprised for a moment, almost shocked, and then laughed merrily. "No, not us!"

"If you are hospitalers . . . nurses . . . where are the doctors?"

She looked at him, biting at her lip, as if trying to decide something. Roland found her doubt utterly charming, and he realized that, sick or not, he was looking at a woman *as* a woman for the first time since Susan Delgado had died, and that had been long ago. The whole world had changed since then, and not for the better.

"Would you really know?"

"Yes, of course," he said, a little surprised. A little disquieted, too. He kept waiting for her face to shimmer and change, as the faces of the others had done. It didn't. There was none of that unpleasant dead earth smell about her, either.

Wait, he cautioned himself. *Believe nothing here, least of all your senses. Not yet.*

"I suppose you must," she said with a sigh. It tinkled the bells at her forehead, which were darker in color than those the others wore—not black like her hair but charry, somehow, as if they had been hung in the smoke of a campfire. Their sound, however, was brightest silver. "Promise me you'll not scream and wake the pube in yonder bed."

"Pube?"

"The boy. Do ye promise?"

"Aye," he said, falling into the half-forgotten patois of the Outer Arc without even being aware of it. Susan's dialect. "It's been long since I screamed, pretty."

She colored more definitely at that, roses more natural and lively than the one on her breast mounting in her cheeks.

"Don't call pretty what ye can't properly see," she said.

"Then push back the wimple you wear."

Her face he could see perfectly well, but he badly wanted to see her hair—hungered for it, almost. A full flood of black in all this dreaming white. Of course it might be cropped, those of her order might wear it that way, but he somehow didn't think so.

"No, 'tis not allowed."

"By who?"

"Big Sister."

"She who calls herself Mary?"

"Aye, her." She started away, then paused and looked back over her shoulder. In another girl her age, one as pretty as this, that look back would have been flirtatious. This girl's was only grave.

"Remember your promise."

"Aye, no screams."

She went to the bearded man, skirt swinging. In the dimness, she cast only a blur of shadow on the empty beds she passed. When she reached the man (this one was unconscious, Roland thought, not just sleeping), she looked back at Roland once more. He nodded.

Sister Jenna stepped close to the suspended man's side on the far side of his bed, so that Roland saw her through the twists and loops of woven white silk. She placed her hands lightly on the left side of his chest, bent over him . . . and shook her head from side to side, like one expressing a brisk negative. The bells she wore on her forehead rang sharply, and Roland once more felt that weird stirring up his back, accompanied by a low ripple of pain. It was as if he had shuddered without actually shuddering, or shuddered in a dream.

What happened next almost *did* jerk a scream from him; he had to bite his lips against it. Once more the unconscious man's legs seemed to move without moving . . . because it was what was *on* them that moved. The man's hairy shins, ankles, and feet were exposed below the hem of his bed-dress. Now a black wave of bugs moved down them. They were singing fiercely, like an army column that sings as it marches.

Roland remembered the black scar across the man's cheek and nose—the scar that had disappeared. More such as these, of course. And they were on *him*, as well. That was how he could shiver without shivering. They were all over his back. *Battening* on him.

No, keeping back a scream wasn't as easy as he had expected it to be.

The bugs ran down to the tips of the suspended man's toes, then leaped off them in waves, like creatures leaping off an embankment and into a swimming hole. They organized themselves quickly and easily on the bright white sheet below, and began to march down to the floor in a battalion about a foot wide. Roland couldn't get a good look at them, the distance was too far and the light too dim, but he thought they were perhaps twice the size of ants, and a little smaller than the fat honeybees which had swarmed the flower beds back home.

They sang as they went.

The bearded man didn't sing. As the swarms of bugs that had coated his twisted legs began to diminish, he shuddered and groaned. The young woman put her hand on his brow and soothed him, making Roland a little jealous even in his revulsion at what he was seeing.

And was what he was seeing really so awful? In Gilead, leeches had been used for certain ailments—swellings of the brain, the armpits, and the groin, primarily. When it came to the brain, the leeches, ugly as they were, were certainly preferable to the next step, which was trepanning.

Yet there *was* something loathsome about them, perhaps only because he couldn't see them well, and something awful about trying to imagine them all over his back as he hung here, helpless. Not singing, though. Why? Because they were feeding? Sleeping? Both at once?

The bearded man's groans subsided. The bugs marched away across the floor, toward one of the mildly rippling silken walls. Roland lost sight of them in the shadows.

Jenna came back to him, her eyes anxious. "Ye did well. Yet I see how ye feel; it's on your face."

"The doctors," he said.

"Yes. Their power is very great, but . . ." She dropped her voice. "I believe that drover is beyond their help. His legs are a little better, and the wounds on his face are all but healed, but he has injuries where the doctors cannot reach." She traced a hand across her midsection, suggesting the location of these injuries, if not their nature.

"And me?" Roland asked.

"Ye were ta'en by the green folk," she said. "Ye must have angered them powerfully, for them not to kill ye outright. They roped ye and dragged ye, instead. Tamra, Michela, and Louise were out gathering herbs. They saw the green folk at play with ye, and bade them stop, but—"

"Do the muties always obey you, Sister Jenna?"

She smiled, perhaps pleased he remembered her name. "Not always, but mostly. This time they did, or ye'd have now found the clearing in the trees."

"I suppose so."

"The skin was stripped almost clean off your back—red ye were from nape to waist. Ye'll always bear the scars, but the doctors have gone far toward healing ye. And their singing is passing fair, is it not?"

"Yes," Roland said, but the thought of those black things all over his back, roosting in his raw flesh, still revolted him. "I owe you thanks, and give it freely. Anything I can do for you—"

"Tell me your name, then. Do that."

"I'm Roland of Gilead. A gunslinger. I had revolvers, Sister Jenna. Have you seen them?"

"I've seen no shooters," she said, but cast her eyes aside. The roses bloomed in her cheeks again. She might be a good nurse, and fair, but Roland thought her a poor liar. He was glad. Good liars were common. Honesty, on the other hand, came dear.

Let the untruth pass for now, he told himself. *She speaks it out of fear, I think.*

"Jenna!" The cry came from the deeper shadows at the far end of the infirmary—today it seemed longer than ever to the gunslinger—and Sister Jenna jumped guiltily. "Come away! Ye've passed words enough to entertain twenty men! Let him sleep!"

"Aye!" she called, then turned back to Roland. "Don't let on that I showed you the doctors."

"Mum is the word, Jenna."

She paused, biting her lip again, then suddenly swept back her wimple. It fell against the nape of her neck in a soft chiming of bells. Freed from its confinement, her hair swept against her cheeks like shadows.

"*Am* I pretty? *Am* I? Tell me the truth, Roland

55

of Gilead—no flattery. For flattery's kind only a candle's length."

"Pretty as a summer night."

What she saw in his face seemed to please her more than his words, because she smiled radiantly. She pulled the wimple up again, tucking her hair back in with quick little finger-pokes. "Am I decent?"

"Decent as fair," he said, then cautiously lifted an arm and pointed at her brow. "One curl's out . . . just there."

"Aye, always that one to devil me." With a comical little grimace, she tucked it back. Roland thought how much he would like to kiss her rosy cheeks . . . and perhaps her rosy mouth, for good measure.

"All's well," he said.

"*Jenna!*" The cry was more impatient than ever. "Meditations!"

"I'm coming just now!" she called, and gathered her voluminous skirts to go. Yet she turned back once more, her face now very grave and very serious. "One more thing," she said in a voice only a step above a whisper. She snatched a quick look around. "The gold medallion ye wear—ye wear it because it's yours. Do'ee understand . . . James?"

"Yes." He turned his head a bit to look at the sleeping boy. "This is my brother."

"If they ask, yes. To say different would be to get Jenna in serious trouble."

How serious he did not ask, and she was gone in any case, seeming to flow along the aisle between all the empty beds, her skirt caught up in one hand. The roses had fled from her face, leaving her cheeks and brow ashy. He remembered the greedy look on the faces of the others, how they had gathered around him in a tightening knot . . . and the way their faces had shimmered.

Six women, five old and one young.

Doctors that sang and then crawled away across the floor when dismissed by jingling bells.

And an improbable hospital ward of perhaps a hundred beds, a ward with a silk roof and silk walls . . .

. . . and all the beds empty save three.

Roland didn't understand why Jenna had taken the dead boy's medallion from his pants pocket and put it around his neck, but he had an idea that if they found out she had done so, the Little Sisters of Eluria might kill her.

Roland closed his eyes, and the soft singing of the doctor-insects once again floated him off into sleep.

IV. A Bowl of Soup. The Boy in the Next Bed. The Night-Nurses.

Roland dreamed that a very large bug (a doctor-bug, mayhap) was flying around his head and banging repeatedly into his nose—collisions which were annoying rather than painful. He swiped at the bug repeatedly, and although his hands were eerily fast under ordinary circumstances, he kept missing it. And each time he missed, the bug giggled.

I'm slow because I've been sick, he thought.

No, ambushed. Dragged across the ground by slow mutants, saved by the Little Sisters of Eluria.

Roland had a sudden, vivid image of a man's shadow growing from the shadow of an overturned freight wagon; heard a rough, gleeful voice cry "Booh!"

He jerked awake hard enough to set his body rocking in its complication of slings, and the woman who had been standing beside his head, giggling as she tapped his nose lightly with a wooden spoon, stepped back so quickly that the bowl in her other hand slipped from her fingers.

Roland's hands shot out, and they were as quick as ever—his frustrated failure to catch the bug had been only part of his dream. He caught the bowl before more than a few drops could spill. The woman—Sister Coquina—looked at him with round eyes.

There was pain all up and down his back from the sudden movement, but it was nowhere near as sharp as it had been before, and there was no sensation of movement on his skin. Perhaps the "doctors" were only sleeping, but he had an idea they were gone.

He held out his hand for the spoon Coquina had been teasing him with (he found he wasn't surprised at all that one of these would tease a sick and sleeping man in such a way; it only would have surprised him if it had been Jenna), and she handed it to him, her eyes still big.

"How speedy ye are!" she said. " 'Twas like a magic trick, and you still rising from sleep!"

"Remember it, sai," he said, and tried the soup. There were tiny bits of chicken floating in it. He probably would have considered it bland under other circumstances, but under these, it seemed ambrosial. He began to eat greedily.

"What do'ee mean by that?" she asked. The light was very dim now, the wall panels across the way a pinkish orange that suggested sunset. In this light, Coquina looked quite young and pretty . . . but it was a glamour, Roland was sure; a sorcerous kind of makeup.

"I mean nothing in particular." Roland dismissed the spoon as too slow, preferring to tilt the bowl itself to his lips. In this way he disposed of the soup in four large gulps. "You have been kind to me—"

"Aye, so we *have*!" she said, rather indignantly.

"—and I hope your kindness has no hidden motive. If it does, Sister, remember that I'm quick. And, as for myself, I have not always been kind."

She made no reply, only took the bowl when Roland handed it back. She did this delicately, perhaps not wanting to touch his fingers. Her eyes dropped to where the medallion lay, once more hidden beneath the breast of his bed-dress. He said no more, not wanting to weaken the implied threat by reminding her that the man who made it was unarmed, next to naked, and hung in the air because his back couldn't yet bear the weight of his body.

"Where's Sister Jenna?" he asked.

"Oooo," Sister Coquina said, raising her eyebrows. "We like her, do we? She makes our heart go . . ." She put her hand against the rose on her breast and fluttered it rapidly.

"Not at all, not at all," Roland said, "but she was kind. I doubt she would have teased me with a spoon, as some would."

Sister Coquina's smile faded. She looked both angry and worried. "Say nothing of that to Mary,

if she comes by later. Ye might get me in trouble.''

"Should I care?''

"I might get back at one who caused me trouble by causing little Jenna trouble,'' Sister Coquina said. "She's in Big Sister's black books, just now, anyway. Sister Mary doesn't care for the way Jenna spoke to her about ye . . . nor does she like it that Jenna came back to us wearing the Dark Bells.''

This was no more out of her mouth before Sister Coquina put her hand over that frequently imprudent organ, as if realizing she had said too much.

Roland, intrigued by what she'd said but not liking to show it just now, only replied, "I'll keep my mouth shut about you, if you keep your mouth shut to Sister Mary about Jenna.''

Coquina looked relieved. "Aye, that's a bargain.'' She leaned forward confidingly. "She's in Thoughtful House. That's the little cave in the hillside where we have to go and meditate when Big Sister decides we've been bad. She'll have to stay and consider her impudence until Mary lets her out.'' She paused, then said abruptly, "Who's this beside ye? Do ye know?''

Roland turned his head and saw that the young man was awake, and had been listening. His eyes were as dark as Jenna's.

"Know him?'' Roland asked, with what he

hoped was the right touch of scorn. "Should I not know my own brother?"

"Is he, now, and him so young and you so old?" Another of the sisters materialized out of the darkness: Sister Tamra, who had called herself one-and-twenty. In the moment before she reached Roland's bed, her face was that of a hag who will never see eighty again . . . or ninety. Then it shimmered and was once more the plump, healthy countenance of a thirty-year-old matron. Except for the eyes. They remained yellowish in the corneas, gummy in the corners, and watchful.

"He's the youngest, I the eldest," Roland said. "Betwixt us are seven others, and twenty years of our parents' lives."

"How sweet! And if he's yer brother, then ye'll know his name, won't ye? Know it very well."

Before the gunslinger could flounder, the young man said, "They think you've forgotten such a simple hook as John Norman. What culleens they be, eh, Jimmy?"

Coquina and Tamra looked at the pale boy in the bed next to Roland's, clearly angry . . . and clearly trumped. For the time being, at least.

"You've fed him your muck," the boy (whose medallion undoubtedly proclaimed him 𝔍𝔬𝔥𝔫, 𝓛𝓸𝓿𝓮𝓭 𝓸𝓯 𝓯𝓪𝓶𝓲𝓵𝔂, 𝓛𝓸𝓿𝓮𝓭 𝓸𝓯 𝓖𝓞𝓓) said. "Why don't you go, and let us have a natter?"

"Well!" Sister Coquina huffed. "I like the gratitude around here, so I do!"

"I'm grateful for what's given me," Norman responded, looking at her steadily, "but not for what folk would take away."

Tamra snorted through her nose, turned violently enough for her swirling dress to push a draught of air into Roland's face, and then took her leave. Coquina stayed a moment.

"Be discreet, and mayhap someone ye like better than ye like me will get out of hack in the morning, instead of a week from tonight."

Without waiting for a reply, she turned and followed Sister Tamra.

Roland and John Norman waited until they were both gone, and then Norman turned to Roland and spoke in a low voice. "My brother. Dead?"

Roland nodded. "The medallion I took in case I should meet with any of his people. It rightly belongs to you. I'm sorry for your loss."

"Thankee-sai." John Norman's lower lip trembled, then firmed. "I knew the green men did for him, although these old biddies wouldn't tell me for sure. They did for plenty, and scotched the rest."

"Perhaps the Sisters didn't know for sure."

"They knew. Don't you doubt it. They don't say much, but they know *plenty*. The only one any different is Jenna. That's who the old battle-axe meant when she said 'your friend.' Aye?''

Roland nodded. "And she said something about the Dark Bells. I'd know more of that, if would were could.''

"She's something special, Jenna is. More like a princess—someone whose place is made by blood-line and can't be refused—than like the other Sisters. I lie here and look like I'm asleep—it's safer, I think—but I've heard 'em talking. Jenna's just come back among 'em recently, and those Dark Bells mean something special . . . but Mary's still the one who swings the weight. I think the Dark Bells are only ceremonial, like the rings the old Barons used to hand down from father to son. Was it she who put Jimmy's medal around your neck?''

"Yes.''

"Don't take it off, whatever you do.'' His face was strained, grim. "I don't know if it's the gold or the God, but they don't like to get too close. I think that's the only reason I'm still here.'' Now his voice dropped all the way to a whisper. "They ain't human.''

"Well, perhaps a bit fey and magical, but . . .''

"No!'' With what was clearly an effort, the boy got up on one elbow. He looked at Roland earnestly. "You're thinking about hubber-women, or witches. These ain't hubbers, nor witches, either. *They ain't human!''*

"Then what are they?"

"Don't know."

"How came you here, John?"

Speaking in a low voice, John Norman told Roland what he knew of what had happened to him. He, his brother, and four other young men who were quick and owned good horses had been hired as scouts, riding drogue-and-forward, protecting a long-haul caravan of seven freight wagons taking goods—seeds, food, tools, mail, and four ordered brides—to an unincorporated township called Tejuas some two hundred miles farther west of Eluria. The scouts rode fore and aft of the goods-train in turn-and-turn-about fashion; one brother rode with each party because, Norman explained, when they were together they fought like . . . well . . .

"Like brothers," Roland suggested.

John Norman managed a brief, pained smile. "Aye," he said.

The trio of which John was a part had been riding drogue, about two miles behind the freight wagons, when the green mutants had sprung an ambush in Eluria.

"How many wagons did you see when you got there?" he asked Roland.

"Only one. Overturned."

"How many bodies?"

"Only your brother's."

John Norman nodded grimly. "They wouldn't take him because of the medallion, I think."

"The muties?"

"The Sisters. The muties care nothing for gold or God. These bitches, though . . ." He looked into the dark, which was now almost complete. Roland felt lethargy creeping over him again, but it wasn't until later that he realized the soup had been drugged.

"The other wagons?" Roland asked. "The ones not overturned?"

"The muties would have taken them, and the goods, as well," Norman said. "They don't care for gold or God; the Sisters don't care for goods. Like as not they have their own foodstuffs, something I'd as soon not think of. Nasty stuff . . . like those bugs."

He and the other drogue riders galloped into Eluria, but the fight was over by the time they got there. Men had been lying about, some dead but many more still alive. At least two of the ordered brides had still been alive, as well. Survivors able to walk were being herded together by the green folk—John Norman remembered the one in the bowler hat very well, and the woman in the ragged red vest.

Norman and the other two had tried to fight. He had seen one of his pards gutshot by an arrow, and then he saw no more—someone had cracked him over the head from behind, and the lights had gone out.

Roland wondered if the ambusher had cried ''Booh!'' before he had struck, but didn't ask.

''When I woke up again, I was here,'' Norman said. ''I saw that some of the others—*most* of them—had those cursed bugs on them.''

''Others?'' Roland looked at the empty beds. In the growing darkness, they glimmered like white islands. ''How many were brought here?''

''At least twenty. They healed . . . the bugs healed 'em . . . and then, one by one, they disappeared. You'd go to sleep, and when you woke up there'd be one more empty bed. One by one they went, until only me and that one down yonder was left.''

He looked at Roland solemnly.

''And now you.''

''Norman,'' Roland's head was swimming. ''I—''

''I reckon I know what's wrong with you,'' Norman said. He seemed to speak from far away . . . perhaps from all the way around the curve of the earth. ''It's the soup. But a man has to eat. A woman, too. If she's a natural woman, anyway.

These ones ain't natural. Even Sister Jenna's not natural. Nice don't mean natural.'' Farther and farther away. ''And she'll be like them in the end. Mark me well.''

''Can't move.'' Saying even that required a huge effort. It was like moving boulders.

''No.'' Norman suddenly laughed. It was a shocking sound, and echoed in the growing blackness which filled Roland's head. ''It ain't just sleep medicine they put in their soup; it's can't-move medicine, too. There's nothing much wrong with me, brother . . . so why do you think I'm still here?''

Norman was now speaking not from around the curve of the earth but perhaps from the moon, He said: ''I don't think either of us is ever going to see the sun shining on a flat piece of ground again.''

You're wrong about that, Roland tried to reply, and more in that vein, as well, but nothing came out. He sailed around to the black side of the moon, losing all his words in the void he found there.

Yet he never quite lost awareness of himself. Perhaps the dose of ''medicine'' in Sister Coquina's soup had been badly calculated, or perhaps it was just that they had never had a gunslinger to work their mischief on, and did not know they had one now.

Except, of course, for Sister Jenna—*she* knew.

At some point in the night, whispering, giggling voices and lightly chiming bells brought him back from the darkness where he had been biding, not quite asleep or unconscious. Around him, so constant he now barely heard it, were the singing "doctors."

Roland opened his eyes. He saw pale and chancy light dancing in the black air. The giggles and whispers were closer. Roland tried to turn his head and at first couldn't. He rested, gathered his will into a hard blue ball, and tried again. This time his head *did* turn. Only a little, but a little was enough.

It was five of the Little Sisters—Mary, Louise, Tamra, Coquina, Michela. They came up the long aisle of the black infirmary, laughing together like children out on a prank, carrying long tapers in silver holders, the bells lining the forehead-bands of their wimples chiming little silver runs of sound. They gathered about the bed of the bearded man. From within their circle, candleglow rose in a shimmery column that died before it got halfway to the silken ceiling.

Sister Mary spoke briefly. Roland recognized her voice, but not the words—it was neither low speech nor the High, but some other language entirely. One phrase stood out—*can de lach, mi him en tow*—and he had no idea what it might mean.

He realized that now he could hear only the tinkle of bells—the doctor-bugs had stilled.

"Ras me! On! On!" Sister Mary cried in a harsh, powerful voice. The candles went out. The light that had shone through the wings of their wimples as they gathered around the bearded man's bed vanished, and all was darkness once more.

Roland waited for what might happen next, his skin cold. He tried to flex his hands or feet, and could not. He had been able to move his head perhaps fifteen degrees; otherwise he was as paralyzed as a fly neatly wrapped up and hung in a spider's web.

The low jingling of bells in the black . . . and then sucking sounds. As soon as he heard them, Roland knew he'd been waiting for them. Some part of him had known what the Little Sisters of Eluria were, all along.

If Roland could have raised his hands, he would have put them to his ears to block those sounds out. As it was, he could only lie still, listening and waiting for them to stop.

For a long time—forever, it seemed—they did not. The women slurped and grunted like pigs snuffling half-liquefied feed up out of a trough. There was even one resounding belch, followed by more whispered giggles (these ended when Sister Mary uttered a single curt word—*"Hais!"*). And once there was a low, moaning cry—from the bearded man, Roland was quite sure. If so, it was his last on this side of the clearing.

In time, the sounds of their feeding began to taper off. As it did, the bugs began to sing again—first hesitantly, then with more confidence. The whispering and giggling recommenced. The candles were relit. Roland was by now lying with his head turned in the other direction. He didn't want them to know what he'd seen, but that wasn't all; he had no urge to see more on any account. He had seen and heard enough.

But the giggles and whispers now came his way. Roland closed his eyes, concentrating on the medallion that lay against his chest. *I don't know if it's the gold or the God, but they don't like to get too close,* John Norman had said. It was good to have such a thing to remember as the Little Sisters drew nigh, gossiping and whispering in their strange other tongue, but the medallion seemed a thin protection in the dark.

Faintly, at a great distance, Roland heard the cross-dog barking.

As the Sisters circled him, the gunslinger realized he could smell them. It was a low, unpleasant odor, like spoiled meat. And what else *would* they smell of, such as these?

"Such a pretty man it is." Sister Mary. She spoke in a low, meditative tone.

"But such an ugly *sigul* it wears." Sister Tamra.

"We'll have it off him!" Sister Louise.

"And then we shall have kisses!" Sister Coquina.

"Kisses for all!" exclaimed Sister Michela, with such fervent enthusiasm that they all laughed.

Roland discovered that not *all* of him was paralyzed, after all. Part of him had, in fact, arisen from its sleep at the sound of their voices and now stood tall. A hand reached beneath the bed-dress he wore, touched that stiffened member, encircled it, caressed it. He lay in silent horror, feigning sleep, as wet warmth almost immediately spilled from him. The hand remained where it was for a moment, the thumb rubbing up and down the wilting shaft. Then it let him go and rose a little higher. Found the wetness pooled on his lower belly.

Giggles, soft as wind.

Chiming bells.

Roland opened his eyes the tiniest crack and looked up at the ancient faces laughing down at him in the light of their candles—glittering eyes, yellow cheeks, hanging teeth that jutted over lower lips. Sister Michela and Sister Louise appeared to have grown goatees, but of course that wasn't the darkness of hair but of the bearded man's blood.

Mary's hand was cupped. She passed it from Sister to Sister; each licked from her palm in the candlelight.

Roland closed his eyes all the way and waited for them to be gone. Eventually they were.

I'll never sleep again, he thought, and was five minutes later lost to himself and the world.

V. Sister Mary. A Message. A Visit from Ralph. Norman's Fate. Sister Mary Again.

When Roland awoke, it was full daylight, the silk roof overhead a bright white and billowing in a mild breeze. The doctor-bugs were singing contentedly. Beside him on his left, Norman was heavily asleep with his head turned so far to one side that his stubbly cheek rested on his shoulder.

Roland and John Norman were the only ones here. Farther down on their side of the infirmary, the bed where the bearded man had been was empty, its top sheet pulled up and neatly tucked in, the pillow neatly nestled in a crisp white case. The complication of slings in which his body had rested was gone.

Roland remembered the candles—the way their glow had combined and streamed up in a column, illuminating the Sisters as they gathered around the bearded man. Giggling. Their damned bells jingling.

Now, as if summoned by his thoughts, came Sister Mary, gliding along rapidly with Sister Louise in her wake. Louise bore a tray, and looked nervous. Mary was frowning, obviously not in good temper.

To be grumpy after you've fed so well? Roland thought. *Fie, Sister.*

She reached the gunslinger's bed and looked down at him. "I have little to thank ye for, sai," she said with no preamble.

"Have I asked for your thanks?" he responded in a voice that sounded as dusty and little-used as the pages of an old book.

She took no notice. "Ye've made one who was only impudent and restless with her place outright rebellious. Well, her mother was the same way, and died of it not long after returning Jenna to her proper place. Raise your hand, thankless man."

"I can't. I can't move at all."

"Oh, cully! Haven't you heard it said 'fool not your mother 'less she's out of face'? I know pretty well what ye can and can't do. Now raise your hand."

Roland raised his right hand, trying to suggest more effort than it actually took. He thought that this morning he might be strong enough to slip free

of the slings . . . but what then? Any real walking would be beyond him for hours yet, even without another dose of "medicine" . . . and behind Sister Mary, Sister Louise was taking the cover from a fresh bowl of soup. As Roland looked at it, his stomach rumbled.

Big Sister heard and smiled a bit. "Even lying in bed builds an appetite in a strong man, if it's done long enough. Wouldn't you say so, Jason, brother of John?"

"My name is James. As you well know, Sister."

"Do I?" She laughed angrily. "Oh, la! And if I whipped your little sweetheart hard enough and long enough—until the blood jumped out her back like drops of sweat, let us say—should I not whip a different name out of her? Or didn't ye trust her with it, during your little talk?"

"Touch her and I'll kill you."

She laughed again. Her face shimmered; her firm mouth turned into something that looked like a dying jellyfish. "Speak not of killing to us, cully; lest we speak of it to you."

"Sister, if you and Jenna don't see eye to eye, why not release her from her vows and let her go her course?"

"Such as us can never be released from our vows, nor be let go. Her mother tried and then came back, her dying and the girl sick. Why, it was we nursed Jenna back to health after her mother was nothing but dirt in the breeze the blows out toward End-World, and how little she thanks us! Besides, she bears the Dark Bells, the *sigul* of our sisterhood. Of our *ka-tet*. Now eat—yer belly says ye're hungry!''

Sister Louise offered the bowl, but her eyes kept drifting to the shape the medallion made under the breast of his bed-dress. *Don't like it, do you?* Roland thought, and then remembered Louise by candlelight, the freighter's blood on her chin, her ancient eyes eager as she leaned forward to lick his spend from Sister Mary's hand.

He turned his head aside. ''I want nothing.''

''But ye're hungry!'' Louise protested. ''If'ee don't eat, James, how will'ee get'ee strength back?''

''Send Jenna. I'll eat what she brings.''

Sister Mary's frown was black. ''Ye'll see her no more. She's been released from Thoughtful House only on her solemn promise to double her time of meditation . . . and to stay out of infirmary. Now eat, James, or whoever ye are. Take what's in the soup, or we'll cut ye with knives and rub it in with flannel poultices. Either way, makes no difference to us. Does it, Louise?''

''Nar,'' Louise said. She still held out the bowl. Steam rose from it, and the good smell of chicken.

''But it might make a difference to you.'' Sister Mary grinned humorlessly, baring her unnaturally large teeth. "Flowing blood's risky around here. The doctors don't like it. It stirs them up."

It wasn't just the bugs that were stirred up at the sight of blood, and Roland knew it. He also knew he had no choice in the matter of the soup. He took the bowl from Louise and ate slowly. He would have given much to wipe out the look of satisfaction he saw on Sister Mary's face.

"Good," she said after he had handed the bowl back and she had peered inside to make sure it was completely empty. His hand thumped back into the sling which had been rigged for it, already too heavy to hold up. He could feel the world drawing away again.

Sister Mary leaned forward, the billowing top of her habit touching the skin of his left shoulder. He could smell her, an aroma both ripe and dry, and would have gagged if he'd had the strength.

"Have that foul gold thing off ye when yer strength comes back a little—put it in the pissoir under the bed. Where it belongs. For to be even this close to where it lies hurts my head and makes my throat close."

Speaking with enormous effort, Roland said, "If you want it, take it. How can I stop you, you bitch?"

Once more her frown turned her face into something like a thunderhead. He thought she would have slapped him, if she had dared touch him so close to where the medallion lay. Her ability to touch seemed to end above his waist, however.

"I think you had better consider the matter a little more fully," she said. "I can still have Jenna whipped, if I like. She bears the Dark Bells, but I am the Big Sister. Consider that very well."

She left. Sister Louise followed, casting one look—a strange combination of fright and lust—back over her shoulder.

Roland thought, *I must get out of here—I must.*

Instead, he drifted back to that dark place which wasn't quite sleep. Or perhaps he did sleep, at least for a while; perhaps he dreamed. Fingers once more caressed his fingers, and lips first kissed his ear and then whispered into it: "Look beneath your pillow, Roland . . . but let no one know I was here."

At some point after this, Roland opened his eyes again, half-expecting to see Sister Jenna's pretty young face hovering above him. And that comma of dark hair once more poking out from beneath her wimple. There was no one. The swags of silk overhead were at their brightest, and although it was impossible to tell the hours in here with any real accuracy, Roland guessed it to be around noon. Perhaps three hours since his second bowl of the Sisters' soup.

Beside him, John Norman still slept, his breath whistling out in faint, nasal snores.

Roland tried to raise his hand and slide it under

his pillow. The hand wouldn't move. He could wiggle the tips of his fingers, but that was all. He waited, calming his mind as well as he could, gathering his patience. Patience wasn't easy to come by. He kept thinking about what Norman had said—that there had been twenty survivors of the ambush . . . at least to start with. *One by one they went, until only me and that one down yonder was left. And now you.*

The girl wasn't here. His mind spoke in the soft, regretful tone of Alain, one of his old friends, dead these many years now. *She wouldn't dare, not with the others watching. That was only a dream you had.*

But Roland thought perhaps it had been more than a dream.

Some length of time later—the slowly shifting brightness overhead made him believe it had been about an hour—Roland tried his hand again. This time he was able to get it beneath his pillow. This was puffy and soft, tucked snugly into the wide sling that supported the gunslinger's neck. At first he found nothing, but as his fingers worked their slow way deeper, they touched what felt like a stiffish bundle of thin rods.

He paused, gathering a little more strength (every movement was like swimming in glue), and then burrowed deeper. It felt like a dead bouquet. Wrapped around it was what felt like a ribbon.

Roland looked around to make sure the ward was still empty and Norman still asleep, then drew out what was under the pillow. It was six brittle stems of fading green with brownish reed heads at the tops. They gave off a strange, yeasty aroma that made Roland think of early-morning begging expeditions to the Great House kitchens as a child—forays he had usually made with Cuthbert. The reeds were tied with a wide white silk ribbon, and smelled like burned toast. Beneath the ribbon was a fold of cloth. Like everything else in this cursed place, it seemed, the cloth was of silk.

Roland was breathing hard and could feel drops of sweat on his brow. Still alone, though—good. He took the scrap of cloth and unfolded it. Printed painstakingly in blurred charcoal letters was this message:

NIBBLE HEDS. ONCE EACH HOUR. TOO
MUCH, CRAMPS OR DETH.
TOMORROW NITE. CAN'T BE SOONER.
BE CAREFUL!

No explanation, but Roland supposed none was needed. Nor did he have any option; if he remained here, he would die. All they had to do was have the medallion off him, and he felt sure Sister Mary was smart enough to figure a way to do that.

He nibbled at one of the dry reed heads. The taste was nothing like the toast they had begged from the kitchen as boys; it was bitter in his throat and hot in his stomach. Less than a minute after his nibble, his heart rate had doubled. His muscles awakened, but not in a pleasant way, as after good sleep; they felt first trembly and then hard, as if they were gathered into knots. This feeling passed rapidly, and his heartbeat was back to normal before Norman stirred awake an hour or so later, but he understood why Jenna's note had warned him not to take more than a nibble at a time—this was very powerful stuff.

He slipped the bouquet of reeds back under the pillow, being careful to brush away the few crumbles of vegetable matter which had dropped to the sheet. Then he used the ball of his thumb to blur the painstaking charcoaled words on the bit of silk. When he was finished, there was nothing on the square but meaningless smudges. The square he also tucked back under his pillow.

When Norman awoke, he and the gunslinger spoke briefly of the young scout's home—Delain, it was, sometimes known jestingly as Dragon's Lair, or Liar's Heaven. All tall tales were said to originate in Delain. The boy asked Roland to take his medallion and that of his brother home to their parents, if Roland was able, and explain as well as he could what had happened to James and John, sons of Jesse.

"You'll do all that yourself," Roland said.

"No." Norman tried to raise his hand, perhaps to scratch his nose, and was unable to do even that. The hand rose perhaps six inches, then fell back to the counterpane with a small thump. "I think not. It's a pity for us to have run up against each other this way, you know—I like you."

"And I you, John Norman. Would that we were better met."

"Aye. When not in the company of such fascinating ladies."

He dropped off to sleep again soon after. Roland never spoke with him again . . . although he certainly heard from him. Yes. Roland was lying above his bed, shamming sleep, as John Norman screamed his last.

Sister Michela came with his evening soup just as Roland was getting past the shivery muscles and galloping heartbeat that resulted from his second nibble of brown reed. Michela looked at his flushed face with some concern, but had to accept his assurances that he did not feel feverish; she couldn't bring herself to touch him and judge the heat of his skin for herself—the medallion held her away.

With the soup was a popkin. The bread was leathery and the meat inside it tough, but Roland demolished it greedily, just the same. Michela watched with a complacent smile, hands folded in front of her, nodding from time to time. When he had finished the soup, she took the bowl back from him carefully, making sure their fingers did not touch.

"Ye're healing," she said. "Soon you'll be on yer way, and we'll have just yer memory to keep, Jim."

"Is that true?" he asked quietly.

She only looked at him, touched her tongue against her upper lip, giggled, and departed. Roland closed his eyes and lay back against his pillow, feeling lethargy steal over him again. Her speculative eyes . . . her peeping tongue. He had seen women look at roast chickens and joints of mutton that same way, calculating when they might be done.

His body badly wanted to sleep, but Roland held on to wakefulness for what he judged was an hour, then worked one of the reeds out from under the pillow. With a fresh infusion of their "can't-move medicine" in his system, this took an enormous effort, and he wasn't sure he could have done it at all, had he not separated this one reed from the ribbon holding the others. Tomorrow night, Jenna's note had said. If that meant escape, the idea seemed preposterous. The way he felt now, he might be lying in this bed until the end of the age.

He nibbled. Energy washed into his system,

clenching his muscles and racing his heart, but the burst of vitality was gone almost as soon as it came, buried beneath the Sisters' stronger drug. He could only hope . . . and sleep.

When he woke it was full dark, and he found he could move his arms and legs in their network of slings almost naturally. He slipped one of the reeds out from beneath his pillow and nibbled cautiously. She had left half a dozen, and the first two were now almost entirely consumed.

The gunslinger put the stem back under the pillow, then began to shiver like a wet dog in a downpour. *I took too much,* he thought. *I'll be lucky not to convulse—*

His heart, racing like a runaway engine. And then, to make matters worse, he saw candlelight at the far end of the aisle. A moment later he heard the rustle of their gowns and the whisk of their slippers.

Gods, why now? They'll see me shaking, they'll know—

Calling on every bit of his willpower and control, Roland closed his eyes and concentrated on stilling his jerking limbs. If only he had been in bed instead of in these cursed slings, which seemed to tremble as if with their own ague at every movement!

The Little Sisters drew closer. The light of their

candles bloomed red within his closed eyelids. To-night they were not giggling, nor whispering among themselves. It was not until they were al-most on top of him that Roland became aware of the stranger in their midst—a creature that breathed through its nose in great, slobbery gasps of mixed air and snot.

The gunslinger lay with his eyes closed, the gross twitches and jumps of his arms and legs un-der control, but with his muscles still knotted and crampy, thrumming beneath the skin. Anyone who looked at him closely would see at once that some-thing was wrong with him. His heart was larruping away like a horse under the whip, surely they must see—

But it wasn't him they were looking at—not yet, at least.

"Have it off him," Mary said. She spoke in a bastardized version of the low speech Roland could barely understand. "Then t'other 'un. Go on, Ralph."

"U'se has whik-sky?" the slobberer asked, his dialect even heavier than Mary's. "U'se has 'backky?"

"Yes, yes, plenty whiskey and plenty smoke, but not until you have these wretched things off!" Im-patient. Perhaps afraid, as well.

Roland cautiously rolled his head to the left and cracked his eyelids open.

Five of the six Little Sisters of Eluria were clustered around the far side of the sleeping John Norman's bed, their candles raised to cast their light upon him. It also cast light upon their own faces, faces which would have given the strongest man nightmares. Now, in the ditch of the night, their glamours were set aside, and they were but ancient corpses in voluminous habits.

Sister Mary had one of Roland's guns in her hand. Looking at her holding it, Roland felt a bright flash of hate for her, and promised himself she would pay for her temerity.

The thing standing at the foot of the bed, strange as it was, looked almost normal in comparison with the Sisters. It was one of the green folk. Roland recognized Ralph at once. He would be a long time forgetting that bowler hat.

Now Ralph walked slowly around to the side of Norman's bed closest to Roland, momentarily blocking the gunslinger's view of the Sisters. The mutie went all the way to Norman's head, however, clearing the hags to Roland's slitted view once more.

Norman's medallion lay exposed—the boy had perhaps wakened enough to take it out of his bed-dress, hoping it would protect him better so. Ralph picked it up in his melted-tallow hand. The Sisters watched eagerly in the glow of their candles as the green man stretched it to the end of its chain . . . and then put it down again. Their faces drooped in disappointment.

"Don't care for such as that," Ralph said in his clotted voice. "Want whik-sky! Want 'backky!'"

"You shall have it," Sister Mary said. "Enough for you and all your verminous clan. But first, you must have that horrid thing off him! Off both of them! Do you understand? And you shan't tease us."

"Or what?" Ralph asked. He laughed. It was a choked and gargly sound, the laughter of a man dying from some evil sickness of the throat and lungs, but Roland still liked it better than the giggles of the Sisters. "Or what, Sisser Mary, you'll drink my bluid? My bluid'd drop'ee dead where'ee stand, and glowing in the dark!"

Mary raised the gunslinger's revolver and pointed it at Ralph. "Take that wretched thing, or you die where *you* stand."

"And die after I've done what you want, likely."

Sister Mary said nothing to that. The others peered at him with their black eyes.

Ralph lowered his head, appearing to think. Roland suspected his friend Bowler Hat *could* think, too. Sister Mary and her cohorts might not believe that, but Ralph *had* to be trig to have survived as long as he had. But of course when he came here, he hadn't considered Roland's guns.

"Smasher was wrong to give them shooters to you," he said at last. "Give 'em and not tell me. Did u'se give him whik-sky? Give him 'backky?"

"That's none o' yours," Sister Mary replied. "You have that goldpiece off the boy's neck right now, or I'll put one of yonder man's bullets in what's left of yer brain."

"All right," Ralph said. "Just as you wish, sai."

Once more he reached down and took the gold medallion in his melted fist. That he did slow; what happened after, happened fast. He snatched it away, breaking the chain and flinging the gold heedlessly into the dark. With his other hand he reached down, sank his long and ragged nails into John Norman's neck, and tore it open.

Blood flew from the hapless boy's throat in a jetting, heart-driven gush more black than red in the candlelight, and he made a single bubbly cry. The women screamed—but not in horror. They screamed as women do in a frenzy of excitement. The green man was forgotten; Roland was forgotten; all was forgotten save the life's blood pouring out of John Norman's throat.

They dropped their candles. Mary dropped Roland's revolver in the same hapless, careless fashion. The last the gunslinger saw as Ralph darted away into the shadows (whiskey and tobacco another time, wily Ralph must have thought; tonight he had best concentrate on saving his own life) was the Sisters bending forward to catch as much of the flow as they could before it dried up.

Roland lay in the dark, muscles shivering, heart pounding, listening to the harpies as they fed on the boy lying in the bed next to his own. It seemed to go on forever, but at last they had done with him. The Sisters relit their candles and left, murmuring.

When the drug in the soup once more got the better of the drug in the reeds, Roland was grateful . . . yet for the first time since he'd come here, his sleep was haunted.

In his dream he stood looking down at the bloated body in the town trough, thinking of a line in the book marked REGISTRY OF MISDEEDS AND REDRESS. *Green folk sent hence,* it had read, and perhaps the green folk *had* been sent hence, but then a worse tribe had come. The Little Sisters of Eluria, they called themselves. And a year hence, they might be the Little Sisters of Tejuas, or of Kambero, or some other far western village. They came with their bells and their bugs . . . from where? Who knew? Did it matter?

A shadow fell beside his on the scummy water of the trough. Roland tried to turn and face it. He couldn't; he was frozen in place. Then a green hand grasped his shoulder and whirled him about. It was Ralph. His bowler hat was cocked back on his head; John Norman's medallion, now red with blood, hung around his neck.

"Booh!" cried Ralph, his lips stretching in a toothless grin. He raised a big revolver with worn sandalwood grips. He thumbed the hammer back—

—and Roland jerked awake, shivering all over, dressed in skin both wet and icy cold. He looked at the bed on his left. It was empty, the sheet pulled up and tucked about neatly, the pillow resting above it in its snowy sleeve. Of John Norman there was no sign. It might have been empty for years, that bed.

Roland was alone now. Gods help him, he was the last patient of the Little Sisters of Eluria, those sweet and patient hospitalers. The last human being still alive in this terrible place, the last with warm blood flowing in his veins.

Roland, lying suspended, gripped the gold medallion in his fist and looked across the aisle at the long row of empty beds. After a little while, he brought one of the reeds out from beneath his pillow and nibbled at it.

When Mary came fifteen minutes later, the gunslinger took the bowl she brought with a show of weakness he didn't really feel. Porridge instead of soup this time . . . but he had no doubt the basic ingredient was still the same.

"How well ye look this morning, sai," Big Sister said. She looked well herself—there were no shimmers to give away the ancient *wampir* hiding inside her. She had supped well, and her meal had firmed her up. Roland's stomach rolled over at the thought. "Ye'll be on yer pins in no time, I'll warrant."

"That's shit," Roland said, speaking in an ill-natured growl. "Put me on my pins and you'd be picking me up off the floor directly after. I've started to wonder if you're not putting something in the food."

She laughed merrily at that. "La, you lads! Always eager to blame yer weakness on a scheming woman! How scared of us ye are—aye, way down in yer little boys' hearts, how scared ye are!"

"Where's my brother? I dreamed there was a commotion about him in the night, and now I see his bed's empty."

Her smile narrowed. Her eyes glittered. "He came over fevery and pitched a fit. We've taken him to Thoughtful House, which has been home to contagion more than once in its time."

To the grave is where you've taken him, Roland

thought. *Mayhap that is a Thoughtful House, but little would you know it, sai, one way or another.*

"I know ye're no brother to that boy," Mary said, watching him eat. Already Roland could feel the stuff hidden in the porridge draining his strength once more. "*Sigul* or no *sigul*, I know ye're no brother to him. Why do you lie? 'Tis a sin against God."

"What gives you such an idea, sai?" Roland asked, curious to see if she would mention the guns.

"Big Sister knows what she knows. Why not 'fess up, Jimmy? Confession's good for the soul, they say."

"Send me Jenna to pass the time, and perhaps I'd tell you much," Roland said.

The narrow bone of smile on Sister Mary's face disappeared like chalk-writing in a rainstorm. "Why would ye talk to such as her?"

"She's passing fair," Roland said. "Unlike some."

Her lips pulled back from her overlarge teeth. "Ye'll see her no more, cully. Ye've stirred her up, so you have, and I won't have that."

She turned to go. Still trying to appear weak and hoping he would not overdo it (acting was never his forte), Roland held out the empty porridge bowl. "Do you not want to take this?"

"Put it on your head and wear it as a nightcap, for all of me. Or stick it in your ass. You'll talk before I'm done with ye, cully—talk till I bid you shut up and then beg to talk some more!"

On this note she swept regally away, hands lifting the front of her skirt off the floor. Roland had heard that such as she couldn't go about in daylight, and that part of the old tales was surely a lie. Yet another part was almost true, it seemed: a fuzzy, amorphous shape kept pace with her, running along the row of empty beds to her right, but she cast no real shadow at all.

VI. Jenna. Sister Coquina. Tamra, Michela, Louise. The Cross-Dog. What Happened in the Sage.

That was one of the longest days of Roland's life. He dozed, but never deeply; the reeds were doing their work, and he had begun to believe that he might, with Jenna's help, actually get out of here. And there was the matter of his guns, as well— perhaps she might be able to help there, too.

He passed the slow hours thinking of old times— of Gilead and his friends, of the riddling he had almost won at one Wide Earth Fair. In the end another had taken the goose, but he'd had his chance, aye. He thought of his mother and father; he thought of Abel Vannay, who had limped his way through a life of gentle goodness, and Eldred Jonas, who had limped his way through a life of evil . . . until Roland had blown him loose of his saddle, one fine desert day.

He thought, as always, of Susan.

If you love me, then love me, she'd said . . . and so he had.

So he had.

In this way the time passed. At rough hourly intervals, he took one of the reeds from beneath his pillow and nibbled it. Now his muscles didn't tremble so badly as the stuff passed into his system, nor his heart pound so fiercely. The medicine in the reeds no longer had to battle the Sisters' medicine so fiercely, Roland thought; the reeds were winning.

The diffused brightness of the sun moved across the white silk ceiling of the ward, and at last the dimness which always seemed to hover at bed-level began to rise. The long room's western wall bloomed with the rose-melting-to-orange shades of sunset.

It was Sister Tamra who brought him his dinner that night—soup and another popkin. She also laid a desert lily beside his hand. She smiled as she did it. Her cheeks were bright with color. All of them were bright with color today, like leeches that had gorged until they were full almost to bursting.

"From your admirer, Jimmy," she said. "She's so sweet on ye! The lily means 'Do not forget my promise.' What has she promised ye, Jimmy, brother of Johnny?"

"That she'd see me again, and we'd talk."

Tamra laughed so hard that the bells lining her forehead jingled. She clasped her hands together in a perfect ecstasy of glee. "Sweet as honey! Oh, yes!" She bent her smiling gaze on Roland. "It's sad such a promise can never be kept. Ye'll never see her again, pretty man." She took the bowl. "Big Sister has decided." She stood up, still smiling. "Why not take that ugly gold *sigul* off?"

"I think not."

"Yer brother took his off—look!" She pointed, and Roland spied the gold medallion lying far down the aisle, where it had landed when Ralph threw it.

Sister Tamra looked at him, still smiling.

"He decided it was part of what was making him sick, and cast it away. Ye'd do the same, were ye wise."

Roland repeated, "I think not."

"So," she said dismissively, and left him alone with the empty beds glimmering in the thickening shadows.

Roland hung on, in spite of growing sleepiness,

until the hot colors bleeding across the infirmary's western wall had cooled to ashes. Then he nibbled one of the reeds and felt strength—real strength, not a jittery, heart-thudding substitute—bloom in his body. He looked toward where the castaway medallion gleamed in the last light and made a silent promise to John Norman: he would take it with the other one to Norman's kin, if *ka* chanced that he should encounter them in his travels.

Feeling completely easy in his mind for the first time that day, the gunslinger dozed. When he awoke it was full dark. The doctor-bugs were singing with extraordinary shrillness. He had taken one of the reeds out from under the pillow and had begun to nibble on it when a cold voice said, "So—Big Sister was right. Ye've been keeping secrets."

Roland's heart seemed to stop dead in his chest. He looked around and saw Sister Coquina getting to her feet. She had crept in while he was dozing and hidden under the bed on his right side to watch him.

"Where did ye get that?" she asked. "Was it—"

"He got it from me."

Coquina whirled about. Jenna was walking down the aisle toward them. Her habit was gone. She still wore her wimple with its forehead-fringe of bells, but its hem rested on the shoulders of a simple checkered shirt. Below this she wore jeans and scuffed desert boots. She had something in her hands. It was too dark for Roland to be sure, but he thought—

"*You*," Sister Coquina whispered with infinite hate. "When I tell Big Sister—"

"You'll tell no one anything," Roland said.

If he had planned his escape from the slings that entangled him, he no doubt would have made a bad business of it, but, as always, the gunslinger did best when he thought least. His arms were free in a moment; so was his left leg. His right caught at the ankle, however, twisting, hanging him up with his shoulders on the bed and his leg in the air.

Coquina turned on him, hissing like a cat. Her lips pulled back from teeth that were needle-sharp. She rushed at him, her fingers splayed. The nails at the ends of them looked sharp and ragged.

Roland clasped the medallion and shoved it out toward her. She recoiled from it, still hissing, and whirled back to Sister Jenna in a flare of white skirt. "I'll do for ye, ye interfering trull!" she cried in a low, harsh voice.

Roland struggled to free his leg and couldn't. It was firmly caught, the shitting sling actually wrapped around the ankle somehow, like a noose.

Jenna raised her hands, and he saw he had been right: it was his revolvers she had brought, hol-

stered and hanging from the two old gunbelts he had worn out of Gilead after the last burning.

"Shoot her, Jenna! Shoot her!"

Instead, still holding the holstered guns up, Jenna shook her head as she had on the day when Roland had persuaded her to push back her wimple so he could see her hair. The bells rang with a sharpness that seemed to go into the gunslinger's head like a spike.

The Dark Bells. The sigul *of their* ka-tet. *What—*

The sound of the doctor-bugs rose to a shrill, reedy scream that was eerily like the sound of the bells Jenna wore. Nothing sweet about them now. Sister Coquina's hands faltered on their way to Jenna's throat; Jenna herself had not so much as flinched or blinked her eyes.

"No," Coquina whispered. "You *can't*!"

"I *have*," Jenna said, and Roland saw the bugs. Descending from the legs of the bearded man, he'd observed a battalion. What he saw coming from the shadows now was an army to end all armies; had they been men instead of insects, there might have been more than all the men who had ever carried arms in the long and bloody history of Mid-World.

Yet the sight of them advancing down the boards of the aisle was not what Roland would always remember, nor what would haunt his dreams for a year or more; it was the way they coated the *beds*. These were turning black two by two on both sides of the aisle, like pairs of dim rectangular lights going out.

Coquina shrieked and began to shake her own head, to ring her own bells. The sound they made was thin and pointless compared with the sharp ringing of the Dark Bells.

Still the bugs marched on, darkening the floor, blacking out the beds.

Jenna darted past the shrieking Sister Coquina, dropped Roland's guns beside him, then yanked the twisted sling straight with one hard pull. Roland slid his leg free.

"Come," she said. "I've started them, but staying them could be a different thing."

Now Sister Coquina's shrieks were not of horror but of pain. The bugs had found her.

"Don't look," Jenna said, helping Roland to his feet. He thought that never in his life had he been so glad to be upon them. "Come. We must be quick—she'll rouse the others. I've put your boots and clothes aside up the path that leads away from here—I carried as much as I could. How are ye? Are ye strong?"

"Thanks to you." How long he would stay strong Roland didn't know . . . and right now it wasn't a question that mattered. He saw Jenna snatch up two of the reeds—in his struggle to escape the slings, they had scattered all over the head of the bed—and then they were hurrying up the aisle, away from the bugs and from Sister Coquina, whose cries were now failing.

Roland buckled on his guns and tied them down without breaking stride.

They passed only three beds on each side before reaching the flap of the tent . . . and it *was* a tent, he saw, not a vast pavilion. The silk walls and ceiling were fraying canvas, thin enough to let in the light of a three-quarters Kissing Moon. And the beds weren't beds at all, but only a double row of shabby cots.

He turned and saw a black, writhing hump on the floor where Sister Coquina had been. At the sight of her, Roland was struck by an unpleasant thought.

"I forgot John Norman's medallion!" A keen sense of regret—almost of mourning—went through him like wind.

Jenna reached into the pocket of her jeans and brought it out. It glimmered in the moonlight.

"I picked it up off the floor."

He didn't know which made him gladder—the sight of the medallion or the sight of it in her hand. It meant she wasn't like the others.

Then, as if to dispel that notion before it got too firm a hold on him, she said, "Take it, Roland—I can hold it no more." And, as he took it, he saw unmistakable marks of charring on her fingers.

He took her hand and kissed each burn.

"Thankee-sai," she said, and he saw she was crying. "Thankee, dear. To be kissed so.is lovely, worth every pain. Now . . ."

Roland saw her eyes shift, and followed them. Here were bobbing lights descending a rocky path. Beyond them he saw the building where the Little Sisters had been living—not a convent but a ruined *hacienda* that looked a thousand years old. There were three candles; as they drew closer, Roland saw that there were only three sisters. Mary wasn't among them.

He drew his guns.

"Oooo, it's a gunslinger-man he is!" Louise.

"A *scary* man!" Michela.

"And he's found his ladylove as well as his shooters!" Tamra.

"His slut-whore!" Louise.

Laughing angrily. Not afraid . . . at least, not of *his* weapons.

"Put them away," Jenna told him, and when she looked, saw that he already had.

The others, meanwhile, had drawn closer.

"Ooo, see, she cries!" Tamra.

"Doffed her habit, she has!" Michela. "Perhaps it's her broken vows she cries for."

"Why such tears, pretty?" Louise.

"Because he kissed my fingers where they were

burned," Jenna said. "I've never been kissed before. It made me cry."

"Ooooo!"

"*Luv*-ly!"

"Next he'll stick his thing in her! Even *luv*-lier!"

Jenna bore their japes with no sign of anger. When they were done, she said, "I'm going with him. Stand aside."

They gaped at her, counterfeit laughter disappearing in shock.

"No!" Louise whispered. "Are ye mad? Ye know what'll happen!"

"No, and neither do you," Jenna said. "Besides, I care not." She half-turned and held her hand out to the mouth of the ancient hospital tent. It was a faded olive-drab in the moonlight, with an old red cross drawn on its roof. Roland wondered how many towns the Sisters had been to with this tent, which was so small and plain on the outside, so huge and gloriously dim on the inside. How many towns and over how many years.

Now, cramming the mouth of it in a black, shiny tongue, were the doctor-bugs. They had stopped their singing. Their silence was somehow terrible.

"Stand aside or I'll have them on ye," Jenna said.

"Ye never would!" Sister Michela cried in a low, horrified voice.

"Aye. I've already set them on Sister Coquina. She's a part of their medicine, now."

Their gasp was like cold wind passing through dead trees. Nor was all of that dismay directed toward their own precious hides. What Jenna had done was clearly far outside their reckoning.

"Then you're damned," Sister Tamra said.

"Such ones to speak of damnation! Stand aside."

They did. Roland walked past them and they shrank away from him . . . but they shrank from her more.

"Damned?" he asked after they had skirted the *hacienda* and reached the path beyond it. The Kissing Moon glimmered above a tumbled scree of rocks. In its light Roland could see a small black opening low on the scarp. He guessed it was the cave the Sisters called Thoughtful House. "What did they mean, damned?"

"Never mind. All we have to worry about now is Sister Mary. I like it not that we haven't seen her."

She tried to walk faster, but he grasped her arm and turned her about. He could still hear the singing of the bugs, but faintly; they were leaving the place of the Sisters behind. Eluria, too, if the compass in his head was still working; he thought the town was in the other direction. The husk of the town, he amended.

"Tell me what they meant."

"Perhaps nothing. Ask me not, Roland—what good is it? 'Tis done, the bridge burned. I can't go back. Nor would if I could." She looked down, biting her lip, and when she looked up again, Roland saw fresh tears falling on her cheeks. "I have supped with them. There were times when I couldn't help it, no more than you could help drinking their wretched soup, no matter if you knew what was in it."

Roland remembered John Norman saying *A man has to eat . . . a woman, too.* He nodded.

"I'd go no further down that road. If there's to be damnation, let it be of my choosing, not theirs. My mother meant well by bringing me back to them, but she was wrong." She looked at him shyly and fearfully . . . but met his eyes. "I'd go beside ye on yer road, Roland of Gilead. For as long as I may, or as long as ye'd have me."

"You're welcome to your share of my way," he said. "And I am—"

Blessed by your company, he would have finished, but before he could, a voice spoke from the tangle of moonshadow ahead of them, where the path at last climbed out of the rocky, sterile valley in which the Little Sisters had practiced their glamours.

"It's a sad duty to stop such a pretty elopement, but stop it I must."

Sister Mary came from the shadows. Her fine white habit with its bright red rose had reverted to what it really was: the shroud of a corpse. Caught, hooded in its grimy folds, was a wrinkled, sagging face from which two black eyes stared. They looked like rotted dates. Below them, exposed by the thing's smile, four great incisors gleamed.

Upon the stretched skin of Sister Mary's forehead, bells tinkled . . . but not the Dark Bells, Roland thought. There was that.

"Stand clear," Jenna said. "Or I'll bring the *can tam* on ye."

"No," Sister Mary said, stepping closer, "ye won't. They'll not stray so far from the others. Shake your head and ring those damned bells until the clappers fall out, and still they'll never come."

Jenna did as bid, shaking her head furiously from side to side. The Dark Bells rang piercingly, but without that extra, almost psychic tone-quality that had gone through Roland's head like a spike. And the doctor-bugs—what Big Sister had called the *can tam*—did not come.

Smiling ever more broadly (Roland had an idea Mary herself hadn't been completely sure they wouldn't come until the experiment was made), the corpse-woman closed in on them, seeming to float above the ground. Her eyes flicked toward him. "And put that away," she said.

Roland looked down and saw that one of his guns was in his hand. He had no memory of drawing it.

"Unless 'tis been blessed or dipped in some sect's holy wet—blood, water, semen—it can't harm such as I, gunslinger. For I am more shade than substance . . . yet still the equal to such as yerself, for all that."

She thought he would try shooting her, anyway; he saw it in her eyes. *Those shooters are all ye have*, her eyes said. *Without 'em, you might as well be back in the tent we dreamed around ye, caught up in our slings and awaiting our pleasure.*

Instead of shooting, he dropped the revolver back into its holster and launched himself at her with his hands out. Sister Mary uttered a scream that was mostly surprise, but it was not a long one; Roland's fingers clamped down on her throat and choked the sound off before it was fairly started.

The touch of her flesh was obscene—it seemed not just alive but *various* beneath his hands, as if it was trying to crawl away from him. He could feel it running like liquid, *flowing,* and the sensation was horrible beyond description. Yet he clamped down harder, determined to choke the life out of her.

Then there came a blue flash (not in the air, he would think later; that flash happened inside his head, a single stroke of lightning as she touched off some brief but powerful brainstorm), and his hands flew away from her neck. For one moment his dazzled eyes saw great wet gouges in her gray flesh—gouges in the shapes of his hands. Then he was flung backward, hitting the scree on his back and sliding, hitting his head on a jutting rock hard enough to provoke a second, lesser, flash of light.

"Nay, my pretty man," she said, grimacing at him, laughing with those terrible dull eyes of hers. "Ye don't choke such as I, and I'll take ye slow for'ee impertinence—cut ye shallow in a hundred places to refresh my thirst. First, though, I'll have this vowless girl . . . and I'll have those damned bells off her, in the bargain."

"Come and see if you can!" Jenna cried in a trembling voice, and shook her head from side to side. The Dark Bells rang mockingly, provokingly.

Mary's grimace of a smile fell away. "Oh, I can," she breathed. Her mouth yawned. In the moonlight, her fangs gleamed in her gums like bone needles poked through a red pillow. "I can and I—"

There was a growl from above them. It rose, then

splintered into a volley of snarling barks. Mary turned to her left, and in the moment before the snarling thing left the rock on which it was standing, Roland could clearly read the startled bewilderment on Big Sister's face.

It launched itself at her, only a dark shape against the stars, legs outstretched so it looked like some sort of weird bat, but even before it crashed into the woman, striking her in the chest above her half-raised arms and fastening its own teeth on her throat, Roland knew exactly what it was.

As the shape bore her over onto her back, Sister Mary uttered a gibbering shriek that went through Roland's head like the Dark Bells themselves. He scrambled to his feet, gasping. The shadowy thing tore at her, forepaws on either side of her head, rear paws planted on the grave-shroud above her chest, where the rose had been.

Roland grabbed Jenna, who was looking down at the fallen Sister with a kind of frozen fascination.

"Come on!" he shouted. "Before it decides it wants a bite of you, too!"

The dog took no notice of them as Roland pulled Jenna past. It had torn Sister Mary's head mostly off.

Her flesh seemed to be changing, somehow—decomposing, very likely—but whatever was happening, Roland did not want to see it. He didn't want Jenna to see it, either.

They half-walked, half-ran to the top of the ridge, and when they got there paused for breath in the moonlight, heads down, hands linked, both of them gasping harshly.

The growling and snarling below them had faded, but was still faintly audible when Sister Jenna raised her head and asked him, "What was it? You know—I saw it in your face. And how could it attack her? We all have power over animals, but she has—had—the most."

"Not over that one." Roland found himself recalling the unfortunate boy in the next bed. Norman hadn't known why the medallions kept the Sisters at arms' length—whether it was the gold or the God. Now Roland knew the answer. "It was a dog. Just a town-dog. I saw it in the square, before the green folk knocked me out and took me to the Sisters. I suppose the other animals that could run away *did* run away, but not that one. It had nothing to fear from the Little Sisters of Eluria, and somehow it knew it didn't. It bears the sign of the Jesus-man on its chest. Black fur on white. Just an accident of its birth, I imagine. In any case, it's done for her now. I knew it was lurking around. I heard it barking two or three times."

"Why?" Jenna whispered. "Why would it

come? Why would it stay? And why would it take on her as it did?''

Roland of Gilead responded as he ever had and ever would when such useless, mystifying questions were raised: "*Ka*. Come on. Let's get as far as we can from this place before we hide up for the day.''

As far as they could turned out to be eight miles at most . . . and probably, Roland thought as the two of them sank down in a patch of sweet-smelling sage beneath an overhang of rock, a good deal less. Five, perhaps. It was him slowing them down; or rather, it was the residue of the poison in the soup. When it was clear to him that he could not go farther without help, he asked her for one of the reeds. She refused, saying that the stuff in it might combine with the unaccustomed exercise to burst his heart.

"Besides," she said as they lay back against the embankment of the little nook they had found, "they'll not follow. Those that are left—Michela, Louise, Tamra—will be packing up to move on. They know to leave when the time comes; that's why the Sisters have survived as long as they have. As *we* have. We're strong in some ways, but weak in many more. Sister Mary forgot that. It was her arrogance that did for her as much as the cross-dog, I think.''

She had cached not just his boots and clothes beyond the top of the ridge, but the smaller of his two purses, as well. When she tried to apologize for not bringing his bedroll and the larger purse (she'd tried, she said, but they were simply too heavy), Roland hushed her with a finger to her lips. He thought it a miracle to have as much as he did. And besides (this he did not say, but perhaps she knew it, anyway), the guns were the only things that really mattered. The guns of his father, and his father before him, all the way back to the days of Arthur Eld, when dreams and dragons had still walked the earth.

"Will you be all right?" he asked her as they settled down. The moon had set, but dawn was still at least three hours away. They were surrounded by the sweet smell of the sage. A purple smell, he thought it then . . . and ever after. Already he could feel it forming a kind of magic carpet under him, which would soon float him away to sleep. He thought he had never been so tired.

"Roland, I know not." But even then, he thought she had known. Her mother had brought her back once; no mother would bring her back again. And she had eaten with the others, had taken the communion of the Sisters. *Ka* was a wheel; it was also a net from which none ever escaped.

But then he was too tired to think much of such

things . . . and what good would thinking have done, in any case? As she had said, the bridge was burned. Even if they were to return to the valley, Roland guessed they would find nothing but the cave the Sisters had called Thoughtful House. The surviving Sisters would have packed their tent of bad dreams and moved on, just a sound of bells and singing insects moving down the late night breeze.

He looked at her, raised a hand (it felt heavy), and touched the curl which once more lay across her forehead.

Jenna laughed, embarrassed. "That one always escapes. It's wayward. Like its mistress."

She raised her hand to poke it back in, but Roland took her fingers before she could. "It's beautiful," he said. "Black as night and as beautiful as forever."

He sat up—it took an effort; weariness dragged at his body like soft hands. He kissed the curl. She closed her eyes and sighed. He felt her trembling beneath his lips. The skin of her brow was very cool; the dark curve of the wayward curl like silk.

"Push back your wimple, as you did before," he said.

She did it without speaking. For a moment he only looked at her. Jenna looked back gravely, her eyes never leaving his. He ran his hands through her hair, feeling its smooth weight (like rain, he thought, rain with weight), then took her shoulders and kissed each of her cheeks. He drew back for a moment.

"Would ye kiss me as a man does a woman, Roland? On my mouth?"

"Aye."

And, as he had thought of doing as he lay caught in the silken infirmary tent, he kissed her lips. She kissed back with the clumsy sweetness of one who has never kissed before, except perhaps in dreams. Roland thought to make love to her then—it had been long and long, and she was beautiful—but he fell asleep instead, still kissing her.

He dreamed of the cross-dog, barking its way across a great open landscape. He followed, wanting to see the source of its agitation, and soon he did. At the far edge of that plain stood the Dark Tower, its smoky stone outlined by the dull orange ball of a setting sun, its fearful windows rising in a spiral. The dog stopped at the sight of it and began to howl.

Bells—peculiarly shrill and as terrible as doom—began to ring. Dark bells, he knew, but their tone was as bright as silver. At their sound, the dark windows of the Tower glowed with a deadly red light—the red of poisoned roses. A scream of unbearable pain rose in the night.

The dream blew away in an instant, but the scream remained, now unraveling to a moan. That part was real—as real as the Tower, brooding in its place at the very end of End-World. Roland came back to the brightness of dawn and the soft purple smell of desert sage. He had drawn both his guns, and was on his feet before he had fully realized he was awake.

Jenna was gone. Her boots lay empty beside his purse. A little distance from them, her jeans lay as flat as discarded snakeskins. Above them was her shirt. It was, Roland observed with wonder, still tucked into the pants. Beyond them was her empty wimple, with its fringe of bells lying on the powdery ground. He thought for a moment that they were ringing, mistaking the sound he heard at first.

Not bells but bugs. The doctor-bugs. They sang in the sage, sounding a bit like crickets, but far sweeter.

"Jenna?"

No answer . . . unless the bugs answered. For their singing suddenly stopped.

"Jenna?"

Nothing. Only the wind and the smell of the sage.

Without thinking about what he was doing (like playacting, reasoned thought was not his strong suit), he bent, picked up the wimple, and shook it. The Dark Bells rang.

For a moment there was nothing. Then a thousand small dark creatures came scurrying out of the sage, gathering on the broken earth. Roland thought of the battalion marching down the side of the freighter's bed and took a step back. Then he held his position. As, he saw, the bugs were holding theirs.

He believed he understood. Some of this understanding came from his memory of how Sister Mary's flesh had felt under his hands . . . how it had felt *various,* not one thing but many. Part of it was what she had said: *I have supped with them.* Such as them might never die . . . but they might *change.*

The insects trembled, a dark cloud of them blotting out the white, powdery earth.

Roland shook the bells again.

A shiver ran through them in a subtle wave, and then they began to form a shape. They hesitated as if unsure of how to go on, regrouped, began again. What they eventually made on the whiteness of the sand there between the blowing fluffs of lilac-colored sage was one of the Great Letters: the letter C.

Except it wasn't really a letter, the gunslinger saw; it was a curl.

They began to sing, and to Roland it sounded as if they were singing his name.

The bells fell from his unnerved hand, and when they struck the ground and chimed there, the mass of bugs broke apart, running in every direction. He thought of calling them back—ringing the bells again might do that—but to what purpose? To what end?

Ask me not, Roland. 'Tis done, the bridge burned.

Yet she had come to him one last time, imposing her will over a thousand various parts that should have lost the ability to think when the whole lost its cohesion . . . and yet she *had* thought, somehow—enough to make that shape. How much effort might that have taken?

They fanned wider and wider, some disappearing into the sage, some trundling up the sides of a rock overhang, pouring into the cracks where they would, mayhap, wait out the heat of the day.

They were gone. *She* was gone.

Roland sat down on the ground and put his hands over his face. He thought he might weep, but in time the urge passed; when he raised his head again, his eyes were as dry as the desert he would eventually come to, still following the trail of Walter, the man in black.

If there's to be damnation, she had said, *let it be of my choosing, not theirs.*

He knew a little about damnation himself . . . and he had an idea that the lessons, far from being done, were just beginning.

She had brought him the purse with his tobacco in it. He rolled a cigarette and smoked it hunkered over his knees. He smoked it down to a glowing roach, looking at her empty clothes the while, remembering the steady gaze of her dark eyes. Remembering the scorch-marks on her fingers from the chain of the medallion. Yet she had picked it up, because she had known he would want it; had dared that pain, and Roland now wore both around his neck.

When the sun was fully up, the gunslinger moved on west. He would find another horse eventually, or a mule, but for now he was content to walk. All that day he was haunted by a ringing, singing sound in his ears, a sound like bells. Several times he stopped and looked around, sure he would see a dark following shape flowing over the ground, chasing after as the shadows of our best and worst memories chase after, but no shape was ever there. He was alone in the low hill country west of Eluria.

Quite alone.

MAJIPOOR

〰

Robert Silverberg

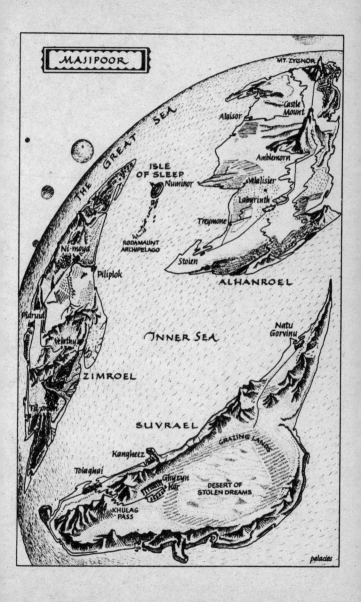

MAJIPOOR

MT. ZYGNOR

THE GREAT SEA

Alaisor

Castle Mount

ISLE OF SLEEP

Numinor

Amblemorn

Velalisier

Labyrinth

Treymone

RODAMAUNT ARCHIPELAGO

Stoien

ALHANROEL

Ni-moya

Piliplok

Piaruid

Velathy

Natu Gorvinu

INNER SEA

ZIMROEL

Til-omon

SUVRAEL

GRAZING LANDS

Kangheez

Tolaghai

Ghyzyn Kor

DESERT OF STOLEN DREAMS

KHULAG PASS

palacios

The giant world of Majipoor, with a diameter at least ten times as great as our own planet's, was settled in the distant past by colonists from Earth, who made a place for themselves amid the Piurivars, the intelligent native beings, whom the intruders from Earth called Shapeshifters or Metamorphs because of their ability to alter their bodily forms. Majipoor is an extraordinarily beautiful planet, with a largely benign climate, and is a place of astonishing zoological, botanical, and geographical wonders. Everything on Majipoor is large-scale—fantastic, marvelous.

Over the course of thousands of years, friction between the human colonists and the Piurivars eventually led to a lengthy war and the defeat of the natives, who were penned up in huge reservations in remote regions of the planet. During those years, also, species from various other worlds came to settle on Majipoor—the tiny gnomish Vroons, the great shaggy four-armed Skandars, the two-headed Su-Suheris race, and several more. Some of these— notably the Vroons and the Su-Suheris—were gifted with extrasensory mental powers that permitted them to practice various forms of wizardry. But throughout the thousands of years of Majipoor history the humans remained the dominant species. They flourished and expanded and eventually the human population of Majipoor came to number in the billions, mainly occupying huge and distinctive cities of ten to twenty million people.

The governmental system that evolved over those years was a kind of nonhereditary dual monarchy. The senior ruler, known as the Pontifex, selects his own junior ruler, the Coronal, when he comes to power. Technically the Coronal is regarded as the adoptive son of the Pontifex, and upon the death of the Pontifex takes his place on the senior throne, naming a new Coronal as his own successor. Both of these rulers make their homes on Alhanroel, the largest and most populous of Majipoor's three continents. The imperial residence of the Pontifex is in the lowest level of a vast subterranean city called the Labyrinth, from which he emerges only at rare intervals. The Coronal, by contrast, lives in an enormous castle at the summit of Castle Mount, a thirty-mile-high peak whose atmosphere is maintained in an eternal springtime by elaborate machinery. From time to time the Coronal descends from the opulence of the Castle to travel across the face of the world in a Grand Processional, an event designed to remind Majipoor of the might and power of its rulers. Such a journey, which in Majipoor's vast distances could take several years, invariably brings the Coronal to Zimroel, the second continent, a place of gigantic cities interspersed among tremendous rivers and great unspoiled forests. More rarely he goes to the torrid third continent in the south, Suvrael, largely a wasteland of Sahara-like deserts.

Two other functionaries became part of the Majipoor governmental system later on. The development of a method of worldwide telepathic communication made possible nightly sendings of oracular advice and occasional therapeutic counsel, which became the responsibility of the mother of the incumbent Coronal, under the title of Lady of the Isle of Sleep. Her headquarters are situated on an island of continental size midway between Alhanroel and Zimroel. Later, a second telepathic authority, the

King of Dreams, was set in place. He employs more powerful telepathic equipment in order to monitor and chastise criminals and other citizens whose behavior deviates from accepted Majipoor norms. This office is the hereditary property of the Barjazid family of Suvrael.

The first of the Majipoor novels, *Lord Valentine's Castle,* tells of a conspiracy that succeeds in overthrowing the legitimate Coronal, Lord Valentine, and replacing him with an impostor. Valentine, stripped of all his memories, is set loose in Zimroel to live the life of a wandering juggler, but gradually regains an awareness of his true role and launches a successful campaign to reclaim his throne. In the sequel, *Valentine Pontifex,* the now mature Valentine, a pacifist at heart, must deal with an uprising among the Metamorphs, who are determined to drive the hated human conquerors from their world at last. Valentine defeats them and restores peace with the help of the giant maritime beasts known as sea-dragons, whose intelligent powers were not previously suspected on Majipoor.

The story collection *Majipoor Chronicles* depicts scenes from many eras and social levels of Majipoor life, providing detailed insight into a number of aspects of the giant world not described in the novels. The short novel *The Mountains of Majipoor,* set five hundred years after Valentine's reign, carries the saga into the icy northlands, where a separate barbaric civilization has long endured. And the most recent of the Majipoor books, *Sorcerers of Majipoor,* begins a new trilogy set a thousand years prior to Valentine's time, in which the powers of sorcery and magic have become rife on Majipoor. The Coronal Lord Prestimion, after being displaced from his throne by the usurping son of the former Coronal with the assistance of mages and warlocks, leads his faction to victory in a civil war in which he too makes use of necromantic powers. The sequel, *Lord Prestimion,* shows him struggling to deal with the day-by-day problems of kingship in a world that has been immensely altered by the wizardry employed at the climax of the war.

The story presented here offers an episode from a period late in Valentine's reign as Pontifex, when the war against the Metamorphs has been over for some years but the process of reconciliation is still incomplete.

THE SEVENTH SHRINE

꧁꧂

Robert Silverberg

One last steep ridge of the rough, boulder-
strewn road lay between the royal party and
the descent into Velalisier Plain. Valentine, who
was leading the way, rode up over it and came to
a halt, looking down with amazement into the valley. The land that lay before him seemed to have
undergone a bewildering transformation since his
last visit. "Look there," the Pontifex said, be-
mused. "This place is always full of surprises, and
here is ours."

The broad shallow bowl of the arid plain spread
out below them. From this vantage point, a little
way east of the entrance to the archaeological site,
they should easily have been able to see a huge

field of sand-swept ruins. There had been a mighty city here once, that notorious Shapeshifter city where, in ancient times, so much dark history had been enacted, such monstrous sacrilege and blasphemy. But—surely it was just an illusion?—the sprawling zone of fallen buildings at the center of the plain was almost completely hidden now by a wondrous rippling body of water, pale pink along its rim and pearly gray at its middle: a great lake where no lake ever had been.

Evidently the other members of the royal party saw it too. But did they understand that it was simply a trick? Some fleeting combination of sunlight and dusty haze and the stifling midday heat must have created a momentary mirage above dead Velalisier, so that it seemed as if a sizable lagoon, of all improbable things, had sprung up in the midst of this harsh desert to engulf the dead city.

It began just a short distance beyond their vantage point and extended as far as the distant gray-blue wall of great stone monoliths that marked the city's western boundary. Nothing of Velalisier could be seen. None of the shattered and timeworn temples and palaces and basilicas, or the red basalt blocks of the arena, the great expanses of blue stone that had been the sacrificial platforms, the tents of the archaeologists who had been at work here at Valentine's behest since late last year. Only the six steep and narrow pyramids that were the tallest surviving structures of the prehistoric Metamorph capital were visible—their tips, at least, jutting out of the gray heart of the ostensible lake like a line of daggers fixed point-upward in its depths.

"Magic," murmured Tunigorn, the oldest of Valentine's boyhood friends, who held the post now of Minister of External Affairs at the Pontifical court. He drew a holy symbol in the air. Tunigorn had grown very superstitious, here in his later years.

"I think not," said Valentine, smiling. "Just an oddity of the light, I'd say."

And, just as though the Pontifex had conjured it up with some countermagic of his own, a lusty gust of wind came up from the north and swiftly peeled the haze away. The lake went with it, vanishing like the phantom it had been. Valentine and his companions found themselves now beneath a bare and merciless iron-blue sky, gazing down at the true Velalisier—that immense dreary field of stony rubble, that barren and incoherent tumble of dun-colored fragments and drab threadbare shards lying in gritty beds of wind-strewn sand, which was all that remained of the abandoned Metamorph metropolis of long ago.

"Well, now," said Tunigorn, "perhaps you were right, majesty. Magic or no, though, I liked it better the other way. It was a pretty lake, and these are ugly stones."

"There's nothing here to like at all, one way or another," said Duke Nascimonte of Ebersinul. He had come all the way from his great estate on the far side of the Labyrinth to take part in this expedition. "This is a sorry place and always has been. If I were Pontifex in your stead, your majesty, I'd throw a dam across the River Glayge and send a raging torrent this way, that would bury this accursed city and its whole history of abominations under two miles of water for all time to come."

Some part of Valentine could almost see the merit of that. It was easy enough to believe that the somber spells of antiquity still hovered here, that this was a territory where ominous enchantments held sway.

But of course Valentine could hardly take Nascimonte's suggestion seriously. "Drown the Metamorphs' sacred city, yes! By all means, let's do that," he said lightly. "Very fine diplomacy, Nascimonte. What a splendid way of furthering harmony between the races that would be!"

Nascimonte, a lean and hard-bitten man of eighty years, with keen sapphire eyes that blazed like fiery gems in his broad furrowed forehead, said pleasantly, "Your words tell us what we already know, majesty: that it's just as well for the world that you are Pontifex, not I. I lack your benign and merciful nature—especially, I must say, when it comes to the filthy Shapeshifters. I know you love them and would bring them up out of their degradation. But to me, Valentine, they are vermin and nothing but vermin. Dangerous vermin at that."

"Hush," said Valentine. He was still smiling, but he let a little annoyance show as well. "The Rebellion's long over. It's high time we put these old hatreds to rest forever."

Nascimonte's only response was a shrug.

Valentine turned away, looking again toward the ruins. Greater mysteries than that mirage awaited them down there. An event as grim and terrible as anything out of Velalisier's doleful past had lately occurred in this city of long-dead stones: a murder, no less.

Violent death at another's hands was no common thing on Majipoor. It was to investigate that murder that Valentine and his friends had journeyed to ancient Velalisier this day.

"Come," he said. "Let's be on our way."

He spurred his mount forward, and the others followed him down the stony road into the haunted city.

The ruins appeared much less dismal at close range than they had on either of Valentine's previous two visits. This winter's rains must have been heavier than usual, for wildflowers were blooming everywhere amidst the dark, dingy waste of ashen dunes and overturned building blocks. They dappled the gray gloominess with startling little bursts of yellow and red and blue and white that were almost musical in their emphatic effect. A host of fragile bright-winged kelebekkos flitted about among the blossoms, sipping at their nectar, and multitudes of tiny gnatlike ferushas moved about in thick swarms, forming broad misty patches in the air that glistened like silvery dust.

But more was happening here than the unfolding of flowers and the dancing of insects. As he made his descent into Velalisier, Valentine's imagination began to teem suddenly with strangenesses, fantasies, marvels. It seemed to him that inexplicable flickers of sorcery and wonder were arising just beyond the periphery of his vision. Sprites and visitations, singing wordlessly to him of Majipoor's infinite past, drifted upward from the broken edge-tilted slabs and capered temptingly about him, leaping to and fro over the porous, limy soil of the site's surface with frantic energy. A subtle shimmer of delicate jade-green iridescence that had not been apparent at a distance rose above everything, tinting the air: some effect of the hot noontime light striking a luminescent mineral in the rocks, he

supposed. It was a wondrous sight all the same, whatever its cause.

These unexpected touches of beauty lifted the Pontifex's mood. Which, ever since the news had reached him the week before of the savage and perplexing death of the distinguished Metamorph archaeologist Huukaminaan amidst these very ruins, had been uncharacteristically bleak. Valentine had had such high hopes for the work that was being done here to uncover and restore the old Shapeshifter capital; and this murder had stained everything.

The tents of his archaeologists came into view now, lofty ones gaily woven from broad strips of green, maroon, and scarlet cloth, billowing atop a low sandy plateau in the distance. Some of the excavators themselves, he saw, were riding toward him down the long rock-ribbed avenues on fat plodding mounts: about half a dozen of them, with chief archaeologist Magadone Sambisa at the head of the group.

"Majesty," she said, dismounting, making the elaborate sign of respect that one would make before a Pontifex. "Welcome to Velalisier."

Valentine hardly recognized her. It was only about a year since Magadone Sambisa had come before him in his chambers at the Labyrinth. He remembered a dynamic, confident, bright-eyed woman, sturdy and strapping, with rounded cheeks florid with life and vigor and glossy cascades of curling red hair tumbling down her back. She seemed oddly diminished now, haggard with fatigue, her shoulders slumped, her eyes dull and sunken, her face sallow and newly lined and no longer full. That great mass of hair had lost its sheen and bounce. He let his amazement show, only for an instant, but long enough for her to see it. She pulled herself upright immediately, trying, it seemed, to project some of her former vigor.

Valentine had intended to introduce her to Duke Nascimonte and Prince Mirigant and the rest of the visiting group. But before he could do it, Tunigorn came officially forward to handle the task.

There had been a time when citizens of Majipoor could not have any sort of direct conversation with the Pontifex. They were required then to channel all intercourse through the court official known as the High Spokesman. Valentine had quickly abolished that custom, and many another stifling bit of imperial etiquette. But Tunigorn, by nature conservative, had never been comfortable with those changes. He did whatever he could to preserve the traditional aura of sanctity in which Pontifices once had been swathed. Valentine found that amusing and charming and only occasionally irritating.

The welcoming party included none of the

Metamorph archaeologists connected with the expedition. Magadone Sambisa had brought just five human archaeologists and a Ghayrog with her. That seemed odd, to have left the Metamorphs elsewhere. Tunigorn formally repeated the archaeologists' names to Valentine, getting nearly every one garbled in the process. Then, and only then, did he step back and allow the Pontifex to have a word with her.

"The excavations," he said. "Tell me, have they been going well?"

"Quite well, majesty. Splendidly, in fact, until —*until*—" She made a despairing gesture: grief, shock, incomprehension, helplessness, all in a single poignant movement of her head and hands.

The murder must have been like a death in the family for her, for all of them here. A sudden and horrifying loss.

"*Until*, yes. I understand."

Valentine questioned her gently but firmly. Had there, he asked, been any important new developments in the investigation? Any clues discovered? Claims of responsibility for the killing? Were there any suspects at all? Had the archaeological party received any threats of further attacks?

But there was nothing new at all. Huukaminaan's murder had been an isolated event, a sudden, jarring, and unfathomable intrusion into the serene progress of work at the site. The slain Metamorph's body had been turned over to his own people for interment, she told him, and a shudder that she made an ineffectual effort to hide ran through the entire upper half of her body as she said it. The excavators were attempting now to put aside their distress over the killing and get on with their tasks.

The whole subject was plainly an uncomfortable one for her. She escaped from it as quickly as she could. "You must be tired from your journey, your majesty. Shall I show you to your quarters?"

Three new tents had been erected to house the Pontifex and his entourage. They had to pass through the excavation zone itself to reach them. Valentine was pleased to see how much progress had been made in clearing away the clusters of pernicious little ropy-stemmed weeds and tangles of woody vines that for so many centuries had been patiently at work pulling the blocks of stone one from another.

Along the way Magadone Sambisa poured forth voluminous streams of information about the city's most conspicuous features as though Valentine were a tourist and she his guide. Over here, the broken but still awesome aqueduct. There, the substantial jagged-sided oval bowl of the arena. And there, the grand ceremonial boulevard, paved with sleek greenish flagstones.

Shapeshifter glyphs were visible on those flag-stones even after the lapse of twenty thousand years, mysterious swirling symbols, carved deep into the stone. Not even the Shapeshifters them-selves were able to decipher them now.

The rush of archaeological and mythological mi-nutia came gushing from her with scarcely a pause for breath. There was a certain frantic, even des-perate, quality about it all, a sign of the uneasiness she must feel in the presence of the Pontifex of Majipoor. Valentine was accustomed enough to that sort of thing. But this was not his first visit to Velalisier and he was already familiar with much of what she was telling him. And she looked so weary, so depleted, that it troubled him to see her expending her energy in such needless outpourings.

But she would not stop. They were passing, now, a huge and very dilapidated edifice of gray stone that appeared ready to fall down if anyone should sneeze in its vicinity. "This is called the Palace of the Final King," she said. "Probably an erroneous name, but that's what the Piurivars call it, and for lack of a better one we do too."

Valentine noted her careful use of the Meta-morphs' own name for themselves. *Piurivars,* yes. University people tended to be very formal about that, always referring to the aboriginal folk of Ma-jipoor that way, never speaking of them as Metamorphs or Shapeshifters, as ordinary people tended to do. He would try to remember that.

As they came to the ruins of the royal palace she offered a disquisition on the legend of the mythical Final King of Piurivar antiquity, he who had presided over the atrocious act of defilement that had brought about the Metamorphs' ancient abandonment of their city. It was a story with which all of them were familiar. Who did not know that dreadful tale?

But they listened politely as she told of how, those many thousands of years ago, long before the first human settlers had come to live on Majipoor, the Metamorphs of Velalisier had in some fit of blind madness hauled two living sea-dragons from the ocean: intelligent beings of mighty size and extraordinary mental powers, whom the Metamorphs themselves had thought of as gods. Had dumped them down on these platforms, had cut them to pieces with long knives, had burned their flesh on a pyre before the Seventh Pyramid as a crazed offering to some even greater gods in whom the King and his subjects had come to believe.

When the simple folk of the outlying provinces heard of that orgy of horrendous massacre, so the legend ran, they rushed upon Velalisier and demolished the temple at which the sacrificial offering had been made. They put to death the Final

King and wrecked his palace, and drove the wicked citizens of the city forth into the wilderness, and smashed its aqueduct and put dams across the rivers that had supplied it with water, so that Velalisier would be thenceforth a deserted and accursed place, abandoned through all eternity to the lizards and spiders and jakkaboles of the fields.

Valentine and his companions moved on in silence when Magadone Sambisa was done with her narrative. The six sharply tapering pyramids that were Velalisier's best-known monuments came now into view, the nearest rising just beyond the courtyard of the Final King's palace, the other five set close together in a straight line stretching to the east. "There was a seventh, once," Magadone Sambisa said. "But the Piurivars themselves destroyed it just before they left here for the last time. Nothing was left but scattered rubble. We were about to start work there early last week, but that was when—when—" She faltered and looked away.

"Yes," said Valentine softly. "Of course."

The road now took them between the two colossal platforms fashioned from gigantic slabs of blue stone that were known to the modern-day Metamorphs as the Tables of the Gods. Even though they were abutted by the accumulated debris of two hundred centuries, they still rose nearly ten feet above the surrounding plain, and the area of their flat-topped surfaces would have been great enough to hold hundreds of people at a time.

In a low sepulchral tone Magadone Sambisa said, "Do you know what these are, your majesty?"

Valentine nodded. "The sacrificial altars, yes. Where the Defilement was carried out."

Magadone Sambisa said, "Indeed. It was also at this site that the murder of Huukaminaan happened. I could show you the place. It would take only a moment."

She indicated a staircase a little way down the road, made of big square blocks of the same blue stone as the platforms themselves. It gave access to the top of the western platform. Magadone Sambisa dismounted and scrambled swiftly up. She paused on the highest step to extend a hand to Valentine as though the Pontifex might be having difficulty in making the ascent, which was not the case. He was still almost as agile as he had been in his younger days. But he reached for her hand for courtesy's sake, just as she—deciding, maybe, that it would be impermissible for a commoner to make contact with the flesh of a Pontifex—began to pull it anxiously back. Valentine, grinning, leaned forward and took the hand anyway, and levered himself upward.

Old Nascimonte came bounding swiftly up just behind him, followed by Valentine's cousin and close counselor, Prince Mirigant, who had the little Vroonish wizard Autifon Deliamber riding on his shoulder. Tunigorn remained below. Evidently this place of ancient sacrilege and infamous slaughter was not for him.

The surface of the altar, roughened by time and pockmarked everywhere by clumps of scruffy weeds and encrustations of red and green lichen, stretched on and on before them, a stupendous expanse. It was hard to imagine how even a great multitude of Shapeshifters, those slender and seemingly boneless people, could ever have hauled so many tremendous blocks of stone into place.

Magadone Sambisa pointed to a marker of yellow tape in the form of a six-pointed star that was affixed to the stone a dozen feet or so away. "We found him here," she said. "Some of him, at any rate. And some here." There was another marker off to the left, about twenty feet farther on. "And here." A third star of yellow tape.

"They dismembered him?" Valentine said, appalled.

"Indeed. You can see the bloodstains all about." She hesitated for an instant. Valentine noticed that she was trembling now.

"All of him was here except his head. We discovered that far away, over in the ruins of the Seventh Pyramid.''

"They know no shame," said Nascimonte vehemently. "They are worse than beasts. We should have eradicated them all.''

"Who do you mean?" asked Valentine.

"You know who I mean, majesty. You know quite well.''

"So you think this was Shapeshifter work, this crime?''

"Oh, no, majesty, no!" Nascimonte said, coloring the words with heavy scorn. "Why would I think such a thing? One of our own archaeologists must have done it, no doubt. Out of professional jealousy, let's say, because the dead Shapeshifter had come upon on some important discovery, maybe, and our own people wanted to take credit for it.—Is that what you think, Valentine? Do you believe any human being would be capable of this sort of loathsome butchery?''

"That's what we're here to discover, my friend," said Valentine amiably. "We are not quite ready for arriving at conclusions, I think.''

Magadone Sambisa's eyes were bulging from her head, as though Nascimonte's audacity in upbraiding a Pontifex to his face was a spectacle beyond her capacity to absorb. "Perhaps we should continue on to your tents now," she said.

*   *   *

It felt very odd, Valentine thought, as they rode on down the rubble-bordered roadway that led to the place of encampment, to be here in this forlorn and eerie zone of age-old ruins once again. But at least he was not in the Labyrinth. So far as he was concerned, any place at all was better than the Labyrinth.

This was his third visit to Velalisier. The first had been long ago when he had been Coronal, in the strange time of his brief overthrow by the usurper Dominin Barjazid. He had stopped off here with his little handful of supporters—Carabella, Nascimonte, Sleet, Ermanar, Deliamber, and the rest—during the course of his northward march to Castle Mount, where he was to reclaim his throne from the false Coronal in the War of Restoration.

Valentine had still been a young man, then. But he was young no longer. He had been Pontifex of Majipoor, senior monarch of the realm, for nine years now, following upon the fourteen of his service as Coronal Lord. There were a few strands of white in his golden hair, and though he still had an athlete's trim body and easy grace he was starting to feel the first twinges of the advancing years.

He had vowed, that first time at Velalisier, to have the weeds and vines that were strangling the ruins cleared away, and to send in archaeologists to excavate and restore the old toppled buildings. And he had intended to allow the Metamorph leaders to play a role in that work, if they were willing. That was part of his plan for giving those once-despised and persecuted natives of the planet a more significant place in Majipoori life; for he knew that Metamorphs everywhere were smoldering with barely contained wrath, and could no longer be shunted into the remote reservations where his predecessors had forced them to live.

Valentine had kept that vow. And had come back to Velalisier years later to see what progress the archaeologists had made.

But the Metamorphs, bitterly resenting Valentine's intrusion into their holy precincts, had shunned the enterprise entirely. That was something he had not expected.

He was soon to learn that although the Shapeshifters were eager to see Velalisier rebuilt, they meant to do the job themselves—after they had driven the human settlers and all other offworld intruders from Majipoor and taken control of their planet once more. A Shapeshifter uprising, secretly planned for many years, erupted just a few years after Valentine had regained the throne. The first group of archaeologists that Valentine had sent to Velalisier could achieve nothing more at the site than some preliminary clearing and mapping before the War of the Rebellion broke out; and then all work there had had to be halted indefinitely.

The war had ended with victory for Valentine's forces. In designing the peace that followed it he had taken care to alleviate as many of the grievances of the Metamorphs as he could. The Danipiur—that was the title of their queen—was brought into the government as a full Power of the Realm, placing her on an even footing with the Pontifex and the Coronal. Valentine had, by then, himself moved on from the Coronal's throne to that of the Pontifex. And now he had revived the idea of restoring the ruins of Velalisier once more; but he had made certain that it would be with the full cooperation of the Metamorph, and that Metamorph archaeologists would work side by side with the scholars from the venerable University of Arkilon in the north to whom he had assigned the task.

In the year just past great things had been done toward rescuing the ruins from the oblivion that had been encroaching on them for so long. But he could take little joy in any of that. The ghastly death that had befallen the senior Metamorph archaeologist atop this ancient altar argued that sinister forces still ran deep in this place. The harmony that he thought his reign had brought to the world might be far shallower than he suspected.

* * *

Twilight was coming on by the time Valentine was settled in his tent. By a custom that even he was reluctant to set aside, he would stay in it alone, since his consort Carabella had remained behind in the Labyrinth on this trip. Indeed, she had tried very strongly to keep him from going himself. Tunigorn, Mirigant, Nascimonte, and the Vroon would share the second tent; the third was occupied by the security forces that had accompanied the Pontifex to Velalisier.

He stepped out into the gathering dusk. A sprinkling of early stars had begun to sparkle overhead, and the Great Moon's bright glint could be seen close to the horizon. The air was parched and crisp, with a brittle quality to it, as though it could be torn in one's hands like dry paper and crumbled to dust between one's fingers. There was a strange stillness in it, an eerie hush.

But at least he was out-of-doors, here, gazing up at actual stars, and the air he breathed here, dry as it was, was *real* air, not the manufactured stuff of the Pontifical city. Valentine was grateful for that.

By rights he had no business being out and abroad in the world at all.

As Pontifex, his place was in the Labyrinth, hidden away in his secret imperial lair deep underground beneath all those coiling levels of subterranean settlement, shielded always from the view of ordinary mortals. The Coronal, the junior king who lived in the lofty castle of forty thousand rooms atop the great heaven-piercing peak that was Castle Mount, was meant to be the active figure of governance, the visible representative of royal majesty on Majipoor. But Valentine loathed the dank Labyrinth where his lofty rank obliged him to dwell. He relished every opportunity he could manufacture to escape from it.

And in fact this one had been thrust unavoidably upon him. The killing of Huukaminaan was serious business, requiring an inquiry on the highest levels; and the Coronal Lord Hissune was many months' journey away just now, touring the distant continent of Zimroel. And so the Pontifex was here in the Coronal's stead.

"You love the sight of the open sky, don't you?" said Duke Nascimonte, emerging from the tent across the way and limping over to stand by Valentine's side. A certain tenderness underlay the harshness of his rasping voice. "Ah, I understand, old friend. I do indeed."

"I see the stars so infrequently, Nascimonte, in the place where I must live."

The duke chuckled. "*Must* live! The most powerful man in the world, and yet he's a prisoner! How ironic that is! How sad!"

"I knew from the moment I became Coronal that I'd have to live in the Labyrinth eventually," Valentine said. "I've tried to make my peace with that. But it was never my plan to be Coronal in the first place, you know. If Voriax had lived—"

"Ah, yes, Voriax—" Valentine's brother, the elder son of the High Counselor Damiandane: the one who had been reared from childhood to occupy the throne of Majipoor. Nascimonte gave Valentine a close look. "It was a Metamorph, was it not, who struck him down in the forest? That has been proven now?"

Uncomfortably Valentine said, "What does it matter now who killed him? He died. And the throne came to me, because I was our father's other son. A crown I had never dreamed of wearing. Everyone knew that Voriax was the one who was destined for it."

"But he had a darker destiny also. Poor Voriax!"

Poor Voriax, yes. Struck down by a bolt out of nowhere while hunting in the forest eight years into his reign as Coronal, a bolt from the bow of some Metamorph assassin skulking in the trees. By accepting his dead brother's crown, Valentine had doomed himself inevitably to descend into the Labyrinth someday, when the old Pontifex died and it became the Coronal's turn to succeed to the greater title, and to the cheerless obligation of underground residence that went with it.

"As you say, it was the decision of fate," Valentine replied, "and now I am Pontifex. Well, so be it, Nascimonte. But I won't hide down there in the darkness all the time. I can't."

"And why should you? The Pontifex can do as he pleases."

"Yes. Yes. But only within our law and custom."

"You shape law and custom to suit yourself, Valentine. You always have."

Valentine understood what Nascimonte was saying. He had never been a conventional monarch. For much of the time during his exile from power in the period of the usurpation he had wandered the world earning a humble living as an intinerant juggler, kept from awareness of his true rank by the amnesia that the usurping faction had induced in him. Those years had transformed him irreversibly; and after his restoration to the royal heights of Castle Mount he had comported himself in a way that few Coronals ever had before—mingling openly with the populace, spreading a cheerful gospel of peace and love even as the Shapeshifters were making ready to launch their long-cherished campaign of war against the conquerors who had taken their world from them.

And then, when the events of that war made Valentine's succession to the Pontificate unavoidable, he had held back as long as possible before relinquishing the upper world to his protégé Lord Hissune, the new Coronal, and descending into the subterranean city that was so alien to his sunny nature.

In his nine years as Pontifex he had found every excuse to emerge from it. No Pontifex in memory had come forth from the Labyrinth more than once a decade or so, and then only to attend high rites at the castle of the Coronal; but Valentine popped out as often as he could, riding hither and thither through the land as though he were still obliged to undertake the formal grand processionals across the countryside that a Coronal must make. Lord Hissune had been very patient with him on each of those occasions, though Valentine had no doubt that the young Coronal was annoyed by the senior monarch's insistence on coming up into public view so frequently.

"I change what I think needs changing," Valentine said. "But I owe it to Lord Hissune to keep myself out of sight as much as possible."

"Well, here you are above ground today, at any rate!"

"It seems that I am. This is one time, though, when I would gladly have forgone the chance to come forth. But with Hissune off in Zimroel—''

"Yes. Clearly you had no choice. You had to lead this investigation yourself." They fell silent. "A nasty mess, this murder," Nascimonte said, after a time. "Pfaugh! Pieces of the poor bastard strewn all over the altar like that!"

"Pieces of the government's Metamorph policy, too, I think," said the Pontifex, with a rueful grin.

"You think there's something political in this, Valentine?"

"Who knows? But I fear the worst."

"You, the eternal optimist!"

"It would be more accurate to call me a realist, Nascimonte. A realist."

The old duke laughed. "As you prefer, majesty." There was another pause, a longer one than before. Then Nascimonte said, more quietly now, "Valentine, I need to ask your forgiveness for an earlier fault. I spoke too harshly, this afternoon, when I talked of the Shapeshifters as vermin who should be exterminated. You know I don't truly believe that. I'm an old man. Sometimes I speak so bluntly that I amaze even myself."

Valentine nodded, but made no other reply.

"—And telling you so dogmatically that it had to be one of his fellow Shapeshifters who killed him, too. As you said, it's out of line for us to be jumping to conclusions that way. We haven't even started to collect evidence yet. At this point we have no justification for assuming—"

"On the contrary. We have *every* reason to assume it, Nascimonte."

The duke stared at Valentine in bewilderment. "Majesty!"

"Let's not play games, old friend. There's no one here right now but you and me. In privacy we're free to speak unvarnished truths, are we not? And you said it truly enough this afternoon. I did tell you then that we mustn't jump to conclusions, yes, but sometimes a conclusion is so obvious that it comes jumping right at *us*. There's no rational reason why one of the human archaeologists—or one of the Ghayrogs, for that matter—would have murdered one of his colleagues. I don't see why anyone else would have done it, either. Murder is such a very rare crime, Nascimonte. We can hardly even begin to understand the motivations of someone who'd be capable of doing it. But someone did."

"Yes."

"Well, and which race's motivations are hardest for us to understand, eh? To my way of thinking the killer almost certainly would have to be a Shapeshifter—either a member of the archaeological team, or one who came in from outside for the particular purpose of carrying out the assassination.''

''So one might assume. But what possible purpose could a Shapeshifter have for killing one of his own kind?''

''I can't imagine. Which is why we're here as investigators,'' said Valentine. ''And I have a nasty feeling that I'm not going to like the answer when we find it.''

At dinner that night in the archaeologists' open-air mess hall, under a clear black sky ablaze now with swirling streams of brilliant stars that cast cold dazzling light on the mysterious humps and mounds of the surrounding ruins, Valentine made the acquaintance of Magadone Sambisa's entire scientific team. There were seventeen in all: six other humans, two Ghayrogs, eight Metamorphs. They seemed, every one of them, to be gentle, studious creatures. Not by the greatest leap of the imagination could Valentine picture any of these people slaying and dismembering their venerable colleague Huukaminaan.

''Are these the only persons who have access to the archaeological zone?'' he asked Magadone Sambisa.

''There are the day laborers also, of course.''

''Ah. And where are they just now?''

"They have a village of their own, over beyond the last pyramid. They go to it at sundown and don't come back until the start of work the next day."

"I see. How many are there altogether? A great many?"

Magadone Sambisa looked across the table toward a pale and long-faced Metamorph with strongly inward-sloping eyes. He was her site supervisor, Kaastisiik by name, responsible for each day's deployment of diggers. "What would you say? About a hundred?"

"One hundred twelve," said Kaastisiik, and clamped his little slit of a mouth in a way that demonstrated great regard for his own precision.

"Mostly Piurivar?" Valentine asked.

"Entirely Piurivar," said Magadone Sambisa. "We thought it was best to use only native workers, considering that we're not only excavating the city but to some extent rebuilding it. They don't appear to have any problem with the presence of non-Piurivar archaeologists, but having humans taking part in the actual reconstruction work would very likely be offensive to them."

"You hired them all locally, did you?"

"There are no settlements of any kind in the immediate vicinity of the ruins, your majesty. Nor are there many Piurivars living anywhere in the surrounding province. We had to bring them in from great distances. A good many from Piurifayne itself, in fact.''

Valentine raised an eyebrow at that. From *Piurifayne?*

Piurifayne was a province of far-off Zimroel, an almost unthinkable distance away on the other side of the Inner Sea. Eight thousand years before, the great conqueror Lord Stiamot—he who had ended for all time the Piurivars' hope of remaining independent on their own world—had driven those Metamorphs who had survived his war against them into Piurifayne's humid jungles and had penned them up in a reservation there. Though the old restrictions had long since been lifted and Metamorphs now were permitted to settle wherever they pleased, more of them still lived in Piurifayne than anywhere else; and it was in the subtropical glades of Piurifayne that the revolutionary Faraataa had founded the underground movement that had sent the War of the Rebellion forth upon peaceful Majipoor like a river of seething lava.

Tunigorn said, ''You've questioned them all, naturally? Established their comings and goings at the time of the murder?''

Magadone Sambisa seemed taken aback. ''You mean, treat them as though they were suspects in the killing?''

"They *are* suspects in the killing," said Tunigorn.

"They are simple diggers and haulers of burdens, nothing more, Prince Tunigorn. There are no murderers among them, that much I know. They *revered* Dr. Huukaminaan. They regarded him as a guardian of their past—almost a sacred figure. It's inconceivable that any one of them could have carried out such a dreadful and hideous crime. Inconceivable!"

"In this very place some twenty thousand years ago," Duke Nascimonte said, looking upward as if he were speaking only to the air, "the King of the Shapeshifters, as you yourself reminded us earlier today, caused two enormous sea-dragons to be butchered alive atop those huge stone platforms back there. It was clear from your words this afternoon that the Shapeshifters of those days must have regarded sea-dragons with even more reverence than you say your laborers had for Dr. Huukaminaan. They called them 'water-kings,' am I not right, and gave them names, and thought of them as holy elder brothers, and addressed prayers to them? Yet the bloody sacrifice took place here in Velalisier even so, the thing that to this very day the Shapeshifters themselves speak of as the Defilement. Is this not true? Permit me to suggest, then, that if the King of the Shapeshifters could have done such a thing back then, it isn't all that inconceivable that one of your own hired Metamorphs here could have found some reason to perpetrate a similar atrocity last week upon the unfortunate Dr. Huukaminaan on the very same altar.''

Magadone Sambisa appeared stunned, as though Nascimonte had struck her in the face. For a moment she could make no reply. Then she said hoarsely, ''How can you use an ancient myth, a fantastic legend, to cast suspicion on a group of harmless, innocent—''

''Ah, so it's a myth and a legend when you want to protect these harmless and innocent diggers and haulers of yours, and absolute historical truth when you want us to shiver with rapture over the significance of these piles of old jumbled stones?''

''Please,'' Valentine said, glaring at Nascimonte. *''Please.''* To Magadone Sambisa he said, ''What time of day did the murder take place?''

''Late at night. Past midnight, it must have been.''

''I was the last to see Dr. Huukaminaan,'' said one of the Metamorph archaeologists, a frail-looking Piurivar whose skin had an elegant emerald hue. Vo-Siimifon was his name; Magadone Sambisa had introduced him as an authority on ancient Piurivar script. ''We sat up late in our tent, he and

I, discussing an inscription that had been found the day before. The lettering was extremely minute; Dr. Huukaminaan complained of a headache, and said finally that he was going out for a walk. I went to sleep.—Dr. Huukaminaan did not return.''

''It's a long way,'' Mirigant observed, ''from here to the sacrificial platforms. *Quite* a long way. It would take at least half an hour to walk there, I'd guess. Perhaps more, for someone his age. He was an old man, I understand.''

''But if someone happened to encounter him just outside the camp, though,'' Tunigorn suggested, ''and *forced* him to go all the way down to the platform area—''

Valentine said, ''Is a guard posted here at the encampment at night?''

''No. There seemed to be no purpose in doing that.''

''And the dig site itself? It's not fenced off, or protected in any way?''

''No.''

''Then anyone at all could have left the day laborers' village as soon as it grew dark,'' Valentine said, ''and waited out there in the road for Dr. Huukaminaan to come out.'' He glanced toward Vo-Siimifon. ''Was Dr. Huukaminaan in the habit of taking a walk before bedtime?''

''Not that I recall.''

"And if he *had* chosen to go out late at night for some reason, would he have been likely to take so long a walk?"

"He was quite a robust man, for his age," said the Piurivar. "But even so that would have been an unusual distance to go just for a stroll before bedtime."

"Yes. So it would seem." Valentine turned again to Magadone Sambisa. "It'll be necessary, I'm afraid, for us to question your laborers. And each member of your expedition, too. You understand that at this point we can't arbitrarily rule anyone out."

Her eyes flashed. "Am I under suspicion too, your majesty?"

"At this point," said Valentine, "nobody here is under suspicion. And everyone is. Unless you want me to believe that Dr. Huukaminaan committed suicide by dismembering himself and distributing parts of himself all over the top of that platform."

The night had been cool, but the sun sprang into the morning sky with incredible swiftness. Almost at once, early as it was in the day, the air began to throb with desert warmth. It was necessary to get a quick start at the site, Magadone Sambisa had told them, since by midday the intense heat would make work very difficult.

Valentine was ready for her when she called for him soon after dawn. At her request he would be accompanied only by some members of his security detachment, not by any of his fellow lords. Tunigorn grumbled about this, as did Mirigant. But she said—and would not yield on the point—that she preferred that the Pontifex alone come with her today, and after he had seen what she had to show him he could make his own decisions about sharing the information with the others.

She was taking him to the Seventh Pyramid. Or what was left of it, rather, for nothing now remained except the truncated base, a square structure about twenty feet long on each side and five or six feet high, constructed from the same reddish basalt from which the great arena and some of the other public buildings had been made. East of that stump the fragments of the pyramid's upper section, smallish broken blocks of the same reddish stone, lay strewn in the most random way across a wide area. It was as though some angry colossus had contemptuously given the western face of the pyramid one furious slap with the back of his ponderous hand and sent it flying into a thousand pieces. On the side of the stump away from the debris Valentine could make out the pointed summit of the still-intact Sixth Pyramid about five hundred feet away, rising above a copse of little contorted trees, and beyond it were the other five, running onward one after another to the edge of the royal palace itself.

"According to Piurivar lore," Magadone Sambisa said, "the people of Velalisier held a great festival every thousand years, and constructed a pyramid to commemorate each one. So far as we've been able to confirm by examining and dating the six undamaged ones, that's correct. This one, we know, was the last in the series. If we can believe the legend"—and she gave Valentine a meaningful look—"it was built to mark the very festival at which the Defilement took place. And had just been completed when the city was invaded and destroyed by those who had come here to punish its inhabitants for what they had done."

She beckoned to him, leading him around toward the northern side of the shattered pyramid. They walked perhaps fifty feet onward from the stump. Then she halted. The ground had been carefully cut away here. Valentine saw a rectangular opening just large enough for a man to enter, and the beginning of a passageway leading underground and heading back toward the foundations of the pyramid.

A star-shaped marker of bright yellow tape was

fastened to a good-sized boulder just to the left of the excavation.

"That's where you found the head, is it?" he asked.

"Not there. Below." She pointed into the opening. "Will you follow me, your majesty?"

Six members of Valentine's security force had gone with Valentine to the pyramid site that morning: the giant warrior-woman Lisamon Hultin, his personal bodyguard, who had accompanied him on all his travels since his juggling days; two shaggy hulking Skandars; a couple of Pontifical officials whom he had inherited from his predecessor's staff; and even a Metamorph, one Aarisiim, who had defected to Valentine's forces from the service of the arch-rebel Faraataa in the final hours of the War of the Rebellion and had been with the Pontifex ever since. All six stepped forward now as if they meant to go down into the excavation with him, though the Skandars and Lisamon Hultin were plainly too big to fit into the entrance. But Magadone Sambisa shook her head fiercely; and Valentine, smiling, signaled to them all to wait for him above.

The archaeologist, lighting a hand torch, entered the opening in the ground. The descent was steep, via a series of precisely chiseled earthen steps that took them downward nine or ten feet. Then, abruptly, the subterranean passageway leveled off. Here there was a flagstone floor made of broad slabs hewn from some glossy green rock. Magadone Sambisa flashed her light at one and Valentine saw that it bore carved glyphs, runes of some kind, reminiscent of those he had seen in the paving of the grand ceremonial boulevard that ran past the royal palace.

"This is our great discovery," she said. "There are shrines, previously unknown and unsuspected, under each of the seven pyramids. We were working near the Third Pyramid about six months ago, trying to stabilize its foundation, when we stumbled on the first one. It had been plundered, very probably in antiquity. But it was an exciting find all the same, and immediately we went looking for similar shrines beneath the other five intact pyramids. And found them: also plundered. For the time being we didn't bother to go digging for the shrine of the Seventh Pyramid. We assumed that there was no hope of finding anything interesting there, that it must have been looted at the time the pyramid was destroyed. But then Huukaminaan and I decided that we might as well check it out too, and we put down this trench that we've been walking through. Within a day or so we reached this flagstone paving. Come."

They went deeper in, entering a carefully constructed tunnel just about wide enough for four people to stand in it abreast. Its walls were fashioned of thin slabs of black stone laid sideways like so many stacked books, leading upward to a vaulted roof of the same stone that tapered into a series of pointed arches. The craftsmanship was very fine, and distinctly archaic in appearance. The air in the tunnel was hot and musty and dry, ancient air, lifeless air. It had a stale, dead taste in Valentine's nostrils.

"We call this kind of underground vault a processional hypogeum," Magadone Sambisa explained. "Probably it was used by priests carrying offerings to the shrine of the pyramid."

Her torch cast a spreading circlet of pallid light that allowed Valentine to perceive a wall of finely dressed white stone blocking the path just ahead of them. "Is that the foundation of the pyramid we're looking at?" he asked.

"No. What we see here is the wall of the shrine, nestling against the pyramid's base. The pyramid itself is on the far side of it. The other shrines were located right up against their pyramids in the same way. The difference is that all the others had been smashed open. This one has apparently never been breached."

Valentine whistled softly. "And what do you think is inside it?"

"We don't have any idea. We were putting off opening it, waiting for Lord Hissune to return from his processional in Zimroel, so that you and he could be on hand when we broke through the wall. But then—the murder—"

"Yes," Valentine said soberly. And, after a moment: "How strange that the destroyers of the city demolished the Seventh Pyramid so thoroughly, but left the shrine beneath it intact! You'd think they would have made a clean sweep of the place."

"Perhaps there was something walled up in the shrine that they didn't want to go near, eh? It's a thought, anyway. We may never know the truth, even after we open it. *If* we open it."

"If?"

"There may be problems about that, majesty. Political problems, I mean. We need to discuss them. But this isn't the moment for that."

Valentine nodded. He indicated a row of small indented apertures, perhaps nine inches deep and about a foot high, that had been chiseled in the wall some eighteen inches above ground level. "Were those for putting offerings in?"

"Exactly." Magadone Sambisa flashed the torch across the row from right to left. "We found microscopic traces of dried flowers in several of them, and potsherds and colored pebbles in others—you can still see them there, actually. And some animal remains." She hesitated. "And then, in the alcove on the far left—"

The torch came to rest on a star of yellow tape attached to the shallow alcove's back wall.

Valentine gasped in shock. "*There*?"

"Huukaminaan's head, yes. Placed very neatly in the center of the alcove, facing outward. An offering of some sort, I suppose."

"To whom? To what?"

The archaeologist shrugged and shook her head.

Then, abruptly, she said, "We should go back up now, your majesty. The air down here isn't good to spend a lot of time in. I simply wanted you to see where the shrine was situated. And where we found the missing part of Dr. Huukaminaan's body."

Later in the day, with Nascimonte and Tunigorn and the rest now joining him, Magadone Sambisa showed Valentine the site of the expedition's other significant discovery: the bizarre cemetery, previously unsuspected, where the ancient inhabitants of Velalisier had buried their dead.

Or, more precisely, had buried certain fragments of their dead. "There doesn't appear to be a complete body anywhere in the whole graveyard. In every interment we've opened, what we've found is mere tiny bits—a finger here, an ear there, a lip, a toe. Or some internal organ, even. Each item carefully embalmed, and placed in a beautiful stone casket and buried beneath one of these gravestones. The part for the whole: a kind of metaphorical burial.''

Valentine stared in wonder and astonishment.

The twenty-thousand-year-old Metamorph cemetery was one of the strangest sights he had seen in all his years of exploring the myriad wondrous strangenesses that Majipoor had to offer.

It covered an area hardly more than a hundred feet long and sixty feet wide, off in a lonely zone of dunes and weeds a short way beyond the end of one of the north-south flagstone boulevards. In that small plot of land there might have been ten thousand graves, all jammed together. A small stela of brown sandstone, a hand's-width broad and about fifteen inches high, jutted upward from each of the grave plots. And each of them crowded in upon the ones adjacent to it in a higgledy-piggledy fashion so that the cemetery was a dense agglomeration of slender close-set gravestones, tilting this way and that in a manner that utterly befuddled the eye.

At one time every stone must have lovingly been set in a vertical position above the casket containing the bit of the departed that had been chosen for interment here. But the Metamorphs of Velalisier had evidently gone on jamming more and more

burials into this little funereal zone over the course
of centuries, until each grave overlapped the next
in the most chaotic manner. Dozens of them were
packed into every square yard of terrain.

As the headstones continued to be crammed one
against another without heed for the damage that
each new burial was doing to the tombs already in
place, the older ones were pushed out of perpen-
dicular by their new neighbors. The slender stones
all leaned precariously one way and another, looking the way a forest might after some monstrous
storm had passed through, or after the ground beneath it had been bent and buckled by the force of
some terrible earthquake. They all stood at crazy
angles now, no two slanting in the same direction.

On each of these narrow headstones a single elegant glyph was carved precisely one-third of the
way from the top, an intricately patterned whorl of
the sort found in other zones of the city. No symbol
seemed like any other one. Did they represent the
names of the deceased? Prayers to some long-
forgotten god?

"We hadn't any idea that this was here," Magadone Sambisa said. "This is the first burial site
that's ever been discovered in Velalisier."

"I'll testify to that," Nascimonte said, with a
great jovial wink. "I did a little digging here myself, you know, long ago. Tomb-hunting, looking

for buried treasure that I might be able to sell somewhere, during the time I was forced from my land
in the reign of the false Lord Valentine and living
like a bandit in this desert. But not a single grave
did any of us come upon then. Not one.''

''Nor did we detect any, though we tried,'' said
Magadone Sambisa. ''When we found this place it
was only by sheer luck. It was hidden deep under
the dunes, ten, twelve, twenty feet below the surface of the sand. No one suspected it was here. But
one day last winter a terrific whirlwind swept
across the valley and hovered right up over this part
of the city for half an hour, and by the time it was
done whirling the whole dune had been picked up
and tossed elsewhere and this amazing collection
of gravestones lay exposed. Here. Look.''

She knelt and brushed a thin coating of sand
away from the base of a gravestone just in front of
her. In moments the upper lid of a small box made
of polished gray stone came into view. She pried
it free and set it to one side.

Tunigorn made a sound of disgust. Valentine,
peering down, saw a thing like a curling scrap of
dark leather lying within the box.

''They're all like this,'' said Magadone Sambisa.
''Symbolic burial, taking up a minimum of space.
An efficient system, considering what a huge pop-
ulation Velalisier must have had in its prime. One

tiny bit of the dead person's body buried here, preserved so artfully that it's still in pretty good condition even after all these thousands of years. The rest of it exposed on the hills outside town, for all we know, to be consumed by natural processes of decay. A Piurivar corpse would decay very swiftly. We'd find no traces, after all this time."

"How does that compare with present-day Shapeshifter burial practices?" Mirigant asked.

Magadone Sambisa looked at him oddly. "We know next to nothing about present-day Piurivar burial practices. They're a pretty secretive race, you know. They've never chosen to tell us anything about such things and evidently we've been too polite to ask, because there's hardly a thing on record about it. Hardly a thing."

"You have Shapeshifter scientists on your own staff," Tunigorn said. "Surely it wouldn't be impolite to consult your own associates about something like that. What's the point of training Shapeshifters to be archaeologists if you're going to be too sensitive of their feelings to make any use of their knowledge of their own people's ways?"

"As a matter of fact," said Magadone Sambisa, "I did discuss this find with Dr. Huukaminaan not long after it was uncovered. The layout of the place, the density of the burials, seemed pretty startling to him. But he didn't seem at all surprised by the concept of burial of body parts instead of entire bodies. He gave me to understand what had been done here wasn't all that different in some aspects from things the Piurivars still do today. There wasn't time just then for him to go into further details, though, and we both let the subject slip. And now—now—''

Once more she displayed that look of stunned helplessness, of futility and confusion in the face of violent death, that came over her whenever the topic of the murder of Huukaminaan arose.

Not all that different in some aspects from things the Piurivars still do today, Valentine repeated silently.

He considered the way Huukaminaan's body had been cut apart, the sundered pieces left in various places atop the sacrificial platform, the head carried down into the tunnel beneath the Seventh Pyramid and carefully laid to rest in one of the alcoves of the underground shrine.

There was something implacably alien about that grisly act of dismemberment that brought Valentine once again to the conclusion, mystifying and distasteful but seemingly inescapable, that had been facing him since his arrival here. *The murderer of the Metamorph archaeologist must have been a Metamorph himself.* As Nascimonte had suggested earlier, there seemed to be a ritual aspect to the butchery that had all the hallmarks of Metamorph work.

But still it made no sense. Valentine had difficulty believing that the old man could have been killed by one of his own people.

"What was Huukaminaan like?" he asked Magadone Sambisa, "I never met him, you know. Was he contentious? Cantankerous?"

"Not in the slightest. A sweet, gentle person. A brilliant scholar. There was no one, Piurivar or human, who didn't love and admire him."

"There must have been one person, at least," said Nascimonte wryly.

Perhaps Nascimonte's theory was worth exploring. Valentine said, "Could there have been some sort of bitter professional disagreement? A dispute over the credit for a discovery, a battle over some piece of theory?"

Magadone Sambisa stared at the Pontifex as though he had gone out of his mind. "Do you think we kill each other over such things, your majesty?"

"It was a foolish suggestion," Valentine said, with a smile. "Well, then," he went on, "suppose Huukaminaan had come into possession of some valuable artifact in the course of his work here, some priceless treasure that would fetch a huge sum in the antiquities market. Might that not have been sufficient cause for murdering him?"

Again the incredulous stare. "The artifacts we find here, majesty, are of the nature of simple sandstone statuettes, and bricks bearing inscriptions, not golden tiaras and emeralds the size of gihorna eggs. Everything worth looting was looted a long, long time ago. And we would no more dream of trying to make a private sale of the little things that we find here than we would—would—than, well, than we would of murdering each other. Our finds are divided equally between the university museum in Arkilon and the Piurivar treasury at Ilirivoyne. In any case—no, no, it's not even worth discussing. The idea's completely absurd." Instantly her cheeks turned flame-red. "Forgive me, majesty, I meant no disrespect."

Valentine brushed the apology aside. "What I'm doing, you see, is groping for some plausible explanation of the crime. A place to begin our investigation, at least."

"*I'll* give you one, Valentine," Tunigorn said suddenly. His normally open and genial face was tightly drawn in a splenetic scowl that brought his heavy eyebrows together into a single dark line. "The basic thing that we need to keep in mind all the time is that there's a curse on this place. You know that, Valentine. A *curse*. The Shapeshifters themselves put the dark word on the city, the Divine knows how many thousands of years ago, when they smashed it up to punish those who had chopped up those two sea-dragons. They intended the place to be shunned forever. Only ghosts have lived here ever since. By sending these archaeologists of yours in here, Valentine, you're disturbing those ghosts. Making them angry. And so they're striking back. Killing old Huukaminaan was the first step. There'll be more, mark my words!''

''And you think, do you, that ghosts are capable of cutting someone into five or six pieces and scattering the parts far and wide?''

Tunigorn was not amused. ''I don't know what sorts of things ghosts may or may not be capable of doing,'' he said staunchly. ''I'm just telling you what has crossed my mind.''

''Thank you, my good old friend,'' said Valentine pleasantly. ''We'll give the thought the examination it deserves.'' And to Magadone Sambisa he said, ''I must tell you what has crossed *my* mind, based on what you've shown me today, here and at the pyramid shrine. Which is that the killing of Huukaminaan strikes me as a ritual murder, and the ritual involved is some kind of Piurivar ritual. I don't say that that's what it was; I just say that it certainly looks that way.''

''And if it does?''

''Then we have our starting point. It's time now to move to the next phase of our work, I think.

Please have the kindness to call your entire group of Piurivar archaeologists together this afternoon. I want to speak with them.''

"One by one, or all together?''

"All of them together at first,'' said Valentine. "After that, we'll see.''

But Magadone Sambisa's people were scattered all over the huge archaeological zone, each one involved with some special project, and she begged Valentine not to have them called in until the working day was over. It would take so long to reach them all, she said, that the worst of the heat would have descended by the time they began their return to camp, and they would be compelled to trek across the ruins in the full blaze of noon, instead of settling in some dark cavern to await the cooler hours that lay ahead. Meet with them at sundown, she implored him. Let them finish their day's tasks.

That seemed only reasonable. He said that he would.

But Valentine himself was unable to sit patiently by until dusk. The murder had jarred him deeply. It was one more symptom of the strange new darkness that had come over the world in his lifetime. Huge as it was, Majipoor had long been a peaceful place where there was comfort and plenty for all, and crime of any sort was an extraordinary rarity.

But, even so, just in this present generation there had been the assassination of the Coronal Lord Voriax, and then the diabolically contrived usurpation that had pushed Voriax's successor—Valentine—from his throne for a time.

The Metamorphs, everyone knew now, had been behind both of those dire acts.

And after Valentine's recovery of the throne had come the War of the Rebellion, organized by the embittered Metamorph Faraataa, bringing with it plagues, famines, riots, a worldwide panic, great destruction everywhere. Valentine had ended that uprising, finally, by reaching out himself to take Faraataa's life—a deed that the gentle Valentine had regarded with horror, but which he had carried out all the same, because it had to be done.

Now, in this new era of worldwide peace and harmony that Valentine, reigning as Pontifex, had inaugurated, an admirable and beloved old Metamorph scholar had been murdered in the most brutal way. Murdered here in the holy city of the Metamorphs themselves, while he was in the midst of archaeological work that Valentine had instituted as one way of demonstrating the newfound respect of the human people of Majipoor for the aboriginal people they had displaced. And there was every indication, at least at this point, that the murderer was himself a Metamorph.

But that seemed insane.

Perhaps Tunigorn was right, that all of this was merely the working out of some ancient curse. That was a hard thing for Valentine to swallow. He had little belief in such things as curses. And yet—yet—

Restlessly he stalked the ruined city all through the worst heat of the day, heedless of the discomfort, pulling his hapless companions along. The sun's great golden-green eye stared unrelentingly down. Heat shimmers danced in the air. The leathery-leaved little shrubs that grew all over the ruins seemed to fold in upon themselves to hide from those torrid blasts of light. Even the innumerable skittering lizards that infested these rocks grew reticent as the temperature climbed.

"I would almost think we had been transported to Suvrael," said Tunigorn, panting in the heat as he dutifully labored along beside the Pontifex. "This is the climate of the miserable southland, not of our pleasant Alhanroel."

Nascimonte gave him a sardonic squinting smirk. "Just one more example of the malevolence of the Shapeshifters, my lord Tunigorn. In the days when the city was alive there were green forests all about this place, and the air was cool and mild. But then the river was turned aside, and the forests died, and nothing was left here but the bare rock that you see, which soaks up the heat of noon and holds it like a sponge. Ask the archaeologist lady, if you don't believe me. This province was deliberately turned into a desert, for the sake of punishing those who had committed great sins in it."

"All the more reason for us to be somewhere else," Tunigorn muttered. "But no, no, this is our place, here with Valentine, now and ever."

Valentine scarcely paid attention to what they were saying. He wandered aimlessly onward, down one weedy byway and another, past fallen columns and shattered façades, past the empty shells of what might once have been shops and taverns, past the ghostly outlines marking the foundation of vanished dwellings that must once have been palatial in their grandeur. Nothing was labeled, and Magadone Sambisa was not with him, now, to bend his ear with endless disquisitions about the former identities of these places. They were bits and pieces of lost Velalisier, that was all he knew: skeletonic remnants of this ancient metropolis.

It was easy enough, even for him, to imagine this place as the lair of ancient phantoms. A glassy glimmer of light shining out of some tumbled mass of broken columns—odd scratchy sounds that might have been those of creatures crawling about where no creatures could be seen—the occasional hiss and slither of shifting sand, sand that moved, so it would appear, of its own volition—

"Every time I visit these ruins," he said to Mirigant, who was walking closest to him now, "I'm astounded by the antiquity of it all. The weight of history that presses down on it."

"History that no one remembers," Mirigant said.

"But its weight remains."

"Not our history, though."

Valentine shot his cousin a scornful look. "So you may believe. But it's Majipoor's history, and what is that if not ours?"

Mirigant shrugged and made no answer.

Was there any meaning, Valentine wondered, in what he had just said? Or was the heat addling his brain?

He pondered it. Into his mind there came, with a force almost like that of an explosion, a vision of the totality of vast Majipoor. Its great continents and overwhelming rivers and immense shining seas, its dense moist jungles and great deserts, its forests of towering trees and mountains rich with strange and wonderful creatures, its multitude of sprawling cities with their populations of many millions. His soul was flooded with an overload of sensation, the perfume of a thousand kinds of flowers, the aromas of a thousand spices, the savory tang of a thousand wondrous meats, the bouquet of a thousand wines. It was a world of infinite richness and variety, this Majipoor of his.

And by a fluke of descent and his brother's bad luck he had come first to be Coronal and now Pontifex of that world. Twenty billion people hailed him as their emperor. His face was on the coinage; the world resounded with his praises; his name would be inscribed forever on the roster of monarchs in the House of Records, an imperishable part of the history of this world.

But once there had been a time when there were no Pontifices and Coronals here. When such wondrous cities as Ni-Moya and Alaisor and the fifty great urban centers of Castle Mount did not exist. And in that time before human settlement had begun on Majipoor, this city of Velalisier already was.

What right did he have to appropriate this city, already thousands of years dead and desolate when the first colonists arrived from space, into the flow of human history here? In truth there was a discontinuity so deep between *their* Majipoor and *our* Majipoor, he thought, that it might never be bridged.

In any case he could not rid himself of the feeling that this place's great legion of ghosts, in whom he did not even believe, were lurking all around him, and that their fury was still unappeased.

Somehow he would have to deal with that fury, which had broken out now, so it seemed, in the form of a terrible act that had cost the life of a studious and inoffensive old man. The logic that infused every aspect of Valentine's soul balked at any comprehension of such a thing. But his own fate, he knew, and perhaps the fate of the world, might depend on his finding a solution to the mystery that had exploded here.

"You will pardon me, good majesty," said Tunigorn, breaking in on Valentine's broodings just as a new maze of ruined streets opened out before them. "But if I take another step in this heat, I will fall down gibbering like a madman. My very brain is melting."

"Why, then, Tunigorn, you should certainly seek refuge quickly, and cool it off! You can ill afford to damage what's left of it, can you, old friend?" Valentine pointed in the direction of the camp. "Go back. Go. But I will continue, I think."

He was not sure why. But something drove him grimly forward across this immense bedraggled sprawl of sand-choked sun-blasted ruins, seeking he knew not what. One by one his other companions dropped away from him, with this apology or that, until only the indefatigable Lisamon Hultin remained. The giantess was ever-faithful. She had protected him from the dangers of Mazadone Forest in the days before his restoration to the Coronal's throne. She had been his guardian in the belly of the sea-dragon that had swallowed them both in the sea off Piliplok, that time when they were shipwrecked sailing from Zimroel to Alhanroel, and she had cut him free and carried him up to safety. She would not leave him now. Indeed she seemed willing to walk on and on with him through the day and the night and the day that followed as well, if that was what he required of her.

But eventually even Valentine had had enough. The sun had long since moved beyond its noon height. Sharp-edged pools of shadow, rose and purple and deepest obsidian, were beginning to reach out all about him. He was feeling a little light-headed now, his head swimming a little and his vision wavering from the prolonged strain of coping with the unyielding glare of that blazing sun, and each street of tumbled-down buildings had come to look exactly like its predecessor. It was time to go back. Whatever penance he had been imposing on himself by such an exhausting journey through this dominion of death and destruction must surely have been fulfilled by now. He leaned on Lisamon Hultin's arm now and again as they made their way toward the tents of the encampment.

Magadone Sambisa had assembled her eight

Metamorph archaeologists. Valentine, having bathed and rested and had a little to eat, met with them just after sundown in his own tent, accompanied only by the little Vroon, Autifon Deliamber. He wanted to form his opinions of the Metamorphs undistracted by the presence of Nascimonte and the rest; but Deliamber had certain Vroonish wizardly skills that Valentine prized highly, and the small many-tentacled being might well be able to perceive things with those huge and keen golden eyes of his that would elude Valentine's own human vision.

The Shapeshifters sat in a semicircle with Valentine facing them and the tiny wizened old Vroon at his left hand. The Pontifex ran his glance down the group, from the site boss Kaastisiik at one end to the paleographer Vo-Siimifon on the other. They looked back at him calmly, almost indifferently, these seven rubbery-faced slope-eyed Piurivars, as he told them of the things he had seen this day, the cemetery and the shattered pyramid and the shrine beneath it, and the alcove where Huukaminaan's severed head had been so carefully placed by his murderer.

"There was, wouldn't you say, a certain formal aspect to the murder?" Valentine said. "The cutting of the body into pieces? The carrying of the head down to the shrine, the placement in the al-

cove of offerings?'' His gaze fastened on Thiuuri-
nen, the ceramics expert, a lithe, diminutive
Metamorph woman with lovely jade-green skin.
''What's your reading on that?'' he asked her.

Her expression was wholly impassive. ''As a
ceramicist I have no opinion at all.''

''I don't want your opinion as a ceramicist, just
as a member of the expedition. A colleague of Dr.
Huukaminaan. Does it seem to you that putting the
head there meant that some kind of offering was
being made?''

''It is only conjecture that those alcoves were
places of offering,'' said Thiuurinen primly. ''I am
not in a position to speculate.''

Nor would she. Nor would any of them. Not
Kaastisiik, not Vo-Siimifon, not the stratigrapher
Pamikuuk, not Hieekraad, the custodian of material
artifacts, nor Driismiil, the architectural specialist,
nor Klelliin, the authority on Piurivar paleotech-
nology, nor Viitaal-Twuu, the specialist in meta-
llurgy.

Politely, mildly, firmly, unshakably, they brushed
aside Valentine's hypotheses about ritual murder.
Was the gruesome dismemberment of Dr. Huukaminaan a hearkening-back to the funereal practices
of ancient Velalisier? Was the placing of his head
in that alcove likely to have been any kind of pro-
pitiation of some supernatural being? Was there

anything in Piurivar tradition that might countenance killing someone in that particular fashion?
They could not say. They would not say. Nor, when
he inquired as to whether their late colleague might
have had an enemy here at the site, did they provide
him with any information.

And they merely gave him the Piurivar equiva-
lent of a shrug when he wondered out loud whether
there could have been some struggle over the discovery of a valuable artifact that might have led to
Huukaminaan's murder; or even a quarrel of a
more abstract kind, a fierce disagreement over the
findings or goals of the expedition. Nobody showed
any sign of outrage at his implication that one of
them might have killed old Huukaminaan over such
a matter. They behaved as though the whole notion
of doing such a thing were beyond their comprehension, a concept too alien even to consider.

During the course of the interview Valentine
took the opportunity to aim at least one direct question at each of them. But the result was always the
same. They were unhelpful without seeming particularly evasive. They were unforthcoming without appearing unusually sly or secretive. There was
nothing overtly suspicious about their refusal to co-
operate. They seemed to be precisely what they
claimed to be: scientists, studious scholars, devoted
to uncovering the buried mysteries of their race's

remote past, who knew nothing at all about the mystery that had erupted right here in their midst. He did not feel himself to be in the presence of murderers here.

And yet—and yet—

They were Shapeshifters. He was the Pontifex, the emperor of the race that had conquered them, the successor across eight thousand years of the half-legendary soldier-king Lord Stiamot, who had deprived them of their independence for all time. Mild and scholarly though they might be, these eight Piurivars before him surely could not help but feel anger, on some level of their souls, toward their human masters. They had no reason to co-operate with him. They would not see themselves under any obligation to tell him the truth. And— was this only his innate and inescapable racial prejudices speaking, Valentine wondered?—intuition told him to take nothing at face value among these people. Could he really trust the impression of apparent innocence that they gave? Was it possible ever for a human to read the things that lay hidden behind a Metamorph's cool impenetrable features?

"What do you think?" he asked Deliamber, when the seven Shapeshifters had gone. "Murderers or not?"

"Probably not," the Vroon replied. "Not these.

Too soft, too citified. But they were holding something back. I'm certain of that.''

''You felt it too, then?''

''Beyond any doubt. What I sensed, your majesty—do you know what the Vroon word *hsirthiir* means?''

''Not really.''

''It isn't easy to translate. But it has to do with questioning someone who doesn't intend to tell you any lies but isn't necessarily going to tell you the truth, either, unless you know exactly how to call it forth. You pick up a powerful perception that there's an important layer of meaning hidden somewhere beneath the surface of what you're being told, but that you won't be allowed to elicit that hidden meaning unless you ask precisely the right question to unlock it. Which means, essentially, that you already have to know the information that you're looking for before you can ask the question that would reveal it. It's a very frustrating sensation, *hsirthiir*: almost painful, in fact. It is like hitting one's beak against a stone wall. I felt myself placed in a state of *hsirthiir* just now. Evidently so did you, your majesty.''

''Evidently I did,'' said Valentine.

There was one more visit to make, though. It had been a long day and a terrible weariness was coming over Valentine now. But he felt some inner need to cover all the basic territory in a single sweep; and so, once darkness had fallen, he asked Magadone Sambisa to conduct him to the village of the Metamorph laborers.

She was unhappy about that. "We don't usually like to intrude on them after they've finished their day's work and gone back there, your majesty."

"You don't usually have murders here, either. Or visits from the Pontifex. I'd rather speak with them tonight than disrupt tomorrow's digging, if you don't mind."

Deliamber accompanied him once again. At her own insistence, so did Lisamon Hultin. Tunigorn was too tired to go—his hike through the ruins at midday had done him in—and Mirigant was feeling feverish from a touch of sunstroke; but formidable old Duke Nascimonte readily agreed to ride with the Pontifex, despite his great age. The final member of the party was Aarisiim, the Metamorph member of Valentine's security staff, whom Valentine brought with him not so much for protection—Lisamon Hultin would look after that—as for the *hsirthiir* problem.

Aarisiim, turncoat though he once had been, seemed to Valentine to be as trustworthy as any Piurivar was likely to be: he had risked his own life to betray his master Faraataa to Valentine in

the time of the Rebellion, when he had felt that
Faraataa had gone beyond all decency by threatening to slay the Metamorph queen. He could be
helpful now, perhaps, detecting things that eluded
even Deliamber's powerful perceptions.

The laborers' village was a gaggle of meager
wickerwork huts outside the central sector of the
dig. In its flimsy makeshift look it reminded Valentine of Ilirivoyne, the Shapeshifter capital in the
jungle of Zimroel, which he had visited so many
years before. But this place was even sadder and
more disheartening than Ilirivoyne. There, at least,
the Metamorphs had had an abundance of tall
straight saplings and jungle vines with which to
build their ramshackle huts, whereas the only construction materials available to them here were the
gnarled and twisted desert shrubs that dotted the
Velalisier plain. And so their huts were miserable
little things, dismally warped and contorted.

They had had advance word, somehow, that the
Pontifex was coming. Valentine found them arrayed in groups of eight or ten in front of their
shacks, clearly waiting for his arrival. They were a
pitiful starved-looking bunch, gaunt and shabby
and ragged, very different from the urbane and cultivated Metamorphs of Magadone Sambisa's archaeological team. Valentine wondered where they
found the strength to do the digging that was re-

quired of them in this inhospitable climate.

As the Pontifex came into view they shuffled forward to meet him, quickly surrounding him and the rest of his party in a way that caused Lisamon Hultin to hiss sharply and put her hand to the hilt of her vibration-sword.

But they did not appear to mean any harm. They clustered excitedly around him and to his amazement offered homage in the most obsequious way, jostling among themselves for a chance to kiss the hem of his tunic, kneeling in the sand before him, even prostrating themselves. "No," Valentine cried, dismayed. "This isn't necessary. It isn't right." Already Magadone Sambisa was ordering them brusquely to get back, and Lisamon Hultin and Nascimonte were shoving the ones closest to Valentine away from him. The giantess was doing it calmly, unhurriedly, efficiently, but Nascimonte was prodding them more truculently, with real detestation apparent in his fiery eyes. Others came pressing forward as fast as the first wave retreated, though, pushing in upon him in frantic determination.

So eager were these weary toil-worn people to show their obeisance to the Pontifex, in fact, that he could not help regarding their enthusiasm as blatantly false, an ostentatious overdoing of whatever might have been appropriate. How likely was it, he wondered, that any group of Piurivars, however lowly and simple, would feel great unalloyed joy at the sight of the Pontifex of Majipoor? Or would, of their own accord, stage such a spontaneous demonstration of delight?

Some, men and women both, were even allowing themselves to mimic the forms of the visitors by way of compliment, so that half a dozen blurry distorted Valentines stood before him, and a couple of Nascimontes, and a grotesque half-sized imitation of Lisamon Hultin. Valentine had experienced that peculiar kind of honor before, in his Ilirivoyne visit, and he had found it disturbing and even chilling then. It distressed him again now. Let them shift shapes if they wished—they had that capacity, to use as they pleased—but there was something almost sinister about this appropriation of the visages of their visitors.

And the jostling began to grow even wilder and more frenzied. Despite himself Valentine started to feel some alarm. There were more than a hundred villagers, and the visitors numbered only a handful. There could be real trouble if things got out of control.

Then in the midst of the hubbub a powerful voice called out, "Back! Back!" And at once the whole ragged band of Shapeshifters shrank away from Valentine as though they had been struck by whips. There was a sudden stillness and silence. Out of the now motionless throng there stepped a tall Metamorph of unusually muscular and powerful build. He made a deep gesticulation and announced, in a dark rumbling tone quite unlike that of any Metamorph voice Valentine had ever heard before, "I am Vathiimeraak, the foreman of these workers. I beg you to feel welcome here among us, Pontifex. We are your servants."

But there was nothing servile about him. He was plainly a man of presence and authority. Briskly he apologized for the uncouth behavior of his people, explaining that they were simple peasants astounded by the presence of a Power of the Realm among them, and this was merely their way of showing respect.

"I know this man," murmured Aarisiim into Valentine's left ear.

But there was no opportunity just then to find out more; for Vathiimeraak, turning away, made a signal with one upraised hand and instantly the scene became one of confusion and noise once again. The villagers went running off in a dozen different directions, some returning almost at once with platters of sausages and bowls of wine for their guests, others hauling lopsided tables and benches from the huts. Platoons of them came crowding in once more on Valentine and his companions, this time urging them to sample the delicacies they had to offer.

"They're giving us their own dinners!" Magadone Sambisa protested. And she ordered Vathiimeraak to call off the feast. But the foreman replied smoothly that it would offend the villagers to refuse their hospitality, and in the end there was no help for it: they must sit down at table and partake of all that the villagers brought for them.

"If you will, majesty," said Nascimonte, as Valentine reached for a bowl of wine. The duke took it from him and sipped it first; and only after a moment did he return it. He insisted also on tasting Valentine's sausages for him, and the scraps of boiled vegetables that went with them.

It had not occurred to Valentine that the villagers would try to poison him. But he allowed old Nascimonte to enact his charming little rite of medieval chivalry without objection. He was too fond of the old man to want to spoil his gesture.

Vathiimeraak said, when the feasting had gone on for some time, "You are here, your majesty, about the death of Dr. Huukaminaan, I assume?"

The foreman's bluntness was startling. "Could it not be," Valentine said good-humoredly, "that I just wanted to observe the progress being made at the excavations?"

Vathiimeraak would have none of that. "I will

do whatever you may require of me in your search for the murderer,'' he said, rapping the table sharply to underscore his words. For an instant the outlines of his broad, heavy-jowled face rippled and wavered as if he were on the verge of undergoing an involuntary metamorphosis. Among the Piurivar, Valentine knew, that was a sign of being swept by some powerful emotion. ''I had the greatest respect for Dr. Huukaminaan. It was a privilege to work beside him. I often dug for him myself, when I felt the site was too delicate to entrust to less skillful hands. He thought that that was improper, at first, that the foreman should dig, but I said, No, no, Dr. Huukaminaan, I beg you to allow me this glory, and he understood, and permitted me. —How may I help you to find the perpetrator of this dreadful crime?''

He seemed so solemn and straightforward and open that Valentine could not help but find himself immediately on guard. Vathiimeraak's strong, booming voice and overly formal choice of phrase had an overly theatrical quality. His elaborate sincerity seemed much like the extreme effusiveness of the villagers' demonstration, all that kneeling and kissing of his hem: unconvincing because it was so excessive.

You are too suspicious of these people, he told himself. *This man is simply speaking as he thinks a Pontifex should be spoken to. And in any case I think he can be useful.*

He said, "How much do you know of how the murder was committed?"

Vathiimeraak responded without hesitation, as if he had been holding a well-rehearsed reply in readiness. "I know that it happened late at night, the week before this, somewhere between the Hour of the Gihorna and the Hour of the Jackal. A person or persons lured Dr. Huukaminaan from his tent and led him to the Tables of the Gods, where he was killed and cut into pieces. We found the various segments of his body the next morning atop the western platform, all but his head. Which we discovered later that day in one of the alcoves along the base of the Shrine of the Downfall."

Pretty much the standard account, Valentine thought. Except for one small detail.

"The Shrine of the Downfall? I haven't heard that term before."

"The shrine of the Seventh Pyramid is what I mean," said Vathiimeraak. "The unopened shrine that Dr. Magadone Sambisa found. The name that I used is what we call it among ourselves. You notice that I do not say she 'discovered' it. We have always known that it was there, adjacent to the broken pyramid. But no one ever asked us, and so we never spoke of it."

Valentine glanced across at Deliamber, who nodded ever so minutely. *Hsirthiir* again, yes.

Something was not quite right, though. Valentine said, "Dr. Magadone Sambisa told me that she and Dr. Huukaminaan came upon the seventh shrine jointly, I think. She indicated that he was just as surprised at finding it there as she had been. Are you claiming that you knew of its existence, but he didn't?"

"There is no Piurivar who does not know of the existence of the Shrine of the Downfall," said Vathiimeraak stolidly. "It was sealed at the time of the Defilement and contains, we believe, evidence of the Defilement itself. If Dr. Magadone Sambisa formed the impression that Dr. Huukaminaan was unaware that it was there, that was an incorrect impression." Once again the edges of the foreman's face flickered and wavered. He looked worriedly toward Magadone Sambisa and said, "I mean no offense in contradicting you, Dr. Magadone Sambisa."

"None taken," she said, a little stiffly. "But if Huukaminaan knew of the shrine before the day we found it, he never said a thing about it to me."

"Perhaps he had hoped it would not be found," Vathiimeraak replied.

This brought a show of barely concealed consternation from Magadone Sambisa; and Valentine himself sensed that there was something here that needed to be followed up. But they were drifting away from the main issue.

"What I need you to do," said Valentine to the foreman, "is to determine the whereabouts of every single one of your people during the hours when the murder was committed." He saw Vathiimeraak's reaction beginning to take form, and added quickly, "I'm not suggesting that we believe at this point that anyone from the village killed Dr. Huukaminaan. No one at all is under suspicion at this point. But we do need to account for everybody who was present in or around the excavation zone that night."

"I will do what I can to find out."

"Your help will be invaluable, I know," Valentine said.

"You will also want to enlist the aid of our khivanivod," Vathiimeraak said. "He is not among us tonight. He has gone off on a spiritual retreat into the farthest zone of the city to pray for the purification of the soul of the killer of Dr. Huukaminaan, whoever that may be. I will send him to you when he returns."

Another little surprise.

A khivanivod was a Piurivar holy man, something midway between a priest and a wizard. They were relatively uncommon in modern Metamorph life, and it was remarkable that there should be one in residence at this scruffy out-of-the-way village. Unless, of course, the high religious leaders of the Piurivars had decided that it was best to install one at Velalisier for the duration of the dig, to insure that everything was done with the proper respect for the holy places. It was odd that Magadone Sambisa hadn't mentioned to him that a khivanivod was present here.

"Yes," said Valentine, a little uneasily. "Send him to me, yes. By all means."

As they rode away from the laborers' village Nascimonte said, "Well, Valentine, I'm pained to confess that I find myself once again forced to question your judgment."

"You do suffer much pain on my behalf," said Valentine, with a twinkling smile. "Tell me, Nascimonte: where have I gone amiss this time?"

"You enlisted that man Vathiimeraak as your ally in the investigation. You treated him, in fact, as though he were a trusted constable of police."

"He seems steady enough to me. And the villagers are terrified of him. What harm is there in asking him to question them for us? If we interrogate them ourselves, they'll just shut up like clams—or at best they'll tell us all kinds of fantastic stories. Whereas Vathiimeraak might just be able to bully the truth out of them. Some useful fraction of it, anyway.''

"Not if he's the murderer himself,'' said Nascimonte.

"Ah, is that it? You've solved the crime, my friend? Vathiimeraak did it?''

"That could very well be.''

"Explain, if you will, then.''

Nascimonte gestured to Aarisiim. "Tell him.''

The Metamorph said, "Majesty, I remarked to you when I first saw Vathiimeraak that I thought I knew that man from somewhere. And indeed I do, though it took me a little while more to place him. He is a kinsman of the rebel Faraataa. In the days when I was with Faraataa in Piurifayne, this Vathiimeraak was often by our side.''

That was unexpected. But Valentine kept his reaction to himself. Calmly he said, "Does that matter? What of our amnesty, Aarisiim? All rebels who agreed to keep the peace after the collapse of Faraataa's campaign have been forgiven and restored to full civil rights. I should hardly need to remind you, of all people, of that.''

"It doesn't mean they all turned into good citizens overnight, does it, Valentine?'' Nascimonte demanded. "Surely it's possible that this Vathiimeraak, a man of Faraataa's own blood, still harbors powerful feelings of—''

Valentine looked toward Magadone Sambisa. "Did you know he was related to Faraataa when you hired him as foreman?"

She seemed embarrassed. "No, majesty, I certainly did not. But I was aware that he had been in the Rebellion and had accepted the amnesty. And he came with the highest recommendation. We're supposed to believe that the amnesty has some meaning, doesn't it? That the Rebellion's over and done with, that those who took part in it and repented deserve to be allowed—"

"And has he truly repented, do you think?" Nascimonte asked. "Can anyone know, really? I say he's a fraud from top to toe. That big booming voice! That high-flown style of speaking! Those expressions of profound reverence for the Pontifex! Phony, every bit of it. And as for killing Huukaminaan, just look at him! Do you think it could have been easy to cut the poor man up in pieces that way? But Vathiimeraak's built like a bull bidlak. In that village of thin flimsy folk he stands out the way a dwikka tree would in a flat meadow."

"Because he has the strength for the crime doesn't yet prove that he's guilty of it," said Valentine in some annoyance. "And this other business, of his being related to Faraataa—what possible motive does that give him for slaughtering that harmless old Piurivar archaeologist? No, Nascimonte. No. No. No. You and Tunigorn between you, I know, would take about five minutes to decree that the man should be locked away for life in the Sangamor vaults that lie deep under the Castle. But we need a little evidence before we proclaim anyone a murderer.'' To Magadone Sambisa he said, ''What about this khivanivod, now? Why weren't we told that there's a khivanivod living in this village?''

''He's been away since the day after the murder, your majesty,'' she said, looking at Valentine apprehensively. ''To be perfectly truthful, I forgot all about him.''

''What kind of person is he? Describe him for me.''

A shrug. ''Old. Dirty. A miserable superstition-monger, like all these tribal shamans. What can I say? I dislike having him around. But it's the price we pay for permission to dig here, I suppose.''

''Has he caused any trouble for you?''

''A little. Constantly sniffing into things, worrying that we'll commit some sort of sacrilege. *Sacrilege,* in a city that the Piurivars themselves destroyed and put a curse on! What possible harm could we do here, after what they've already inflicted on it?''

''This was their capital,'' said Valentine. ''They were free to do with it as they pleased. That doesn't mean they're glad to have us come in here and root around in its ruins.—But has he actually tried to halt any part of your work, this khivanivod?"

"He objects to our unsealing the Shrine of the Downfall."

"Ah. You did say there was some political problem about that. He's filed a formal protest, has he?" The understanding by which Valentine had negotiated the right to send archaeologists into Velalisier included a veto power for the Piurivars over any aspect of the work that was not to their liking.

"So far he's simply told us he doesn't want us to open the shrine," said Magadone Sambisa. "He and I and Dr. Huukaminaan were supposed to have a meeting about it last week and try to work out a compromise, although what kind of middle ground there can be between opening the shrine and *not* opening it is hard for me to imagine. In any event the meeting never happened, for obvious tragic reasons. Now that you're here, perhaps you'll adjudicate the dispute for us when Torkkinuuminaad gets back from wherever he's gone off to."

"Torkkinuuminaad?" Valentine said. "Is that the khivanivod's name?"

"Torkkinuuminaad, yes."

"These jawbreaking Shapeshifter names," Nascimonte said grumpily. "Torkkinuuminaad! Vathii-meraak! Huukaminaan!" He glowered at Aarisiim.

"By the Divine, fellow, was it absolutely necessary for you people to give yourself names that are so utterly impossible to pronounce, when you could just as easily have—"

"The system is very logical," Aarisiim replied serenely. "The doubling of the vowels in the first part of a name implies—"

"Save this discussion for some other time, if you will," said Valentine, making a chopping gesture with his hand. To Magadone Sambisa he said, "Just out of curiosity, what was the khivanivod's relationship with Dr. Huukaminaan like? Difficult? Tense? Did he think it was sacrilegious to pull the weeds off these ruins and set some of the buildings upright again?"

"Not at all," Magadone Sambisa said. "They worked hand in glove. They had the highest respect for each other, though the Divine only knows why Dr. Huukaminaan tolerated that filthy old savage for half a minute.—Why? Are you suggesting that *Torkkinuuminaad* could have been the murderer?"

"Is that so unlikely? You haven't had a single good thing to say about him yourself."

"He's an irritating nuisance and in the matter of the shrine, at least, he's certainly made himself a serious obstacle to our work. But a murderer? Even I wouldn't go that far, your majesty. Anyone could

see that he and Huukaminaan had great affection
for each other."

"We should question him, all the same," said
Nascimonte.

"Indeed," said Valentine. "Tomorrow, I want
messengers sent out through the archaeological
zone in search of him. He's somewhere around the
ruins, right? Let's find him and bring him in. If that
interrupts his spiritual retreat, so be it. Tell him that
the Pontifex commands his presence."

"I'll see to it," said Magadone Sambisa.

"The Pontifex is very tired, now," said Valentine. "The Pontifex is going to go to sleep."

Alone in his grand royal tent at last after the in-
terminable exertions of the busy day, he found himself missing Carabella with surprising intensity:
that small and sinewy woman who had shared his
destiny almost from the beginning of the strange
time when he had found himself at Pidruid, at the
other continent's edge, bereft of all memory, all
knowledge of self. It was she, loving him only for
himself, all unknowing that he was in fact a Coronal in baffled exile from his true identity, who had
helped him join the juggling troupe of Zalzan Ka-
vol; and gradually their lives had merged; and
when he had commenced his astounding return to

the heights of power she had followed him to the summit of the world.

He wished she were with him now. To sit beside him, to talk with him as they always talked before bedtime. To go over with him the twisting ramifications of all that had been set before him this day. To help him make sense out of the tangled mysteries this dead city posed for him. And simply to *be* with him.

But Carabella had not followed him here to Velalisier. It was a foolish waste of his time, she had argued, for him to go in person to investigate this murder. Send Tunigorn; send Mirigant; send Sleet; send any one of a number of high Pontifical officials. But why go yourself?

"Because I must," Valentine had replied. "Because I've made myself responsible for integrating the Metamorphs into the life of this world. The excavations at Velalisier are an essential part of that enterprise. And the murder of the old archaeologist leads me to think that conspirators are trying to interfere with those excavations."

"This is very far-fetched," said Carabella, then.

"And if it is, so be it. But you know how I long for a chance to free myself of the Labyrinth, if only for a week or two. So I will go to Velalisier."

"And I will not. I loathe that place, Valentine. It's a horrid place of death and destruction. I've seen it twice, and its charm isn't growing on me. If you go, you'll go without me."

"I mean to go, Carabella."

"Go, then. If you must." And she kissed him on the tip of the nose, for they were not in the custom of quarreling, or even of disagreeing greatly. But when he went, it was indeed without her. She was in their royal chambers in the Labyrinth tonight, and he was here, in his grand but solitary tent, in this parched and broken city of ancient ghosts.

They came to him that night in his dreams, those ghosts.

They came to him with such intensity that he thought he was having a sending—a lucid and purposeful direct communication in the form of a dream.

But this was like no sending he had ever had. Hardly had he closed his eyes but he found himself wandering in his sleep among the cracked and splintered buildings of dead Velalisier. Eerie ghost-light, mystery-light, came dancing up out of every shattered stone. The city glowed lime-green and lemon-yellow, pulsating with inner luminescence. Glowing faces, ghost-faces, grinned mockingly at him out of the air. The sun itself swirled and leaped in wild loops across the sky.

A dark hole leading into the ground lay open

before him, and unquestioningly he entered it, descending a long flight of massive lichen-encrusted stone steps with archaic twining runes carved in them. Every movement was arduous for him. Though he was going steadily lower, the effort was like that of climbing. Struggling all the way, he made his way ever deeper, but he felt constantly as though he were traveling upward against a powerful pull, ascending some inverted pyramid, not a slender one like those above ground in this city, but one of unthinkable mass and diameter. He imagined himself to be fighting his way up the side of a mountain; but it was a mountain that pointed downward, deep into the world's bowels. And the path was carrying him down, he knew, into some labyrinth far more frightful than the one in which he dwelled in daily life.

The whirling ghost-faces flashed dizzyingly by him and went spinning away. Cackling laughter floated backward to him out of the darkness. The air was moist and hot and rank. The pull of gravity was oppressive. As he descended, traveling through level after endless level, momentary flares of dizzying yellow light showed him caverns twisting away from him on all sides, radiating outward at incomprehensible angles that were both concave and convex.

And now there was sudden numbing brightness.

The throbbing fire of an underground sun streamed upward toward him from the depths ahead of him, a harsh, menacing glare.

Valentine found himself drawn helplessly toward that terrible light; and then, without perceptible transition, he was no longer underground at all, but out in the vastness of Velalisier Plain, standing atop one of the great platforms of blue stone known as the Tables of the Gods.

There was a long knife in his hand, a curving scimitar that flashed like lightning in the brilliance of the noon sun.

And as he looked out across the plain he saw a mighty procession coming toward him from the east, from the direction of the distant sea: thousands of people, hundreds of thousands, like an army of ants on the march. No, two armies; for the marchers were divided into two great parallel columns. Valentine could see, at the end of each column far off near the horizon, two enormous wooden wagons mounted on titanic wheels. Great hawsers were fastened to them, and the marchers, with mighty groaning tugs, were hauling the wagons slowly forward, a foot or two with each pull, into the center of the city.

Atop each of the wagons a colossal water-king lay trussed, a sea-dragon of monstrous size. The great creatures were glaring furiously at their captors but were unable, even with a sea-dragon's prodigious strength, to free themselves from their bonds, strain as they might. And with each tug on the hawsers the wagons bearing them carried them closer to the twin platforms called the Tables of the Gods.

The place of the sacrifice.

The place where the terrible madness of the Defilement was to happen. Where Valentine the Pontifex of Majipoor waited with the long gleaming blade in his hand.

Majesty? Majesty?''

Valentine blinked and came groggily awake. A Shapeshifter stood above him, extremely tall and greatly attenuated of form, his eyes so sharply slanted and narrowed that it seemed at first glance that he had none at all. Valentine began to jump up in alarm; and then, recognizing the intruder after a moment as Aarisiim, he relaxed.

"You cried out," the Metamorph said. "I was on my way to you to tell you some strange news I have learned, and when I was outside your tent I heard your voice. Are you all right, your majesty?"

"A dream, only. A very nasty dream." Which still lingered disagreeably at the edges of his mind. Valentine shivered and tried to shake himself free of its grasp. "What time is it, Aarisiim?"

"The Hour of the Haigus, majesty."

Past the middle of the night, that was. Well along toward dawn.

Valentine forced himself the rest of the way into wakefulness. Eyes fully open now, he stared up into the practically featureless face. "There's news, you say? What news?"

The Metamorph's color deepened from pale green to a rich chartreuse, and his eye slits fluttered swiftly three or four times. "I have had a conversation this night with one of the archaeologists, the woman Hieekraad, she who keeps the records of the discovered artifacts. The foreman of the diggers brought her to me, the man Vathiimeraak, from the village. He and this Hieekraad are lovers, it seems."

Valentine stirred impatiently. "Get to the point, Aarisiim."

"I approach it, sir. The woman Hieekraad, it seems, has revealed things to the man Vathiimeraak about the excavations that a mere foreman might otherwise not have known. He has told those things to me this evening."

"Well?"

"They have been lying to us, majesty—all the archaeologists, the whole pack of them, deliberately concealing something important. Something *quite* important, a major discovery. Vathiimeraak, when he learned from this Hieekraad that we had been deceived in this way, made the woman come with him to me, and compelled her to reveal the whole story to me.''

''Go on.''

''It was this,'' said Aarisiim. He paused a moment, swaying a little as though he were about to plunge into a fathomless abyss. ''Dr. Huukamínaan, two weeks before he died, uncovered a burial site that had never been detected before. This was in an otherwise desolate region out at the western edge of the city. Magadone Sambisa was with him. It was a post-abandonment site, dating from the historic era. From a time not long after Lord Stiamot, actually.''

''But how could that be?'' said Valentine, frowning. ''Completely aside from the little matter that there was a curse on this place and no Piurivar would have dared to set foot in it after it was destroyed, there weren't any Piurivars living on this continent at that time anyway. Stiamot had sent them all into the reservations on Zimroel. You know that very well, Aarisiim. Something's wrong here.''

''This was not a Piurivar burial, your majesty.''

''What?''

''It was the tomb of a human,'' Aarisiim said.

"The tomb of a *Pontifex*, according to the woman Hieekraad."

Valentine would not have been more surprised if Aarisiim had set off an explosive charge. "A Pontifex?" he repeated numbly. "The tomb of a Pontifex, here in Velalisier?"

"So did this Hieekraad say. A definite identification. The symbols on the wall of the tomb—the Labyrinth sign, and other things of that sort—the ceremonial objects found lying next to the body— inscriptions—everything indicated that this was a Pontifex's grave, thousands of years old. So she said; and I think she was telling the truth. Vathi- imeraak was standing over her, scowling, as she spoke. She was too frightened of him to have ut- tered any falsehoods just then."

Valentine rose and paced fiercely about the tent. "By the Divine, Aarisiim! If this is true, it's some- thing that should have been brought to my attention as soon as it came to light. Or at least mentioned to me upon my arrival here. The tomb of some ancient Pontifex, and they hide it from me? Un- believable. Unbelievable!"

"It was Magadone Sambisa herself who ordered that all news of the discovery was to be suppressed. There would be no public announcement whatever. Not even the diggers were told what had been uncovered. It was to be a secret known to the ar- chaeologists of the dig, only."

"This according to Hieekraad also?"

"Yes, majesty. She said that Magadone Sambisa gave those orders the very day the tomb was found. This Hieekraad furthermore told me that Dr. Huukaminaan disagreed strenuously with Magadone Sambisa's decision, that indeed they had a major quarrel over it. But in the end he gave in. And when the murder happened, and word came that you were going to visit Velalisier, Magadone Sambisa called a meeting of the staff and reiterated that nothing was to be said to you about it. Everyone involved with the dig was specifically told to keep all knowledge of it from you."

"Absolutely incredible," Valentine muttered.

Earnestly Aarisiim said, "You must protect the woman Hieekraad, majesty, as you investigate this thing. She will be in great trouble if Magadone Sambisa learns that she's the one who let the story of the tomb get out."

"Hieekraad's not the only one who's going to be in trouble," Valentine said. He slipped from his nightclothes and started to dress.

"One more thing, majesty. The khivanivod—Torkkinuuminaad? He's at the tomb site right now. That's where he went to make his prayer retreat. I have this information from the foreman Vathiimeraak."

"Splendid," Valentine said. His head was whirling. "The village khivanivod mumbling Piurivar prayers in the tomb of a Pontifex! Beautiful! Wonderful!—Get me Magadone Sambisa, right away, Aarisiim."

"Majesty, the hour is very early, and—"

"Did you hear me, Aarisiim?"

"Majesty," said the Shapeshifter, more subserviently this time. He bowed deeply. And went out to fetch Magadone Sambisa.

An ancient Pontifex's tomb, Magadone Sambisa, and no announcement is made? An ancient Pontifex's tomb, and when the current Pontifex comes to inspect your dig, you go out of your way to keep him from learning about it? This is all extremely difficult for me to believe, let me assure you."

Dawn was still an hour away. Magadone Sambisa, called from her bed for this interview, looked even paler and more haggard than she had yesterday, and now there might have been a glint of fear in her eyes as well. But for all that, she still was capable of summoning some of the unrelenting strength that had propelled her to the forefront of her profession: there was even a steely touch of defiance in her voice as she said, "Who told you about this tomb, your majesty?"

Valentine ignored the sally. "It was at your order, was it, that the story was suppressed?"

"Yes."

"Over Dr. Huukaminaan's strong objections, so I understand."

Now fury flashed across her features. "They've told you everything, haven't they? Who was it? Who?"

"Let me remind you, lady, that I am the one asking the questions here.—It's true, then, that Huukaminaan disagreed with you about concealing the discovery?"

"Yes." In a very small voice.

"Why was that?"

"He saw it as a crime against the truth," Magadone Sambisa said, still speaking very quietly now. "You have to understand, majesty, that Dr. Huukaminaan was utterly dedicated to his work. Which was, as it is for us all, the recovery of the lost aspects of our past through rigorous application of formal archaeological disciplines. He was totally committed to this, a true and pure scientist."

"Whereas you are not committed quite so totally?"

Magadone Sambisa reddened and glanced shamefacedly to one side. "I admit that my actions may make it seem that way. But sometimes even the pursuit of truth has to give way, at least for a time, before tactical realities. Surely you, a Pontifex, would not deny that. And I had reasons, reasons that seemed valid enough to me, for not wanting to let news of this tomb reach the public. Dr. Huukaminaan didn't agree with my position; and he and I battled long and hard over it. It was the only occasion in our time as co-leaders of this expedition that we disagreed over anything.''

"And finally it became necessary, then, for you to have him murdered? Because he yielded to you only grudgingly, and you weren't sure he really would keep quiet?''

"*Majesty!*'' It was a cry of almost inexpressible shock.

"A motive for the killing can be seen there. Isn't that so?''

She looked stunned. She waved her arms helplessly about, the palms of her hands turned outward in appeal. A long moment passed before she could bring herself to speak. But she had recovered much of her composure when she did.

"Majesty, what you have just suggested is greatly offensive to me. I am guilty of hiding the tomb discovery, yes. But I swear to you that I had nothing to do with Dr. Huukaminaan's death. I can't possibly tell you how much I admired that

man. We had our professional differences, but—''
She shook her head. She looked drained. Very quietly she said, "I didn't kill him. I have no idea who did.''

Valentine chose to accept that, for now. It was hard for him to believe that she was merely play-acting her distress.

"Very well, Magadone Sambisa. But now tell me why you decided to conceal the finding of that tomb.''

"I would have to tell you, first, an old Piurivar legend, a tale out of their mythology, one that I heard from the khivanivod Torkkinuuminaad on the day that we found the tomb.''

"Must you?''

"I must, yes.''

Valentine sighed. "Go ahead, then.''

Magadone Sambisa moistened her lips and drew a deep breath.

"There once was a Pontifex, so the story goes,'' she said, "who lived in the years soon after the conquest of the Piurivars by Lord Stiamot. This Pontifex had fought in the War of the Conquest himself when he was a young man, and had had charge over a camp of Piurivar prisoners, and had listened to some of their campfire tales. Among which was the story of the Defilement at Velalisier—the sacrifice by the Final King of the two sea-dragons, and the destruction of the city that followed it. They told him also of the broken Seventh Pyramid, and of the shrine beneath it, the Shrine of the Downfall, as they called it. In which, they said, certain artifacts dating from the day of the Defilement had been buried—artifacts that would, when properly used, grant their wielder godlike power over all the forces of space and time. This story stayed with him, and many years later when he had become Pontifex he came to Velalisier with the intention of locating the shrine of the Seventh Pyramid, the Shrine of the Downfall, and opening it."

"For the purpose of bringing forth these magical artifacts, and using them to gain godlike power over the forces of space and time?"

"Exactly," said Magadone Sambisa.

"I think I see where this is heading."

"Perhaps you do, majesty. We are told that he went to the site of the shattered pyramid. He drove a tunnel into the ground; he came upon the stone passageway that leads to the wall of the shrine. He found the wall and made preparations for breaking through it."

"But the seventh shrine, you told me, is intact. Since the time of the abandonment of the city no one has ever entered it. Or so you believe."

"No one ever has. I'm sure of that."

"This Pontifex, then—?"

"Was just at the moment of breaching the shrine wall when a Piurivar who had hidden himself in the tunnel overnight rose up out of the darkness and put a sword through his heart."

"Wait a moment," said Valentine. Exasperation began to stir in him. "A Piurivar popped out of nowhere and killed him, you say? A *Piurivar*? I've just gone through this same thing with Aarisiim. Not only weren't there any Piurivars anywhere in Alhanroel at that time, because Stiamot had locked them all up in reservations over in Zimroel, but there was supposed to be a curse on this place that would have prevented members of their race from going near it."

"Except for the guardians of the shrine, who were exempted from the curse," said Magadone Sambisa.

"Guardians?" Valentine said. "What guardians? I've never heard anything about Piurivar guardians here."

"Nor had I, until Torkkinuuminaad told me this story. But at the time of the city's destruction and abandonment, evidently, a decision was made to post a small band of watchmen here, so that nobody would be able to break into the seventh shrine and gain access to whatever's in there. And that guard force remained on duty here throughout the centuries. There were still guardians here when the Pontifex came to loot the shrine. One of them tucked himself away in the tunnel and killed the Pontifex just as he was about to chop through the wall.''

"And his people buried him *here*? Why in the world would they do that?"

Magadone Sambisa smiled. "To hush things up, of course. Consider, majesty: A Pontifex comes to Velalisier in search of forbidden mystical knowledge, and is assassinated by a Piurivar who has been sneaking around undetected in the supposedly abandoned city. If word of that got around, it would make everyone look bad."

"I suppose that it would."

"The Pontifical officials certainly wouldn't have wanted to let it be known that their master had been struck down right under their noses. Nor would they be eager to advertise the story of the secret shrine, which might lead others to come here looking for it too. And surely they'd never want anyone to know that the Pontifex had died at the hand of a Piurivar, something that could reopen all the wounds of the War of the Conquest and perhaps touch off some very nasty reprisals."

"And so they covered everything up," said Valentine.

"Exactly. They dug a tomb off in a remote corner of the ruins and buried the Pontifex in it with some sort of appropriate ritual, and went back to the Labyrinth with the news that his majesty had very suddenly been stricken down at the ruins by an unknown disease and it had seemed unwise to bring his body back from Velalisier for the usual kind of state funeral—Ghorban, was his name. There's an inscription in the tomb that names him. Ghorban Pontifex, three Pontifexes after Stiamot. He really existed. I did research in the House of Records. You'll see him listed there.''

''I'm not familiar with the name.''

''No. He's not exactly one of the famous ones. But who can remember them all, anyway? Hundreds and hundreds of them, across all those thousands of years. Ghorban was Pontifex only a short while, and the only event of any importance that occurred during his reign was something that was carefully obliterated from the records. I'm speaking of his visit to Velalisier.''

Valentine nodded. He had paused by the great screen outside the Labyrinth's House of Records often enough, and many times had stared at that long list of his predecessors, marveling at the names of all-but-forgotten monarchs, Meyk and Spurifon and Heslaine and Kandibal and dozens more. Who must have been great men in their day, but their day was thousands of years in the past.

No doubt there was a Ghorban on the list, if Magadone Sambisa said there had been: who had reigned in regal grandeur for a time as the Coronal Lord Ghorban atop Castle Mount, and then had succeeded to the Pontificate in the fullness of his years, and for some reason had paid a visit to this accursed city of Velalisier, where he died, and was buried, and fell into oblivion.

"A curious tale," Valentine said. "But what is there in it that would have made you want to suppress the discovery of this Ghorban's tomb?"

"The same thing that made those ancient Pontifical officials suppress the real circumstances of his death," replied Magadone Sambisa. "You surely know that most ordinary people already are sufficiently afraid of this city. The horrible story of the Defilement, the curse, all the talk of ghosts lurking in the ruins, the general spookiness of the place—well, you know what people are like, your majesty. How timid they can be in the face of the unknown. And I was afraid that if the Ghorban story came out—the secret shrine, the search for mysterious magical lore by some obscure ancient Pontifex, the murder of that Pontifex by a Piurivar—there'd be such public revulsion against the whole idea of excavating Velalisier that the dig would be shut down. I didn't want that to happen. That's all it was, your majesty. I was trying to preserve my own job, I suppose. Nothing more than that.''

It was a humiliating confession. Her tone, which had been vigorous enough during the telling of the tale, now was flat, weary, almost lifeless. To Valentine it had the sound of complete sincerity.

''And Dr. Huukaminaan didn't agree with you that revealing the discovery of the tomb could be a threat to the continuation of your work here?''

''He saw the risk. He didn't care. For him the truth came first and foremost, always. If public opinion forced the dig to be shut down, and nobody worked here again for fifty or a hundred or five hundred years, that was all right with him. His integrity wouldn't permit hiding a startling piece of history like that, not for any reason. So we had a big battle and finally I pushed him into giving in. You've seen how stubborn I can be. But I didn't kill him. If I had wanted to kill anybody, it wouldn't have been Dr. Huukaminaan. It would have been the khivanivod, who actually *does* want the dig shut down.''

''He does? You said he and Huukaminaan worked hand in glove.''

''In general, yes. As I told you yesterday, there was one area where he and Huukaminaan diverged: the issue of opening the shrine. Huukaminaan and I, you know, were planning to open it as soon as we could arrange for you and Lord Hissune to be present at the work. But the khivanivod was passionately opposed. The rest of our work here was acceptable to him, but not that. The Shrine of the Downfall, he kept saying, is the holy of holies, the most sacred Piurivar place.''

"He might just have a point there," Valentine said.

"You also don't think we should look inside that shrine?"

"I think that there are certain important Piurivar leaders who might very much not want that to happen."

"But the Danipiur herself has given us permission to work here! Not only that, but she and all the rest of the Piurivar leaders understand that we've come here to restore the city—that we hope to undo as much as we can of the harm that thousands of years of neglect have caused. They have no quarrel with that. But just to be completely certain that our work would give no offense to the Piurivar community, we all agreed that the expedition would consist of equal numbers of Piurivar and non-Piurivar archaeologists, and that Dr. Huukaminaan and I would share the leadership on a co-equal basis."

"Although you turned out to be somewhat more co-equal than he was when there happened to be a significant disagreement between the two of you, didn't you?"

"In that one instance of the Ghorban tomb, yes," said Magadone Sambisa, looking just a little out of countenance. "But only that one. He and I were in complete agreement at all times on everything else. On the issue of opening the shrine, for example."

"A decision which the khivanivod then vetoed."

"The khivanivod has no power to veto anything, majesty. The understanding we had was that any Piurivar who objected to some aspect of our work on religious grounds could appeal to the Danipiur, who would then adjudicate the matter in consultation with you and Lord Hissune."

"Yes. I wrote that decree myself, actually."

Valentine closed his eyes a moment and pressed the tips of his fingers against them. He should have realized, he told himself, that problems like these would inevitably crop up. This city had too much tragic history. Terrible things had happened here. The mysterious aura of Piurivar sorcery still hovered over the place, thousands of years after its destruction.

He had hoped to dispel some of that aura by sending in these scientists. Instead he had only enmeshed himself in its dark folds.

After a time he looked up and said, "I understand from Aarisiim that where your khivanivod has gone to make his spiritual retreat is in fact the Ghorban tomb that you've taken such pains to hide from me, and that he's there at this very moment. Is that true?''

''I believe it is.''

The Pontifex walked to the tent entrance and peered outside. The first bronze streaks of the desert dawn were arching across the great vault of the sky.

''Last night,'' he said, ''I asked you to send messengers out looking for him, and you said that you would. You didn't, of course, tell me that you knew where he was. But since you do know, get your messengers moving. I want to speak with him first thing this morning.''

''And if he refuses to come, your majesty?''

''Then have him brought.''

The khivanivod Torkkinuuminaad was every bit as disagreeable as Magadone Sambisa had led Valentine to expect, although the fact that it had been necessary for Valentine's security people to threaten to drag him bodily from the Ghorban tomb must not have improved his temper. Lisamon Hultin was the one who had ordered him out of there, heedless of his threats and curses. Piurivar witcheries and spells held little dread for her, and she let him know that if he didn't go to Valentine more or less willingly on his own two feet, she would carry him to the Pontifex herself.

The Shapeshifter shaman was an ancient, emaciated man, naked but for some wisps of dried grass around his waist and a nasty-looking amulet, fashioned of interwoven insect legs and other such things, that dangled from a frayed cord about his neck. He was so old that his green skin had faded to a faint gray, and his slitted eyes, bright with rage, glared balefully at Valentine out of sagging folds of rubbery skin.

Valentine began on a conciliatory note. "I ask your pardon for interrupting your meditations. But certain urgent matters must be dealt with before I return to the Labyrinth, and your presence was needed for that."

Torkkinuuminaad said nothing.

Valentine proceeded regardless. "For one thing, a serious crime has been committed in the archaeological zone. The killing of Dr. Huukaminaan is an offense not only against justice but against knowledge itself. I'm here to see that the murderer is identified and punished."

"What does this have to do with me?" asked the khivanivod, glowering sullenly. "If there has been a murder, you should find the murderer and punish him, yes, if that is what you feel you must do. But why must a servant of the Gods That Are be compelled by force to break off his sacred communion like this? Because the Pontifex of Majipoor commands it?'' Torkkinuuminaad laughed harshly. ''The Pontifex! Why should the commands of the Pontifex mean anything to me? I serve only the Gods That Are.''

''You also serve the Danipiur,'' said Valentine in a calm, quiet tone. ''And the Danipiur and I are colleagues in the government of Majipoor.'' He indicated Magadone Sambisa and the other archaeologists, both human and Metamorph, who stood nearby. ''These people are at work in Velalisier this day because the Danipiur has granted her permission for them to be here. You yourself are here at the Danipiur's request, I believe. To serve as spiritual counselor for those of your people who are involved in the work.''

''I am here because the Gods That Are require me to be here, and for no other reason.''

''Be that as it may, your Pontifex stands before you, and he has questions to ask you, and you will answer.''

The shaman's only response was a sour glare.

''A shrine has been discovered near the ruins of the Seventh Pyramid,'' Valentine went on. ''I understand that the late Dr. Huukaminaan intended to open that shrine. You had strong objections to that, am I correct?"

"You are."

"Objections on what grounds?"

"That the shrine is a sacred place not to be disturbed by profane hands."

"How can there be a sacred place," asked Valentine, "in a city that had a curse pronounced on it?"

"The shrine is sacred nevertheless," the khivanivod said obdurately.

"Even though no one knows what may be inside it?"

"*I* know what is inside it," said the khivanivod.

"You? How?"

"I am the guardian of the shrine. The knowledge is handed down from guardian to guardian."

Valentine felt a chill traveling along his spine. "Ah," he said. "The guardian. Of the shrine." He was silent a moment. "As the officially designated successor, I suppose, of the guardian who murdered a Pontifex here once thousands of years ago. The place where you were found praying just now, so I've been told, was the tomb of that very Pontifex. Is that so?"

"It is."

"In that case," said Valentine, allowing a little smile to appear at the corners of his mouth, "I need to ask my guards to keep very careful watch on you. Because the next thing I'm going to do, my friend, is to instruct Magadone Sambisa and her people to proceed at once with the opening of the seventh shrine. And I see now that that might place me in some danger at your hands.''

Torkkinuuminaad looked astounded. Abruptly the Metamorph shaman began to go through a whole repertoire of violent changes of form, contracting and elongating wildly, the borders of his body blurring and recomposing with bewildering speed.

But the archaeologists too, both the human ones and the two Ghayrogs and the little tight-knit group of Shapeshifters, were staring at Valentine as though he had just said something beyond all comprehension. Even Tunigorn and Mirigant and Nascimonte were flabbergasted. Tunigorn turned to Mirigant and said something, to which Mirigant replied only with a shrug, and Nascimonte, standing near them, shrugged also in complete bafflement.

Magadone Sambisa said in hoarse choking tones, ''Majesty? Do you mean that? I thought you said only a little while ago that the best thing would be to leave the shrine unopened!''

''I said that? I?'' Valentine shook his head. ''Oh, no. No. How long will it take you to get started on the job?''

"Why—let me see—" He heard her murmur, "The recording devices, the lighting equipment, the masonry drills—" She grew quiet, as if counting additional things off in her mind. Then she said, "We could be ready to begin in half an hour."

"Good. Let's get going, then."

"No! This will not be!" cried Torkkinuuminaad, a wild screech of rage.

"It will," said Valentine. "And you'll be there to watch it. As will I." He beckoned toward Lisamon Hultin. "Speak with him, Lisamon. Tell him in a persuasive way that it'll be much better for him if he remains calm."

Magadone Sambisa said, wonderingly, "Are you serious about all this, Pontifex?"

"Oh, yes. Yes. Very serious indeed."

The day seemed a hundred hours long.

Opening any sealed site for the first time would ordinarily have been a painstaking process. But this one was so important, so freighted with symbolic significance, so potentially explosive in its political implications, that every task was done with triple care.

Valentine himself waited at surface level during the early stages of the work. What they were doing down there had all been explained to him—running cables for illumination and ventilating pipes for the excavators; carefully checking with sonic probes to make sure that opening the shrine wall would not cause the ceiling of the vault to collapse; sonic testing of the interior of the shrine itself to see if there was anything important immediately behind the wall that might be imperiled by the drilling operation.

All that took hours. Finally they were ready to start cutting into the wall.

"Would you like to watch, majesty?" Magadone Sambisa asked.

Despite the ventilation equipment, Valentine found it hard work to breathe inside the tunnel. The air had been hot and stale enough on his earlier visit; but now, with all these people crowded into it, it was thin, feeble stuff, and he had to strain his lungs to keep from growing dizzy.

The close-packed archaeologists parted ranks to let him come forward. Bright lights cast a brilliant glare on the white stone façade of the shrine. Five people were gathered there, three Piurivars, two humans. The actual drilling seemed to be the responsibility of the burly foreman Vathiimeraak. Kaasti-siik, the Piurivar archaeologist who was the site boss, was assisting. Just behind them was Driismiil, the Piurivar architectural expert, and a human woman named Shimrayne Gelvoin, who also was an architect, evidently. Magadone Sambisa stood to the rear, quietly issuing orders.

They were peeling the wall back stone by stone. Already an area of the façade perhaps three feet square had been cleared just above the row of offering alcoves. Behind it lay rough brickwork, no more than one course thick. Vathiimeraak, muttering to himself in Piurivar as he worked, now was chiseling away at one of the bricks. It came loose in a crumbling mass, revealing an inner wall made of the same fine black stone slabs as the tunnel wall itself.

A long pause, now, while the several layers of the wall were measured and photographed. Then Vathiimeraak resumed the inward probing. Valentine was at the edge of queasiness in this foul, acrid atmosphere, but he forced it back.

Vathiimeraak cut deeper, halting to allow Kaastisiik to remove some broken pieces of the black stone. The two architects came forward and inspected the opening, conferring first with each other, then with Magadone Sambisa; and then Vathiimeraak stepped toward the breach once again with his drilling tool.

"We need a torch," Magadone Sambisa said suddenly. "Give me a torch, someone!"

A hand torch was passed up the line from the crowd in the rear of the tunnel. Magadone Sambisa thrust it into the opening, peered, gasped.

"Majesty? Majesty, would you come and look?"

By that single shaft of light Valentine made out a large rectangular room, which appeared to be completely empty except for a large square block of dark stone. It was very much like the glossy block of black opal, streaked with veins of scarlet ruby, from which the glorious Confalume Throne at the castle of the Coronal had been carved.

There were things lying on that block. But what they were was impossible to tell at this distance.

"How long will it take to make an opening big enough for someone to enter the room?" Valentine asked.

"Three hours, maybe."

"Do it in two. I'll wait aboveground. You call me when the opening is made. Be certain that no one enters it before me."

"You have my word, majesty."

Even the dry desert air was a delight after an hour or so of breathing the dank stuff below. Valentine could see by the lengthening shadows creeping across the deep sockets of the distant dunes that the afternoon was well along. Tunigorn, Mirigant, and Nascimonte were pacing about amidst the rubble of the fallen pyramid. The Vroon Deliamber stood a little distance apart.

"Well?" Tunigorn asked.

"They've got a little bit of the wall open. There's something inside, but we don't know what, yet."

"Treasure?" Tunigorn asked, with a lascivious grin. "Mounds of emeralds and diamonds and jade?"

"Yes," said Valentine. "All that and more. Treasure. An enormous treasure, Tunigorn." He chuckled and turned away. "Do you have any wine with you, Nascimonte?"

"As ever, my friend. A fine Muldemar vintage."

He handed his flask to the Pontifex, who drank deep, not pausing to savor the bouquet at all, guzzling as though the wine were water.

The shadows deepened. One of the lesser moons crept into the margin of the sky.

"Majesty? Would you come below?"

It was the archaeologist Vo-Siimifon. Valentine followed him into the tunnel.

The opening in the wall was large enough now to admit one person. Magadone Sambisa, her hand trembling, handed Valentine the torch.

"I must ask you, your majesty, to touch nothing, to make no disturbance whatever. We will not deny you the privilege of first entry, but you must bear in mind that this is a scientific enterprise. We have to record everything just as we find it before anything, however trivial, can be moved."

"I understand," said Valentine.

He stepped carefully over the section of the wall below the opening and clambered in.

The shrine's floor was of some smooth glistening stone, perhaps rosy quartz. A fine layer of dust covered it. *No one has walked across this floor for twenty thousand years,* Valentine thought. *No human foot has ever come in contact with it at all.*

He approached the broad block of black stone in the center of the room and turned the torch full on it. Yes, a single dark mass of ruby-streaked opal, just like the Confalume Throne. Atop it, with only the faintest tracery of dust concealing its brilliance, lay a flat sheet of gold, engraved with intricate Piurivar glyphs and inlaid with cabochons of what looked like beryl and carnelian and lapis lazuli. Two long, slender objects that could have been daggers carved from some white stone lay precisely in the center of the gold sheet, side by side.

Valentine felt a tremor of the deepest awe. He knew what those two things were.

"Majesty? Majesty?" Magadone Sambisa called. "Tell us what you see! Tell us, please!"

But Valentine did not reply. It was as though Magadone Sambisa had not spoken. He was deep in memory, traveling back eight years to the climactic hour of the War of the Rebellion.

He had, in that hour, held in his hand a dagger-like thing much like these two, and had felt the strange coolness of it, a coolness that gave a hint of a fiery core within, and had heard a complex far-off music emanating from it into his mind, a turbulent rush of dizzying sound.

It had been the tooth of a sea-dragon that he had been grasping then. Some mystery within that tooth had placed his mind in communion with the mind of the mighty water-king Maazmoorn, a dragon of the distant Inner Sea. And with the aid of the mind of Maazmoorn had Valentine Pontifex reached across the world to strike down the unrepentent rebel Faraataa and bring that sorry uprising to an end.

Whose teeth were these, now?

He thought he knew. This was the Shrine of the Downfall, the Place of the Defilement. Not far from here, long ago, two water-kings had been brought from the sea to be sacrificed on platforms of blue stone. That was no myth. It had actually happened. Valentine had no doubt of that, for the sea-dragon Maazmoorn had shown it to him with the full communion of his mind, in a manner that admitted of no question. He knew their names, even: one was the water-king Niznorn and the other the water-king Domsitor. Was this tooth here Niznorn's, and this one Domsitor's?

Twenty thousand years.

"Majesty? Majesty?"

"One moment," Valentine said, speaking as though from halfway around the world.

He picked up the left-hand tooth. Grasped it tightly. Hissed as its fiery chill stung the palm of his hand. Closed his eyes, allowed his mind to be pervaded by its magic. Felt his spirit beginning to soar outward and outward and outward, toward some waiting dragon of the sea—Maazmoorn again, for all he could know, or perhaps some other one of the giants who swam in those waters out there—while all the time he heard the sounding bells, the tolling music of that sea-dragon's mind.

And was granted a vision of the ancient sacrifice of the two water-kings, the event known as the Defilement.

He already knew, from Maazmoorn in that meeting of minds years ago, that that traditional name was a misnomer. There had been no defilement whatever. It had been a voluntary sacrifice; it had been the formal acceptance by the sea-dragons of the power of That Which Is, which is the highest of all the forces of the universe.

The water-kings had given themselves gladly to those Piurivars of long-ago Velalisier to be slain. The slayers themselves had understood what they were doing, perhaps, but the simple Piurivars of the outlying provinces had not; and so those simpler

Piurivars had called it a Defilement, and had put the Final King of Velalisier to death and smashed the Seventh Pyramid and then had wrecked all the rest of this great capital, and had laid a curse on the city forever. But the shrine of these teeth they had not dared to touch.

Valentine, holding the tooth, beheld the sacrifice once more. Not with the bound sea-dragons writhing in fury as they were brought to the knife, the way he had seen it in his nightmare of the previous night. No. He saw it now as a serene and holy ceremony, a benign yielding up of the living flesh. And as the knives flashed, as the great sea-creatures died, as their dark flesh was carried to the pyres for burning, a resounding wave of triumphant harmony went rolling out to the boundaries of the universe.

He put the tooth down and picked up the other one. Grasped. Felt. Surrendered himself to its power.

This time the music was more discordant. The vision that came to him was that of some unknown man of middle years, garbed in a rich costume of antique design, clothing befitting to a Pontifex. He was moving cautiously by the smoky light of a flickering torch down the very passageway outside this room where Magadone Sambisa and her archaeologists now clustered. Valentine watched that

Pontifex of long ago approaching the white unsullied wall of the shrine. Saw him press the flat of his hand against it, pushing as though he hoped to penetrate it by his own strength alone. Turning from it, then, beckoning to workmen with picks and spades, indicating that they should start hacking their way through it.

And a figure uncoiling out of the darkness, a Shapeshifter, long and lean and grim-faced, taking one great step forward and in a swift unstoppable lunge driving a knife upward and inward beneath the heart of the man in the brocaded Pontifical robes—

Majesty, I beg you!"

Magadone Sambisa's voice, ripe with anguish.

"Yes," said Valentine, in the distant tone of one who has been lost in a dream. "I'm coming."

He had had enough visions, for the moment. He set the torch down on the floor, aiming it toward the opening in the wall to light his way. Carefully he picked up the two dragon teeth—letting them rest easily on the palms of his hands, taking care not to touch them so tightly as to activate their powers, for he did not want now to open his mind to them—and made his way back out of the shrine.

Magadone Sambisa stared at him in horror. "I asked you, your majesty, not to touch the objects in the vault, not to cause any disturbance to—"

"Yes. I know that. You will pardon me for what I have done."

It was not a request.

The archaeologists melted back out of his way as he strode through their midst, heading for the exit to the upper world. Every eye was turned to the things that rested on Valentine's upturned hands.

"Bring the khivanivod to me here," he said quietly to Aarisiim. The light of day was nearly gone now, and the ruins were taking on the greater mysteriousness that came over them by night, when moonlight's cool gleam danced across the shattered city's ancient stones.

The Shapeshifter went rushing away. Valentine had not wanted the khivanivod anywhere near the shrine while the opening of the wall was taking place; and so, over his violent objections, Torkkinuuminaad had been bundled off to the archaeologists' headquarters in the custody of some of Valentine's security people. The two immense woolly Skandars brought him forth now, holding him by the arms.

Anger and hatred were bubbling up from the shaman like black gas rising from a churning marsh. And, staring into that jagged green wedge of a face, Valentine had a powerful sense of the ancient magic of this world, of mysteries reaching toward him out of the timeless misty Majipoor dawn, when Shapeshifters had moved alone and unhindered through this great planet of marvels and splendors.

The Pontifex held the two sea-dragon teeth aloft.

"Do you know what these are, Torkkinuuminaad?"

The rubbery eye-folds drew back. The narrow eyes were yellow with rage. "You have committed the most terrible of all sacrileges, and you will die in the most terrible of agonies."

"So you do know what they are, eh?"

"They are the holiest of holies! You must return them to the shrine at once!"

"Why did you have Dr. Huukaminaan killed, Torkkinuuminaad?"

The khivanivod's only answer was an even more furiously defiant glare.

He would kill me with his magic, if he could, thought Valentine. *And why not? I know what I represent to Torkkinuuminaad. For I am Majipoor's emperor and therefore I am Majipoor itself, and if one thrust would send us all to our doom he would strike that thrust.*

Yes. Valentine was in his own person the embodiment of the Enemy: of those who had come out of the sky and taken the world away from the

Piurivars, who had built their own gigantic sprawling cities over virgin forests and glades, had intruded themselves by the billions into the fragile fabric of the Piurivars' trembling web of life. And so Torkkinuuminaad would kill him, if he could, and by killing the Pontifex kill, by the symbolism of magic, all of human-dominated Majipoor.

But magic can be fought with magic, Valentine thought.

"Yes, look at me," he told the shaman. "Look right into my eyes, Torkkinuuminaad."

And let his fingers close tightly about the two talismans he had taken from the shrine.

The double force of the teeth struck into Valentine with a staggering impact as he closed the mental circuit. He felt the full range of the sensations all at once, not simply doubled, but multiplied many times over. He held himself upright nevertheless; he focused his concentration with the keenest intensity; he aimed his mind directly at that of the khivanivod.

Looked. Entered. Penetrated the khivanivod's memories and quickly found what he was seeking.

Midnight *darkness. A sliver of moonlight. The sky ablaze with stars. The billowing tent of the archaeologists. Someone coming out of it, a Piurivar, very thin, moving with the caution of age.*

Dr. Huukaminaan, surely.

A slender figure stands in the road, waiting: another Metamorph, also old, just as gaunt, raggedly and strangely dressed.

The khivanivod, that one is. Viewing himself in his own mind's eye.

Shadowy figures moving about behind him, five, six, seven of them. Shapeshifters all. Villagers, from the looks of them. The old archaeologist does not appear to see them. He speaks with the khivanivod; the shaman gestures, points. There is a discussion of some sort. Dr. Huukaminaan shakes his head. More pointing. More discussion. Gestures of agreement. Everything seems to be resolved.

As Valentine watches, the khivanivod and Huukaminaan start off together down the road that leads to the heart of the ruins.

The villagers, now, emerging from the shadows that have concealed them. Surrounding the old man; seizing him; covering his mouth to keep him from crying out. The khivanivod approaches him.

The khivanivod has a knife.

Valentine did not need to see the rest of the scene. Did not *want* to see that monstrous ceremony of dismemberment at the stone platform, nor the weird ritual afterward in the excavation leading to the

Shrine of the Downfall, the placing of the dead man's head in that alcove.

He released his grasp on the two sea-dragon teeth and set them down with great care beside him on the ground.

"Now," he said to the khivanivod, whose expression had changed from one of barely controllable wrath to one that might almost have been resignation. "There's no need for further pretending here, I think. Why did you kill Dr. Huukaminaan?"

"Because he would have opened the shrine." The khivanivod's tone was completely flat, no emotion in it at all.

"Yes. Of course. But Magadone Sambisa also was in favor of opening it. Why not kill her instead?"

"He was one of us, and a traitor," said Torkinuuminaad. "She did not matter. And he was more dangerous to our cause. We know that she might have been prevented from opening the shrine, if we objected strongly enough. But nothing would stop him."

"The shrine was opened anyway, though," Valentine said.

"Yes, but only because you came here. Otherwise the excavations would have been closed down. The outcry over Huukaminaan's death would demonstrate to the whole world that the curse of this place still had power. You came, and you opened the shrine; but the curse will strike you just as it struck the Pontifex Ghorban long ago."

"There is no curse," Valentine said calmly. "This is a city that has seen much tragedy, but there is no curse, only misunderstanding piled on misunderstanding."

"The Defilement—"

"There was no Defilement either, only a sacrifice. The destruction of the city by the people of the provinces was a vast mistake."

"So you understand our history better than we do, Pontifex?"

"Yes," said Valentine. "Yes. I do." He turned away from the shaman and said, glancing toward the village foreman, "Vathiimeraak, there are murderers living in your settlement. I know who they are. Go to the village now and announce to everyone that if the guilty ones will come forward and confess their crime, they'll be pardoned after they undergo a full cleansing of their souls."

Turning next to Lisamon Hultin, he said, "As for the khivanivod, I want him handed over to the Danipiur's officials to be tried in her own courts. This falls within her area of responsibility. And then—"

"Majesty!" someone called. "Beware!"

* * *

Valentine swung around. The Skandar guards had stepped back from the khivanivod and were staring at their own trembling hands as though they had been burned in a fiery furnace. Torkkinuuminaad, freed of their grasp, thrust his face up into Valentine's. His expression was one of diabolical intensity.

"Pontifex!" he whispered. "Look at me, Pontifex! Look at me!"

Taken by surprise, Valentine had no way of defending himself. Already a strange numbness had come over him. The dragon teeth went tumbling from his helpless hands. Torkkinuuminaad was shifting shape, now, running through a series of grotesque changes at a frenzied rate, so that he appeared to have a dozen arms and legs at once, and half a dozen bodies; and he was casting some sort of spell. Valentine was caught in it like a moth in a spider's cunningly woven strands. The air seemed thick and blurred before him, and a wind had come up out of nowhere. Valentine stood perplexed, trying to force his gaze away from the khivanivod's fiery eyes, but he could not. Nor could he find the strength to reach down and seize hold of the two dragon teeth that lay at his feet. He stood as though frozen, muddled, dazed, tottering. There was a burning sensation in his breast and it was a struggle simply to draw breath.

There seemed to be phantoms all around him.

A dozen Shapeshifters—a hundred, a thousand—

Grimacing faces. Glowering eyes. Teeth; claws; knives. A horde of wildly cavorting assassins surrounded him, dancing, bobbing, gyrating, hissing, mocking him, calling his name derisively—

He was lost in a whirlwind of ancient sorceries.

"Lisamon?" Valentine cried, baffled. "Deliamber? Help me—help—" But he was not sure that the words had actually escaped his lips.

Then he saw that his guardians had indeed perceived his danger. Deliamber, the first to react, came rushing forward, flinging his own many tentacles up hastily in a counterspell, a set of gesticulations and thrusts of mental force intended to neutralize whatever was emanating from Torkkinuuminaad. And then, as the little Vroon began to wrap the Piurivar shaman in his web of Vroonish wizardry, Vathiimeraak advanced on Torkkinuuminaad from the opposite side, boldly seizing the shaman in complete indifference to his spells, forcing him down to the ground, bending him until his forehead was pressing against the soil at Valentine's feet.

Valentine felt the grip of the shaman's wizardry

beginning to ebb, then easing further, finally losing its last remaining hold on his soul. The contact between Torkkinuuminaad's mind and his gave way with an almost audible snap.

Vathiimeraak released the khivanivod and stepped back. Lisamon Hultin now came to the shaman's side and stood menacingly over him. But the episode was over. The shaman remained where he was, absolutely still now, staring at the ground, scowling bitterly in defeat.

"Thank you," Valentine said simply to Deliamber and Vathiimeraak. And, with a dismissive gesture: "Take him away."

Lisamon Hultin threw Torkkinuuminaad over her shoulder like a sack of calimbots and went striding off down the road.

A long stunned silence followed. Magadone Sambisa broke it, finally. In a hushed voice she said, "Your majesty, are you all right?"

He answered only with a nod.

"And the excavations," she said anxiously, after another moment. "What will happen to them? Will they continue?"

"Why not?" Valentine replied. "There's still much work to be done." He took a step or two away from her. He touched his hands to his chest, to his throat. He could still almost feel the pressure of those relentless invisible hands.

Magadone Sambisa was not finished with him, though.

"And these?" she asked, indicating the sea-dragon teeth. She spoke more aggressively now, taking charge of things once again, beginning to recover her vigor and poise. "If I may have them now, majesty—"

Angrily Valentine said, "Take them, yes. But put them back in the shrine. And then seal up the hole you made today."

The archaeologist stared at him as though he had turned into a Piurivar himself. With a note of undisguised asperity in her voice she said, "What, your majesty? What? Dr. Huukaminaan died for those teeth! Finding that shrine was the pinnacle of his work. If we seal it up now—"

"Dr. Huukaminaan was the perfect scientist," Valentine said, not troubling to conceal his great weariness now. "His love of the truth cost him his life. Your own love of truth, I think, is less than perfect, and therefore you will obey me in this."

"I beg you, majesty—"

"No. Enough begging. I don't pretend to be a scientist at all, but I understand my own responsibilities. Some things should remain buried. These teeth are not things for us to handle and study and put on display at a museum. The shrine is a holy place to the Piurivars, even if they don't understand its own holiness. It's a sad business for us all that it ever was uncovered. The dig itself can continue, in other parts of the city. But put these back. Seal that shrine and stay away from it. Understood?"

She looked at him numbly, and nodded.

"Good. Good."

The full descent of darkness was settling upon the desert now. Valentine could feel the myriad ghosts of Velalisier hovering around him. It seemed that bony fingers were plucking at his tunic, that eerie whispering voices were murmuring perilous magics in his ears.

Most heartily he yearned to be quit of these ruins. He had had all he cared to have of them for one lifetime.

To Tunigorn he said, "Come, old friend, give the orders, make things ready for our immediate departure."

"Now, Valentine? At this late hour?"

"Now, Tunigorn. Now." He smiled. "Do you know, this place has made the Labyrinth seem almost appealing to me! I feel a great desire to return to its familiar comforts. Come: get everything organized for leaving. We've been here quite long enough."

TALES OF
ALVIN MAKER

Orson Scott Card

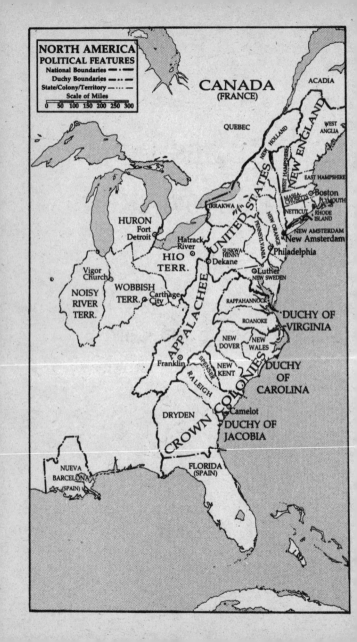

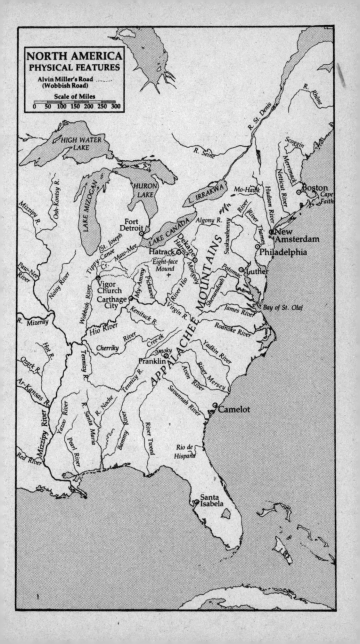

NORTH AMERICA
PHYSICAL FEATURES

Alvin Miller's Road ....
(Wobbish Road)

Scale of Miles

0   50 100 150 200 250 300

HIGH WATER LAKE

Osh-Kontsy R.

R. Seine

R. St. Denis

R. Rhone

Scoggin R.

Merrimack

Nettical River

Boston
Cape Faith

HURON LAKE

LAKE MIZOGAN

L. IRRAKWA

Mo-Hauk

Hudson River

Mizzipy R.

Paw-Nee River

Noisy River

Fort Detroit

LAKE CANADA

St. Joseph

Tippy-Canoe C.

Matu-Mee

Hatrack

DekaNee

Hanky Panky

Pickaweeqy

Algony R.

River Thames

Susquehenny

New Amsterdam

Philadelphia

Luther

Eight-face Mound

Vigor Church

Carthage City

Wobbish River

Pickaweeqy

Virgin R. River Hio

Shenandoah

Potomac

Bay of St. Olaf

Mizeray R.

Kentuck R.

Hio River

Cherriky

Creek

APPALACHEE MOUNTAINS

James River

Roanoke River

Hot R.

Ozark R.

Tennizy R.

Franklin

Smoky

Tennizy R.

Yadkin River

River Mersey

Ar-Kansas R.

R. Noche

Avon River

Camelot

Red River

Mizzipy River

Yocoo River

R. Santa Maria

Katy

Bammy

River Tweed

Savannah River

Pearl River

Rio de Hispann

Santa Isabela

In the Tales of Alvin Maker series, an alternate-history view of an America that never was, Orson Scott Card postulated what the world might have been like if the Revolutionary War had never happened, and if folk magic actually worked.

America is divided into several provinces, with the Spanish and French still having a strong presence in the New World. The emerging scientific revolution in Europe has led many people with "talent," that is, magical ability, to emigrate to North America, bringing their prevailing magic with them. The books chronicle the life of Alvin, the seventh son of a seventh son—a fact that marks him right away as a person of great power. It is

Alvin's ultimate destiny to become a Maker, an adept being of a kind that has not existed for a thousand years. However, there exists an Unmaker for every Maker—a being of great supernatural evil—who is Alvin's adversary, and strives to use Alvin's brother Calvin against him.

During the course of his adventures, Alvin explores the world around him and encounters such problems as slavery and the continued enmity between the settlers and the Native Americans who control the western half of the continent. The series appears to be heading toward an ultimate confrontation between Alvin and the Unmaker, with the fate of the entire continent, perhaps even the world, hinging on the outcome.

GRINNING MAN

∾

Orson Scott Card

The first time Alvin Maker ran across the grinning man was in the steep woody hills of eastern Kenituck. Alvin was walking along with his ward, the boy Arthur Stuart, talking either deep philosophy or the best way for travelers to cook beans, I can't bring to mind now which, when they come upon a clearing where a man was squatting on his haunches looking up into a tree. Apart from the unnatural grin upon his face, there wasn't all that much remarkable about him, for that time and place. Dressed in buckskin, a cap made of coonhide on his head, a musket lying in the grass ready to hand—plenty of men of such youth and roughness walked the game trails of the unsettled forest in those days.

Though come to think of it, eastern Kenituck wasn't all that unsettled by then, and most men gave up buckskin for cotton during summer, less they was too poor to get them none. So maybe it *was* partly his appearance that made Alvin stop up short and look at the fellow. Arthur Stuart, of course, he did what he saw Alvin do, till he had some good reason to do otherwise, so he stopped at the meadow's edge too, and fell silent too, and watched.

The grinning man had his gaze locked on the middle branches of a scruffy old pine that was getting somewhat choked out by slower-growing flat-leaf trees. But it wasn't no tree he was grinning at. No sir, it was the bear.

There's bears and there's bears, as everyone knows. Some little old brown bears are about as dangerous as a dog—which means if you beat it with a stick you deserve what you get, but otherwise it'll leave you alone. But some black bears and some grizzlies, they have a kind of bristle to the hair on their backs, a kind of spikiness like a porcupine that tells you they're just spoiling for a fight, hoping you'll say a cross word so's they can take a swipe at your head and suck your lunch back up through your neck. Like a likkered-up riverman.

This was that kind of bear. A little old, maybe, but as spiky as they come, and it wasn't up that tree cause it was afraid, it was up there for honey, which it had plenty of, along with bees that were now so tired of trying to sting through that matted fur that they were mostly dead, all stung out. There was no shortage of buzzing, though, like a choir of folks as don't know the words to the hymn so they just hum, only the bees was none too certain of the tune, neither.

But there sat that man, grinning at the bear. And there sat the bear, looking down at him with its teeth showing.

Alvin and Arthur stood watching for many a minute while nothing in the tableau changed. The man squatted on the ground, grinning up; the bear squatted on a branch, grinning down. Neither one showed the slightest sign that he knew Alvin and Arthur was even there.

So it was Alvin broke the silence. "I don't know who started the ugly contest, but I know who's going to win."

Without breaking his grin, through clenched teeth the man said, "Excuse me for not shaking your hands but I'm a-busy grinning this bear."

Alvin nodded wisely—it certainly seemed to be a truthful statement. "And from the look of it," says Alvin, "that bear thinks he's grinning you, too."

"Let him think what he thinks," said the grinning man. "He's coming down from that tree."

Arthur Stuart, being young, was impressed. "You can do that just by grinning?"

"Just hope I never turn my grin on *you*," said the man. "I'd hate to have to pay your master the purchase price of such a clever blackamoor as you."

It was a common mistake, to take Arthur Stuart for a slave. He was half-Black, wasn't he? And south of the Hio was all slave country then, where a Black man either was, or used to be, or sure as shooting was bound to become somebody's property. In those parts, for safety's sake, Alvin didn't bother correcting the assumption. Let folks think Arthur Stuart already had an owner, so folks didn't get their hearts set on volunteering for the task.

"That must be a pretty strong grin," said Alvin Maker. "My name's Alvin. I'm a journeyman blacksmith."

"Ain't much call for a smith in these parts. Plenty of better land farther west, more settlers, you ought to try it." The fellow was still talking through his grin.

"I might," said Alvin. "What's your name?"

"Hold still now," says the grinning man. "Stay

right where you are. He's a-coming down.''

The bear yawned, then clambered down the trunk and rested on all fours, his head swinging back and forth, keeping time to whatever music it is that bears hear. The fur around his mouth was shiny with honey and dotted with dead bees. Whatever the bear was thinking, after a while he was done, whereupon he stood on his hind legs like a man, his paws high, his mouth open like a baby showing its mama it swallowed its food.

The grinning man rose up on *his* hind legs, then, and spread *his* arms, just like the bear, and opened his mouth to show a fine set of teeth for a human, but it wasn't no great shakes compared to bear teeth. Still, the bear seemed convinced. It bent back down to the ground and ambled away without complaint into the brush.

''That's my tree now,'' said the grinning man.

''Ain't much of a tree,'' said Alvin.

''Honey's about all et up,'' added Arthur Stuart.

''My tree and all the land round about,'' said the grinning man.

''And what you plan to do with it? You don't look to be a farmer.''

''I plan to sleep here,'' said the grinning man. ''And my intention was to sleep without no bear coming along to disturb my slumber. So I had to tell him who was boss.''

"And that's all you do with that knack of yours?" asked Arthur Stuart. "Make bears get out of the way?"

"I sleep under bearskin in winter," said the grinning man. "So when I grin a bear, it stays grinned till I done what I'm doing."

"Don't it worry you that someday you'll meet your match?" asked Alvin mildly.

"I got no match, friend. My grin is the prince of grins. The king of grins."

"The emperor of grins," said Arthur Stuart. "The Napoleon of grins!"

The irony in Arthur's voice was apparently not subtle enough to escape the grinning man. "Your boy got him a mouth."

"Helps me pass the time," said Alvin. "Well, now you done us the favor of running off that bear, I reckon this is a good place for us to stop and build us a canoe."

Arthur Stuart looked at him like he was crazy. "What do we need a canoe for?"

"Being a lazy man," said Alvin, "I mean to use it to go downstream."

"Don't matter to me," said the grinning man. "Float it, sink it, wear it on your head, or swallow it for supper, you ain't building nothing right here." The grin was still on his face.

"Look at that, Arthur," said Alvin. "This fellow

hasn't even told us his name, and he's a-grinning *us*."

"Ain't going to work," said Arthur Stuart. "We been grinned at by politicians, preachers, witchers, and lawyers, and you ain't got teeth enough to scare us."

With that, the grinning man brought his musket to bear right on Alvin's heart. "I reckon I'll stop grinning then," he said.

"I think this ain't canoe-building country," said Alvin. "Let's move along, Arthur."

"Not so fast," said the grinning man. "I think maybe I'd be doing all my neighbors a favor if I kept you from ever moving away from this spot."

"First off," said Alvin, "you got no neighbors."

"All mankind is my neighbor," said the grinning man. "Jesus said so."

"I recall he specified Samaritans," said Alvin, "and Samaritans got no call to fret about me."

"What I see is a man carrying a poke that he hides from my view."

That was true, for in that sack was Alvin's golden plow, and he always tried to keep it halfway hid behind him so folks wouldn't get troubled if they happened to see it move by itself, which it was prone to do from time to time. Now, though, to answer the challenge, Alvin moved the sack around in front of him.

"I got nothing to hide from a man with a gun," said Alvin.

"A man with a poke," said the grinning man, "who *says* he's a blacksmith but his only companion is a boy too scrawny and stubby to be learning his trade. But the boy is just the right size to skinny his way through an attic window or the eaves of a loose-made house. So I says to myself, this here's a second-story man, who lifts his boy up with those big strong arms so he can sneak into houses from above and open the door to the thief. So shooting you down right now would be a favor to the world."

Arthur Stuart snorted. "Burglars don't get much trade in the woods."

"I never said you-all looked smart," said the grinning man.

"Best point your gun at somebody else now," said Arthur Stuart quietly. "Iffen you want to keep the use of it."

The grinning man's answer was to pull the trigger. A spurt of flame shot out as the barrel of the gun exploded, splaying into iron strips like the end of a worn-out broom. The musket ball rolled slowly down the barrel and plopped out into the grass.

"Look what you done to my gun," said the grinning man.

"Wasn't me as pulled the trigger," said Alvin. "And you was warned."

"How come you still grinning?" asked Arthur Stuart.

"I'm just a cheerful sort of fellow," said the grinning man, drawing his big old knife.

"Do you like that knife?" asked Arthur Stuart.

"Got it from my friend Jim Bowie," said the grinning man. "It's took the hide off six bears and I can't count how many beavers."

"Take a look at the barrel of your musket," said Arthur Stuart, "and then look at the blade of that knife you like so proud, and think real hard."

The grinning man looked at the gun barrel and then at the blade. "Well?" asked the man.

"Keep thinking," said Arthur Stuart. "It'll come to you."

"You let him talk to White men like that?"

"A man as fires a musket at me," said Alvin, "I reckon Arthur Stuart here can talk to him any old how he wants."

The grinning man thought that over for a minute, and then, though no one would have believed it possible, he grinned even wider, put away his knife, and stuck out his hand. "You got some knack," he said to Alvin.

Alvin reached out and shook the man's hand. Arthur Stuart knew what was going to happen next, because he'd seen it before. Even though Alvin was announced as a blacksmith and any man with eyes could see the strength of his arms and hands, this grinning man just had to brace foot-to-foot against him and try to pull him down.

Not that Alvin minded a little sport. He let the grinning man work himself up into quite a temper of pulling and tugging and twisting and wrenching. It would have looked like quite a contest, except that Alvin could've been fixing to nap, he looked so relaxed.

Finally Alvin got interested. He squished down hard and the grinning man yelped and dropped to his knees and began to beg Alvin to give him back his hand. "Not that I'll ever have the use of it again," said the grinning man, "but I'd at least like to have it so I got a place to store my second glove."

"I got no plan to keep your hand," said Alvin.

"I know, but it crossed my mind you might be planning to leave it here in the meadow and send me somewheres else," said the grinning man.

"Don't you ever stop grinning?" asked Alvin.

"Don't dare try," said the grinning man. "Bad stuff happens to me when I don't smile."

"You'd be doing a whole lot better if you'd've

frowned at me but kept your musket pointed at the ground and your hands in your pockets," said Alvin.

"You got my fingers squished down to one, and my thumb's about to pop off," said the grinning man. "I'm willing to say uncle."

"Willing is one thing. Doing's another."

"Uncle," said the grinning man.

"Nope, that won't do," said Alvin. "I need two things from you."

"I got no money and if you take my traps I'm a dead man."

"What I want is your name, and permission to build a canoe here," said Alvin.

"My name, if it don't become 'One-handed Davy,' is Crockett, in memory of my daddy," said the grinning man. "And I reckon I was wrong about this tree. It's your tree. Me and that bear, we're both far from home and got a ways to travel before nightfall."

"You're welcome to stay," said Alvin. "Room for all here."

"Not for me," said Davy Crockett. "My hand, should I get it back, is going to be mighty swoll up, and I don't think there's room enough for it in this clearing."

"I'll be sorry to see you go," said Alvin. "A new friend is a precious commodity in these parts." He let go. Tears came to Davy's eyes as he gingerly felt the sore palm and fingers, testing to see if any of them was about to drop off.

"Pleased to meet you, Mr. Journeyman Smith," said Davy. "You too, boy." He nodded cheerfully, grinning like an innkeeper. "I reckon you couldn't possibly be no burglar. Nor could you possibly be the famous Prentice Smith what stole a golden plow from his master and run off with the plow in a poke."

"I never stole nothing in my life," said Alvin. "But now you ain't got a gun, what's in my poke ain't none of your business."

"I'm pleased to grant you full title to this land," said Davy, "and all the rights to minerals under the ground, and all the rights to rain and sunlight on top of it, plus the lumber and all hides and skins."

"You a lawyer?" asked Arthur Stuart suspiciously.

Instead of answering, Davy turned tail and slunk out of the clearing just like that bear done, and in the same direction. He kept on slinking, too, though he probably wanted to run; but running would have made his hand bounce and that would hurt too much.

"I think we'll never see *him* again," said Arthur Stuart.

"I think we will," said Alvin.

"Why's that?"

"Cause I changed him deep inside, to be a little more like the bear. And I changed that bear to be a little bit more like Davy."

"You shouldn't go messing with people's insides like that," said Arthur Stuart.

"The Devil makes me do it," said Alvin.

"You don't believe in the Devil."

"Do so," said Alvin. "I just don't think he looks the way folks say he does."

"Oh? What does he look like then?" demanded the boy.

"Me," said Alvin. "Only smarter."

Alvin and Arthur set to work making them a dugout canoe. They cut down a tree just the right size—two inches wider than Alvin's hips—and set to burning one surface of it, then chipping out the ash and burning it deeper. It was slow, hot work, and the more they did of it, the more puzzled Arthur Stuart got.

"I reckon you know your business," he says to Alvin, "but we don't need no canoe."

"*Any* canoe," says Alvin. "Miss Larner'd be right peeved to hear you talking like that."

"First place," says Arthur Stuart, "you learned from Tenskwa-Tawa how to run like a Red man through the forest, faster than any canoe can float, and with a lot less work than this.''

"Don't feel like running," said Alvin.

"Second place," Arthur Stuart continued, "water works against you every chance it gets. The way Miss Larner tells it, water near killed you sixteen times before you was ten."

"It wasn't the water, it was the Unmaker, and these days he's about give up on using water against me. He mostly tries to kill me now by making me listen to fools with questions."

"Third," says Arthur Stuart, "in case you're keeping count, we're supposed to be meeting up with Mike Fink and Verily Cooper, and making this canoe ain't going to help us get there on time."

"Those are two boys as need to learn patience," says Alvin calmly.

"Fourth," says Arthur Stuart, who was getting more and more peevish with every answer Alvin gave, "*fourth* and final reason, you're a *Maker,* dagnabbit, you could just think this tree hollow and float it over to the water light as a feather, so even if you had a reason to make this canoe, which you don't, and a safe place to float it, which you don't, you sure don't have to put me through this work to make it by hand!"

"You working too hard?" asked Alvin.

"Harder than is needed is always too hard," said Arthur.

"Needed by whom and for what?" asked Alvin. "You're right that I'm not making this canoe because we need to float down the river, and I'm not making it because it'll hurry up our travel."

"Then why? Or have you give up altogether on doing things for reasons?"

"I'm not making a canoe at all," says Alvin.

There knelt Arthur Stuart, up to his elbows in a hollowed-out log, scraping ash. "This sure ain't a house!"

"Oh, *you're* making a canoe," said Alvin. "And we'll float in that canoe down that river over there. But *I'm* not making a canoe."

Arthur Stuart kept working while he thought this over. After a few minutes he said, "I know what you're making."

"Do you?"

"You're making *me* do what you want."

"Close."

"You're making me make this tree into something, but you're also using this tree to make me into something."

"And what would I be trying to make *you* into?"

"Well, I think *you* think you're making me into a maker," said Arthur Stuart. "But all you're making me into is a *canoe*-maker, which ain't the same thing as being an all-around all-purpose Maker like yourself."

"Got to start somewhere."

"You didn't," says Arthur. "You was born knowing how to make stuff."

"I was born, with a knack," says Alvin. "But I wasn't born knowing how to use it, or when, or why. I learned to love making for its own sake. I learned to love the feel of the wood and the stone under my hands, and from that I learned to see inside it, to feel how it felt, to know how it worked, what held it together, and how to help it come apart in just the right way."

"But I'm not learning any of that," says Arthur.

"Yet."

"No sir," says Arthur Stuart. "I'm not seeing inside nothing, I'm not feeling inside nothing except how my back·aches and my whole body's pouring off sweat and I'm getting more and more annoyed at being made to labor on a job you could do with a wink of your eye."

"Well, that's something," says Alvin. "At least you're learning to see inside yourself."

Arthur Stuart fumed a little more, chipping away burnt wood as he did. "Someday I'm going to get fed up with your smugness," he says to Alvin, "and I won't follow you anymore."

Alvin shook his head. "Arthur Stuart, I tried to get you not to follow me this time, if you'll recall."

"Is *that* what this is about? You're punishing me for following you when you told me not to?"

"You said you wanted to learn everything about being a Maker," says Alvin. "And when I try to teach you, all I get is pissing and moaning."

"You also get work from me," says Arthur. "I never stopped working the whole time we talked."

"That's true," says Alvin.

"And here's something you didn't consider," says Arthur Stuart. "All the time we're making a canoe, we're also *un*making a tree."

Alvin nodded. "That's how it's done. You never make something out of nothing. You always make it out of something else. When it becomes the new thing, it ceases to be what it was before."

"So every time you do a making, you do an unmaking, too," says Arthur Stuart.

"Which is why the Unmaker always knows where I am and what I'm doing," says Alvin. "Because along with doing my work, I'm also doing a little bit of his."

That didn't sound right or true to Arthur Stuart, but he couldn't figure out an argument to answer it, and while he was trying to think one up, they kept on a-burning and a-chipping and lo and behold, they had them a canoe. They dragged it to the stream and put it in and got inside it and it tipped them right over. Spilled them into the water three times, till Alvin finally gave up and used his knack to feel the balance of the thing and then re-shape it just enough that it had a good balance to it.

Arthur Stuart had to laugh at him then. "What lesson am I supposed to learn from *this*? How to make a *bad* canoe?"

"Shut up and row," said Alvin.

"We're going downstream," said Arthur Stuart, "and I don't have to row. Besides which all I've got is this stick, which is no kind of paddle."

"Then use it to keep us from running into the bank," said Alvin, "which we're about to do thanks to your babbling."

Arthur Stuart fended the canoe away from the bank of the stream, and they kept on floating down until they joined a larger stream, and a larger, and then a river. All the time, Arthur kept coming back to the things Alvin said to him, and what he was trying to teach, and as usual Arthur Stuart de-spaired of learning it. And yet he couldn't help but think he had learned *something*, even if he had no idea at present what the thing he learned might be.

Because folks build towns on rivers, when you float down a river you're likely as not to come upon a town, which they did one morning with mist still on the river and sleep still in their eyes. It wasn't much of a town, but then it wasn't much of a river, and they weren't in much of a boat. They put in to shore and dragged the canoe onto the bank, and Alvin shouldered his poke with the plow inside and they trudged on into town just as folks was getting up and about their day.

First thing they looked for was a roadhouse, but the town was too small and too new. Only a dozen houses, and the road so little traveled that grass was growing from one front door to the next. But that didn't mean there was no hope of breakfast. If there's light in the sky, somebody's up, getting a start on the day's work. Passing one house with a barn out back, they heard the ping-ping-ping of a cow getting milked into a tin pail. At another house, a woman was coming in with the night's eggs from a chicken coop. That looked promising.

"Got anything for a traveler?" asked Alvin.

The woman looked them up and down. Without a word she walked on into her house.

"If you wasn't so ugly," said Arthur Stuart, "she would have asked us in."

"Whereas looking at you is like seeing an angel," said Alvin.

They heard the front door of the house opening.

"Maybe she was just hurrying in to cook them eggs for us," said Arthur Stuart.

But it wasn't the woman who came out. It was a man, looking like he hadn't had much time to fasten his clothing. In fact, his trousers were kind of droopy, and they might have started laying bets on how quick they'd drop to the porch if he hadn't been aiming a pretty capable-looking blunderbuss at them.

"Move along," the man said.

"We're moving," said Alvin. He hoisted his poke to his back and started walking across in front of the house. The barrel of the shotgun followed them. Sure enough, just as they were about even with the front door, the trousers dropped. The man looked embarrassed and angry. The barrel of the blunderbuss dipped. The loose birdshot rolled out of the barrel, dozens of tiny lead balls hitting the porch like rain. The man looked confused now.

"Got to be careful loading up a big-barrel gun like that," Alvin said. "I always wrap the shot in paper so it don't do that."

The man glared at him. "I did."

"Why, I know you did," said Alvin.

But there sat the shot on the porch, a silent refutation. Nevertheless, Alvin was telling the simple truth. The paper was still in the barrel, as a matter of fact, but Alvin had persuaded it to break open at the front, freeing the shot.

"Your pants is down," said Arthur Stuart.

"Move along," said the man. His face was turning red. His wife was watching from the doorway behind him.

"Well, you know, we was already planning to," said Alvin, "but as long as you can't quite kill us, for the moment at least, can I ask you a couple of questions?"

"No," said the man. He set down the gun and pulled up his trousers.

"First off, I'd like to know the name of this town. I reckon it must be called 'Friendly' or 'Welcome.'"

"It ain't."

"Well, that's two down," said Alvin. "We got to keep guessing, or you think you can just tell us like one fellow to another?"

"How about 'Pantsdown Landing'?" murmured Arthur Stuart.

"This here is Westville, Kenituck," said the man. "Now move along."

"My second question is, seeing as how you folks don't have enough to share with a stranger, is there somebody who's prospering a bit more and might have something to spare for travelers as have a bit of silver to pay for it?"

"Nobody here got a meal for the likes of you," said the man.

"I can see why this road got grass growing on it," said Alvin. "But your graveyard must be full of strangers as died of hunger hoping for breakfast here."

On his knees picking up loose shot, the man didn't answer, but his wife stuck her head out the door and proved she had a voice after all. "We're as hospitable as anybody else, except to known burglars and thieving prentices."

Arthur Stuart let out a low whistle. "What you want to bet Davy Crockett came this way?" he said softly.

"I never stole a thing in my life," said Alvin.

"What you got in that poke, then?" demanded the woman.

"I wish I could say it was the head of the last man who pointed a gun at me, but unfortunately I left it attached to his neck, so he could come here and tell lies about me."

"So you're ashamed to show the golden plow you stole?"

"I'm a blacksmith, ma'am," said Alvin, "and I got my tools here. You're welcome to look, if you want."

He turned to address the other folks who were

gathering, out on their porches or into the street, a couple of them armed.

"I don't know what you folks heard tell," said Alvin, setting down his poke, "but you're welcome to look at my tools." He drew open the mouth of the poke and let the sides drop so his hammer, tongs, bellows, and nails lay exposed in the street. Not a sign of a plow.

Everyone looked closely, as if taking inventory.

"Well, maybe you ain't the one we heared tell of," said the woman.

"No, ma'am, I'm the exact one, if it was a certain trapper in a coonskin cap named Davy Crockett who was telling the tale."

"So you confess to being that Prentice Smith who stole the plow? And a burglar?"

"No, ma'am, I just confess to being a fellow as got himself on the wrong side of a trapper who talks a man harm behind his back." He gathered up his bag over the tools and drew the mouth closed. "Now, if you-all want to turn me away, go ahead, but don't go thinking you turned away a thief, because it ain't so. You pointed a gun at me and turned me away without a bite to eat for me or this hungry boy, without so much as a trial or a scrap of evidence, just on the word of a traveler who was as much a stranger here as me."

The accusation made them all sheepish. One old

woman, though, wasn't having any of it. "We know Davy, I reckon," she said. "It's you we never set eyes on."

"And never will again, I promise you," said Alvin. "You can bet I'll tell this tale wherever I travel—Westville, Kenituck, where a stranger can't get a bite to eat, and a man is guilty before he even hears the accusation."

"If there's no truth to it," said the old woman, "how did you know it was Davy Crockett a-telling the tale?"

The others nodded and murmured as if this were a telling point.

"Cause Davy Crockett accused me of it to my face," said Alvin, "and he's the only one who ever looked at me and my boy and thought of burglaring. I'll tell you what I told him. If we're burglars, why ain't we in a big city with plenty of fine houses to rob? A burglar could starve to death, trying to find something to steal in a town as poor as this one."

"We ain't poor," said the man on the porch.

"You got no food to spare," said Alvin. "And there ain't a house here with a door that even locks."

"See?" cried the old woman. "He's already checked our doors to see how easy they'll be to break into!"

Alvin shook his head. "Some folks see sin in sparrows and wickedness in willow trees." He took Arthur Stuart by the shoulder and turned to head back out of town the way they came.

"Hold, stranger!" cried a man behind them. They turned to see a large man on horseback approaching slowly along the road. The people parted to make way for him.

"Quick, Arthur," Alvin murmured. "Who do you reckon this is?"

"The miller," said Alvin Stuart.

"Good morning to you, Mr. Miller!" cried Alvin in greeting.

"How did you know my trade?" asked the miller.

"The boy here guessed," said Alvin.

The miller rode nearer, and turned his gaze to Arthur Stuart. "And how did you guess such a thing?"

"You spoke with authority," said Arthur Stuart, "and you're riding a horse, and people made way for you. In a town this size, that makes you the miller."

"And in a bigger town?" asked the miller.

"You'd be a lawyer or a politician," said Arthur Stuart.

"The boy's a clever one," said the miller.

"No, he just runs on at the mouth," said Alvin.

"I used to beat him but I plumb gave out the last time. Only thing I've found that shuts him up is a mouthful of food, preferably pancakes, but we'd settle for eggs, boiled, scrambled, poached, or fried."

The miller laughed. "Come along to my house, not three rods beyond the commons and down the road toward the river."

"You know," said Alvin, "my father's a miller."

The miller cocked his head. "Then how does it happen you don't follow his trade?"

"I'm well down the list of eight boys," said Alvin. "Can't all be millers, so I got put out to a smith. I've got a ready hand with mill equipment, though, in case you'll let me help you to earn our breakfast."

"Come along and we'll see how much you know," said the miller. "As for these folks, never mind them. If some wanderer came through and told them the sun was made of butter, you'd see them all trying to spread it on their bread." His mirth at this remark was not widely appreciated among the others, but that didn't faze him. "I've got a shoeing shed, too, so if you ain't above a little farrier work, I reckon there's horses to be shod."

Alvin nodded his agreement.

"Well, go on up to the house and wait for me," said the miller. "I won't be long. I come to pick up my laundry." He looked at the woman that Alvin had first spoken to. Immediately she ducked back inside the house to fetch the clothes the miller had come for.

On the road to the mill, once they were out of sight of the villagers, Alvin began to chuckle.

"What's so funny?" asked Arthur Stuart.

"That fellow with his pants around his ankles and birdshot dribbling out of his blunderbuss."

"I don't like that miller," said Arthur Stuart.

"Well, he's giving us breakfast, so I reckon he can't be all bad."

"He's just showing up the town folks," said Arthur Stuart.

"Well, excuse me, but I don't think that'll change the flavor of the pancakes."

"I don't like his voice."

That made Alvin perk up and pay attention. Voices were part of Arthur Stuart's knack. "Something wrong with the way he talks?"

"There's a meanness in him," said Arthur Stuart.

"May well be," said Alvin. "But his meanness is better than hunting for nuts and berries again, or taking another squirrel out of the trees."

"Or another fish." Arthur made a face.

"Millers get a name for meanness sometimes," he said. "People need their grain milled, all right, but they always think the miller takes too much. So millers are used to having folks accuse them. Maybe that's what you heard in his voice."

"Maybe," said Arthur Stuart. Then he changed the subject. "How'd you hide the plow when you opened your poke?"

"I kind of opened up a hole in the ground under the poke," said Alvin, "and the plow sank down out of sight."

"You going to teach me how to do things like *that*?"

"I'll do my best to teach," said Alvin, "if you do your best to learn."

"What about making shot spill out of a gun that's pointed at you?"

"My knack opened the paper, but his own trousers, that's what made the barrel dip and spill out the shot."

"And you didn't make his trousers fall?"

"If he'd pulled up his suspenders, his pants would've stayed up just fine," said Alvin.

"It's all Unmaking though, isn't it?" said Arthur Stuart. "Spilling shot, dropping trousers, making them folks feel guilty for not taking you in."

"So I should've let them drive us away without breakfast?"

"I've skipped breakfasts before."

"Well, aren't you the prissy one," said Alvin. "Why are you suddenly so critical of the way I do things?"

"You're the one made me dig out a canoe with my own hands," said Arthur Stuart. "To teach me Making. So I keep looking to see how much Making *you* do. And all I see is how you Unmake things."

Alvin took that a little hard. Didn't get mad, but he was kind of thoughtful and didn't speak much the rest of the way to the miller's house.

So nearly a week later, there's Alvin working in a mill for the first time since he left his father's place in Vigor Church and set out to be a Prentice Smith in Hatrack River. At first he was happy, running his hands over the machinery, analyzing how the gears all meshed. Arthur Stuart, watching him, could see how each bit of machinery he touched ran a little smoother—a little less friction, a little tighter fit—so more and more of the power from the water flowing over the wheel made it to the rolling millstone. It ground faster and smoother, less inclined to bind and jerk. Rack Miller, for that was his name, also noticed, but since he hadn't been watching Alvin work, he assumed that he'd done something with tools and lubricants. "A good can of oil and a keen eye do wonders for machinery,'' said Rack, and Alvin had to agree.

But after those first few days, Alvin's happiness faded, for he began to see what Arthur Stuart had noticed from the beginning: Rack was one of the reasons why millers had a bad name. It was pretty subtle. Folks would bring in a sack of corn to be ground into meal, and Rack would cast it in handfuls onto the millstone, then brush the corn flour into a tray and back into the same sack they brought it in. That's how all millers did it. No one bothered with weighing before and after, because everyone knew there was always some corn flour lost on the millstone.

What made Rack's practice a little different was the geese he kept. They had free rein in the millhouse, the yard, the millrace, and—some folks said—Rack's own house at night. Rack called them his daughters, though this was a perverse kind of thing to say, seeing as how only a few laying geese and a gander or two ever lasted out the winter. What Arthur Stuart saw at once, and Alvin finally noticed when he got over his love scene with the machinery, was how those geese were fed. It was expected that a few kernels of corn would drop; couldn't be helped. But Rack always took the sack and held it, not by the top, but by the shank of the sack, so kernels of corn dribbled out the whole way to the millstone. The geese were on that corn like—well, like geese on corn. And then he'd take big sloppy handfuls of corn to throw onto the millstone. A powerful lot of kernels hit the side of the stone instead of the top, and of course they dropped and ended up in the straw on the floor, where the geese would have them up in a second.

"Sometimes as much as a quarter of the corn," Alvin told Arthur Stuart.

"You counted the kernels? Or are you weighing corn in your head now?" asked Arthur.

"I can tell. Never less than a tenth."

"I reckon he figures he ain't stealing, it's the geese doing it," said Arthur Stuart.

"Miller's supposed to keep his tithe of the ground corn, not double or triple it or more in gooseflesh."

"I don't reckon it'll do much good for me to point out to you that this ain't none of our business," said Arthur Stuart.

"I'm the adult here, not you," said Alvin.

"You keep saying that, but the things you do, I keep wondering," said Arthur Stuart. "I'm not the one gallivanting all over creation while my pregnant wife is resting up to have the baby back in Hatrack River. I'm not the one keeps getting himself thrown in jail or guns pointed at him."

"You're telling me that when I see a thief I got to keep my mouth shut?"

"You think these folks are going to thank you?"

"They might."

"Put their miller in jail? Where they going to get their corn ground then?"

"They don't put the *mill* in jail."

"Oh, you going to stay here, then? You going to run this mill for them, till you taught the whole works to a prentice? How about me? You can bet they'll love paying their miller's tithe to a free half-Black prentice. What are you *thinking*?"

Well, that was always the question, wasn't it? Nobody ever knew, really, what Alvin was thinking. When he talked, he pretty much told the truth, he wasn't much of a one for fooling folks. But he also knew how to keep his mouth shut so you didn't know what was in his head. Arthur Stuart knew, though. He might've been just a boy, though more like a near-man these days, height coming on him kind of quick, his hands and feet getting big even faster than his legs and arms was getting long, but Arthur Stuart was an expert, he was a bona fide certified scholar on one subject, and that was Alvin, journeyman blacksmith, itinerant all-purpose dowser and doodlebug, and secret maker of golden plows and reshaper of the universe. He knew Alvin had him a plan for putting a stop to this thievery without putting anybody in jail.

Alvin picked his time. It was a morning getting on toward harvest time, when folks was clearing out a lot of last year's corn to make room for the new. So a lot of folks, from town and the nearby farms, was queued up to have their grain ground. And Rack Miller, he was downright exuberant in sharing that corn with the geese. But as he was handing the sack of corn flour to the customer, less about a quarter of its weight in goose fodder, Alvin scoops up a fine fat gosling and hands it to the customer right along with the grain.

The customer and Rack just looks at him like he's crazy, but Alvin pretends not to notice Rack's consternation at all. It's the customer he talks to. "Why, Rack Miller told me it was bothering him how much corn these geese've been getting, so this year he was giving out his goslings, one to each regular customer, as long as they last, to make up for it. I think that shows Rack to be a man of real honor, don't you?"

Well, it showed *something,* but what could Rack say after that? He just grinned through clenched teeth and watched as Alvin gave away gosling after gosling, making the same explanation, so everybody, wide-eyed and happy as clams, gave profuse thanks to the provider of their Christmas feast about four months off. Them geese would be monsters by then, they were already so big and fat.

Of course, Arthur Stuart noticed how, as soon as Rack saw how things was going, suddenly he started holding the sacks by the top, and taking smaller handfuls, so most of the time not a kernel fell to the ground. Why, that fellow had just learned himself a marvelous species of efficiency, returning corn to the customer diminished by nought but the true miller's tithe. It was plain enough that Rack Miller wasn't about to feed no corn to geese that somebody else was going to be feasting on that winter!

And when the day's work ended, with every last gosling gone, and only two ganders and five layers left, Rack faced Alvin square on and said, "I won't have no liar working for me."

"Liar?" asked Alvin.

"Telling them fools I meant to give them goslings!"

"Well, when I first said it, it wasn't true *yet,* but the minute you didn't raise your voice to argue with me, it became true, didn't it?" Alvin grinned, looking for all the world like Davy Crockett grinning him a bear.

"Don't chop no logic with me," said Rack. "You know what you was doing."

"I sure do," said Alvin. "I was making your customers happy with you for the first time since you come here, and making an honest man out of you in the meantime.''

''I already *was* an honest man,'' said Rack. ''I never took but what I was entitled to, living in a godforsaken place like this.''

''Begging your pardon, my friend, but God ain't forsaken this place, though now and then a soul around here might have forsaken *Him*.''

''I'm done with your help,'' said Rack icily. ''I think it's time for you to move on.''

''But I haven't even looked at the machinery you use for weighing the corn wagons,'' said Alvin. Rack hadn't been in a hurry for Alvin to check them over—the heavy scales out front was only used at harvest time, when farmers brought in whatever corn they meant to sell. They'd roll the wagons onto the scales, and through a series of levers the scale would be balanced with much lighter weights. Then the wagon would be rolled back on empty and weighed, and the difference between the two weights was the weight of the corn. Later on the buyers would come, roll on their empty wagons and weigh them, then load them up and weigh them again. It was a clever bit of machinery, a scale like that, and it was only natural that Alvin wanted to get his hands on it.

But Rack wasn't having none of it. ''My scales

is my business, stranger,'' he says to Alvin.

"I've et at your table and slept in your house,'' says Alvin. "How am I a stranger?''

"Man who gives away my geese, he's a stranger here forever.''

"Well, then, I'll be gone from here.'' Still smiling, Alvin turned to his young ward. "Let's be on our way, Arthur Stuart.''

"No sir,'' says Rack Miller. "You owe me for thirty-six meals these last six days. I didn't notice this Black boy eating one whit less than you. So you owe me in service.''

"I gave you due service,'' says Alvin. "You said yourself that your machinery was working smooth.''

"You didn't do nought but what I could have done myself with an oilcan.''

"But the fact is I did it, and you didn't, and that was worth our keep. The boy's worked, too, sweeping and fixing and cleaning and hefting.''

"I want six days' labor out of your boy. Harvest is upon us, and I need an extra pair of hands and a sturdy back. I've seen he's a good worker and he'll do.''

"Then take three days' service from me *and* the boy. I won't give away any more geese.''

"I don't have any more geese to give, except the

layers. Anyway I don't want no miller's son, I just want the boy's labor.''

"Then we'll pay you in silver money.''

"What good is silver money here? Ain't nothing to spend it on. Nearest city of any size is Carthage, across the Hio, and hardly anybody goes there.''

"I don't use Arthur Stuart to discharge my debts. He's not my—''

Well, long before those words got to Alvin's lips, Arthur Stuart knew what he was about to do— he was going to declare that Arthur wasn't his slave. And that would be about as foolish a thing as Alvin could do. So Arthur Stuart spoke right up before the words could get away. "I'm happy to work off the debt,'' he says. "Except I don't think it's possible. In six days I'll eat eighteen more meals and then I'll owe another three days, and in those three days I'll eat nine meals and I'll owe a day and a half, and at that rate I reckon I'll never pay off that debt.''

"Ah yes,'' says Alvin. "Zeno's paradox.''

"And you told me there was never any practical use for that 'bit of philosophical balderdash,' as I recall you saying,'' says Arthur Stuart. It was an argument from the days they both studied with Miss Larner, before she became Mrs. Alvin Smith.

"What the Sam Hill you boys talking about?'' asked Rack Miller.

Alvin tried to explain. "Each day that Arthur Stuart works for you, he'll build up half again the debt that he pays off by his labor. So he only covers half the distance toward freedom. Half and half and half again, only he never quite gets to the goal."

"I don't get it," says Rack. "What's the joke?"

By this point, though, Arthur Stuart had another idea in mind. Mad as Rack Miller was about the goslings, if he truly needed help at harvest time he'd keep Alvin on for it, unless there was some other reason for getting rid of him. There was something Rack Miller planned to do that he didn't want Alvin to see. What he didn't reckon on was that this half-Black "servant" boy was every bit smart enough to figure it out himself. "I'd like to stay and see how we solve the paradox," says Arthur Stuart.

Alvin looks at him real close. "Arthur, I got to go see a man about a bear."

Well, that tore Arthur Stuart's resolve a bit. If Alvin was looking for Davy Crockett, to settle things, there might be scenes that Arthur wanted to see. At the same time, there was a mystery here at the millhouse, too, and with Alvin gone Arthur Stuart had a good chance at solving it all by himself. The one temptation was greater than the other. "Good luck," said Arthur Stuart. "I'll miss you."

Alvin sighed. "I don't plan to leave you here at the tender mercy of a man with a peculiar fondness for geese."

"What does *that* mean?" Rack said, growing more and more certain that they were making fun of him underneath all their talk.

"Why, you call them your daughters and then cook them and eat them," says Alvin. "What woman would ever marry you? She wouldn't dare leave you alone with the children!"

"Get out of my millhouse!" Rack bellowed.

"Come on, Arthur Stuart," said Alvin.

"I *want* to stay," Arthur Stuart insisted. "It can't be no worse than the time you left me with that schoolmaster." (Which is another story, not to be told right here.)

Alvin looked at Arthur Stuart real steady. He was no Torch, like his wife. He couldn't look into Arthur's heartfire and see a blame thing. But somehow he saw something that let him make up his mind the way Arthur Stuart wanted him to. "I'll go for now. I'll be back, though, in six days, and I'll have an accounting with you. You don't raise a hand or a stick against this boy, and you feed him and treat him proper."

"What do you think I am?" asked Rack.

"A man who gets what he wants," said Alvin.

"I'm glad you recognize that about me," said Rack.

"Everybody knows that about you," said Alvin. "It's just that you aren't too good at picking what you ought to be wanting." With another grin, Alvin tipped his hat and left Arthur Stuart.

Well, Rack was as good as his word. He worked Arthur Stuart hard, getting ready for the harvest. A late-summer rain delayed the corn in the field, but they put the time to good account, and Arthur was given plenty to eat and a good night's rest, though it was the millhouse loft he slept in now, and not the house; he had only been allowed inside as Alvin's personal servant, and with Alvin gone, there was no excuse for a half-Black boy sleeping in the house.

What Arthur noticed was that all the customers were in good cheer when they came to the millhouse for whatever business they had, especially during the rain when there wasn't no field work to be done. The story of the goslings had spread far and wide, and folks pretty much believed that it really had been Rack's idea, and not Alvin's doing at all. So instead of being polite but distant, the way folks usually was with a miller, they gave him hail-fellow-well-met and he heard the kind of jokes and gossip that folks shared with their friends. It was a new experience for Rack, and Arthur Stuart could see that this change was one Rack Miller didn't mind.

Then, the last day before Alvin was due to return, the harvest started up, and farmers from miles around began to bring in their corn wagons. They'd line up in the morning, and the first would pull his wagon onto the scale. The farmer would unhitch the horses and Rack would weigh the whole wagon. Then they'd hitch up the horses, pull the wagon to the dock, the waiting farmers would help unload the corn sacks—of course they helped, it meant they'd be home all the sooner themselves— and then back the wagon onto the scale and weigh it again, empty. Rack would figure the difference between the two weighings, and that difference was how many pounds of corn the farmer got credit for.

Arthur Stuart went over the figures in his head, and Rack wasn't cheating them with his arithmetic. He looked carefully to see if Rack was doing something like standing on the scale when the empty wagon was being weighed, but no such thing.

Then, in the dark of that night, he remembered something one of the farmers grumbled as they were backing an empty wagon onto the scale. "Why didn't he build this scale right at the loading dock, so we could unload the wagon and reweigh it without having to move the durn thing?" Arthur Stuart didn't know the mechanism of it, but he

thought back over the day and remembered that
another time a farmer had asked if he could get his
full wagon weighed while the previous farmer's
wagon was being unloaded. Rack glared at the
man. "You want to do things your way, go build
your own mill."

Yes sir, the only thing Rack cared about was that
every wagon get two weighings, right in a row.
And the same system would work just as well in
reverse when the buyers came with their empty
wagons to haul corn east for the big cities. Weigh
the empty, load it, and weigh it again.

When Alvin got back, Arthur Stuart would be
ready with the mystery mostly solved.

Meanwhile, Alvin was off in the woods, looking
for Davy Crockett, that grinning man who was
single-handedly responsible for getting two separate guns pointed at Alvin's heart. But it wasn't
vengeance that was on Alvin's mind. It was rescue.

For he knew what he'd done to Davy and the
bear, and kept track of their heartfires. He couldn't
see into heartfires the way Margaret could, but he
could see the heartfires themselves, and keep track
of who was who. In fact, knowing that no gun
could shoot him and no jail could hold him, Alvin
had deliberately come to the town of Westville because he knew Davy Crockett had come through

that town, the bear not far behind him, though Davy wouldn't know that, not at the time.

He knew it now, though. What Alvin saw back in Rack's millhouse was that Davy and the bear had met again, and this time it might come out a little different. For Alvin had found the place deep in the particles of the body where knacks were given, and he had taken the bear's best knack and given as much to Davy, and Davy's best knack and given the same to the bear. They were evenly matched now, and Alvin figured he had some responsibility to see to it that nobody got hurt. After all, it was partly Alvin's fault that Davy didn't have a gun to defend himself. Mostly it was Davy's fault for pointing it at him, but Alvin hadn't had to wreck the gun the way he did, making the barrel blow apart.

Running lightly through the woods, leaping a stream or two, and stopping to eat from a fine patch of wild strawberries on a riverbank, Alvin got to the place well before nightfall, so he had plenty of time to reconnoiter. There they were in the clearing, just as Alvin expected, Davy and the bear, not five feet apart, both of them a-grinning, staring each other down, neither one budging. That bear was all spiky, but he couldn't get past Davy's grin; and Davy matched the bear's single-minded tenacity, oblivious to pain, so even though his butt was already sore and he was about out of his mind with sleepiness, he didn't break his grin.

Just as the sun set, Alvin stepped out into the clearing behind the bear. "Met your match, Davy?" he asked.

Davy didn't have an ounce of attention to spare for chat. He just kept grinning.

"I think this bear don't mean to be your winter coat this year," said Alvin.

Davy just grinned.

"In fact," said Alvin, "I reckon the first one of you to fall asleep, that's who the loser is. And bears store up so much sleep in the winter, they just flat out don't need as much come summertime."

Grin.

"So there you are barely keeping your eyelids up, and there's the bear just happy as can be, grinning at you out of sincere love and devotion."

Grin. With maybe a little more desperation around the eyes.

"But here's the thing, Davy," said Alvin. "Bears is better than people, mostly. You got your bad bears, sometimes, and your good people, but on average, I'd trust a bear to do what he thinks is right before I'd trust a human. So now what you got to wonder is, what does that bear think will be the right thing to do with you, once he's grinned you down?"

Grin grin grin.

"Bears don't need no coats of human skin. They do need to pile on the fat for winter, but they don't generally eat meat for that. Lots of fish, but you ain't a swimmer and the bear knows that. Besides, that bear don't think of you as meat, or he wouldn't be grinning you. He thinks of you as a rival. He thinks of you as his equal. What *will* he do. Don't you kind of wonder? Don't you have some speck of curiosity that just wants to know the answer to that question?"

The light was dimming now, so it was hard to see much more of either Davy or the bear than their white, white teeth. And their eyes.

"You've already stayed up one whole night," said Alvin. "Can you do it again? I don't think so. I think pretty soon you're going to understand the mercy of bears."

Only now, in his last desperate moments before succumbing to sleep, did Davy dare to speak. "Help me," he said.

"And how would I do that?" asked Alvin.

"Kill that bear."

Alvin walked up quietly behind the bear and gently rested his hand on the bear's shoulder. "Why would I do that? This bear never pointed no gun at me."

"I'm a dead man," Davy whispered. The grin

faded from his face. He bowed his head, then toppled forward, curled up on the ground, and waited to be killed.

But it didn't happen. The bear came up, nosed him, snuffled him all over, rolled him back and forth a little, all the time ignoring the little whimpering sounds Davy was making. Then the bear lay down beside the man, flung one arm over him, and dozed right off to sleep.

Unbelieving, Davy lay there, terrified yet hopeful again. If he could just stay awake a little longer.

Either the bear was a light sleeper in the summertime, or Davy made his move too soon, but no sooner did his hand slide toward the knife at his waist than the bear was wide awake, slapping more or less playfully at Davy's hand.

"Time for sleep," said Alvin. "You've earned it, the bear's earned it, and come morning you'll find things look a lot better."

"What's going to happen to me?" asked Davy.

"Don't you think that's kind of up to the bear?"

"You're controlling him somehow," said Davy. "This is all your doing."

"He's controlling himself," said Alvin, careful not to deny the second charge, seeing how it was true. "And he's controlling you. Because that's what grinning is all about—deciding who is master. Well, that bear is master here, and I reckon tomorrow we'll find out what bears do with domesticated humans.''

Davy started to murmur a prayer.

The bear laid a heavy paw on Davy's mouth.

"Prayers are done," intoned Alvin. "Gone the sun. Shadows creep. Go to sleep."

That's how it came about that when Alvin returned to Westville, he did it with two friends along—Davy Crockett and a big old grizzly bear. Oh, folks was alarmed when that bear come into town, and ran for their guns, but the bear just grinned at them and they didn't shoot. And when the bear gave Davy a little poke, why, he'd step forward and say a few words. "My friend here doesn't have much command of the American language," said Davy, "but he'd just as soon you put that gun away and didn't go pointing it at him. Also, he'd be glad of a bowl of corn mush or a plate of corn bread, if you've got any to spare."

Why, that bear plumb ate his way through Westville, setting down to banquets without raising a paw except to poke at Davy Crockett, and folks didn't even mind it, it was such a sight to see a man serve gruel and corn bread to a bear. And that wasn't all, either. Davy Crockett spent a good little while picking burrs out of the bear's fur, especially in the rumpal area, and singing to the bear whenever it crooned in a high-pitched tone. Davy sang pert near every song that he ever heard, even if he only heard it once, or didn't hear the whole thing, for there's nothing to bring back the memory of tunes and lyrics like having an eleven-foot bear poking you and whining to get you to sing, and when he flat out couldn't remember, why, he made something up, and since the bear wasn't altogether particular, the song was almost always good enough.

As for Alvin, he'd every now and then pipe up and ask Davy to mention whether it was true that Alvin was a burglar and a plow-stealing prentice, and each time Davy said no, it wasn't true, that was just a made-up lie because Davy was mad at Alvin and wanted to get even. And whenever Davy told the truth like that, the bear rumbled its approval and stroked Davy's back with his big old paw, which Davy was just barely brave enough to endure without wetting himself much.

Only when they'd gone all through the town and some of the outlying houses did this parade come to the millhouse, where the horses naturally complained a little at the presence of a bear. But Alvin spoke to each of them and put them at ease, while the bear curled up and took him a nap, his belly being full of corn in various forms. Davy didn't go far, though, for the bear kept sniffing, even in his sleep, to make sure Davy was close by.

Davy was putting the best face on things, though. He had his pride.

"A man does things for a friend, and this here bear's my friend," said Davy. "I'm done with trapping, as you can guess, so I'm looking for a line of work that can help my friend get ready for the winter. What I mean is, I got to earn some corn, and I hope some of you have jobs for me to do. The bear just watches, I promise, he's no danger to your livestock."

Well, they heard him out, of course, because one tends to listen for a while at least to a man who's somehow got himself hooked up as a servant to a grizzly bear. But there wasn't a chance in hell that they were going to let no bear anywhere near their pigsties, nor their chicken coops, especially not when the bear clearly showed no disposition to earn its food honestly. If it would beg, they figured, it would steal, and they'd have none of it.

Meanwhile, as the bear napped and Davy talked to the farmers, Alvin and Arthur had their reunion, with Arthur Stuart telling him what he'd figured out. "Some mechanism in the scale makes it weigh light when the wagon's full, and heavy when it's empty, so the farmers get short weight. But then, without changing a thing, it'll weight light on the buyers' empty wagons, and heavy when they're full, so Rack gets extra weight when he's selling the same corn."

Alvin nodded. "You find out if this theory is actually true?"

"The only time he ain't watching me is in the dark, and in the dark I can't sneak down and see a thing. I'm not crazy enough to risk getting myself caught sneaking around the machinery in the dark, anyway."

"Glad to know you got a brain."

"Says the man who keeps getting himself put in jail."

Alvin made a face at him, but in the meantime he was sending out his doodlebug to probe the machinery of the scale underground. Sure enough, there was a ratchet that engaged on one weighing, causing the levering to shift a little, making short weight; and on the next weighing, the ratchet would disengage and the levers would move back, giving long weight. No wonder Rack didn't want Alvin looking over the machinery of the scale.

The solution, as Alvin saw it, was simple enough. He told Arthur Stuart to stand near the scale but not to step on it. Rack wrote down the weight of the empty wagon, and while it was being pulled off the scale, he stood there calculating the difference. The moment the wagon was clear of the scale, Alvin rounded on Arthur Stuart, speaking loud enough for all to hear.

"Fool boy! What were you doing! Didn't you see you was standing on that scale?"

"I wasn't!" Arthur Stuart cried.

"I don't think he was," said a farmer. "I worried about that, he was so close, so I looked."

"And I say I saw him stand on it," said Alvin. "This farmer shouldn't be out the cost of a boy's weight in corn, I think!"

"I'm sure the boy didn't stand on the scale," Rack said, looking up from his calculation.

"Well, there's a simple enough test," said Alvin. "Let's get that empty wagon back onto the scale."

Now Rack grew alarmed. "Tell you what," he said to the farmer, "I'll just *give* you credit for the boy's weight."

"Is this scale sensitive enough to weigh the boy?" asked Alvin.

"Well, I don't know," said Rack. "Let's just estimate."

"No!" cried Alvin. "This farmer doesn't want any more than his fair credit, and it's not right for him to receive any less. Haul the wagon back on and let's weigh it again."

Rack was about to protest again, when Alvin said, "Unless there's something wrong with the scale. There wouldn't be something wrong with the scale, now, would there?''

Rack got a sick look on his face. He couldn't very well confess. ''Nothing wrong with the scale,'' he said gruffly.

''Then let's weigh this wagon and see if my boy's weight made any difference.''

Well, you guessed it. As soon as the wagon was back on the scale, it showed near a hundred pounds lighter than it did the first time. The other witnesses were flummoxed. ''Could have sworn the boy never stepped on that scale,'' said one. And another said, ''I don't know as I would have guessed that boy to weigh a hundred pounds.''

''Heavy bones,'' says Alvin.

''No sir, it's my brain that weighs heavy,'' said Arthur Stuart, winning a round of laughter.

And Rack, trying to put a good face on it, pipes up, ''No, it's the food he's been eating at my table—that's fifteen pounds of it right there!''

In the meantime, though, the farmer's credit was being adjusted by a hundred pounds.

And the next wagon to come on the scale was a full one, while the scale was set to read heavy. In vain did Rack try to beg off early—Alvin simply offered to keep on weighing for him, with the farmers as witnesses so he wrote down everything square. ''You don't want any of these men to have to wait an extra day to sell you their market grain, do you?'' Alvin said. ''Let's weigh it all!''

And weigh it all they did, thirty wagons before the day was done, and the farmers was all remarking to each other about what a good corn year it was, the kernels heavier than usual. Arthur Stuart did hear one man start to grumble that his wagon seemed to be lighter this year than in any previous year, but Arthur immediately spoke up loud enough for all to hear. ''It don't matter if the scale is weighing light or heavy—it's the difference between the full weight and the empty weight that matters, and as long as it's the same scale, it's going to be correct.'' The farmers thought that over and it sounded right to them, while Rack couldn't very well explain.

Arthur Stuart figured it all out in his head and he realized that Alvin hadn't exactly set things to rights. On the contrary, this year Rack was getting cheated royally, recording credits for these farmers that were considerably more than the amount of corn they actually brought in. He could bear such losses for one day; and by tomorrow, Alvin and Arthur both knew, Rack meant to have the scale back in its regular pattern—light for the full wagons, heavy for the empty ones.

Still, Alvin and Arthur cheerfully bade Rack

farewell, not even commenting on the eagerness he showed to be rid of them.

That night, Rack Miller's lantern bobbed across the yard between his house and the mill. He closed the mill door behind him and headed for the trapdoor leading down to the scale mechanism. But to his surprise, there was something lying on top of that trapdoor. A bear. And nestled in to sleep with the bear wrapped around him was Davy Crockett.

"I hope you don't mind," said Davy, "but this here bear took it into his head to sleep right here, and I'm not inclined to argue with him."

"Well, he can't, so that's that," said the miller.

"You tell him," said Davy. "He just don't pay no heed to my advice."

The miller argued and shouted, but the bear paid no mind. Rack got him a long stick and poked at the bear, but the bear just opened one eye, slapped the stick out of Rack's hand, then took it in his mouth and crunched it up like a cracker. Rack Miller proposed to bring a gun out, but Davy drew his knife then. "You'll have to kill me along with the bear," he said, "cause if you harm him, I'll carve you up like a Christmas goose."

"I'll be glad to oblige you," said Rack.

"But then you'll have to explain how I came to be dead. If you manage to kill the bear with one shot, that is. Sometimes these bears can take a half-dozen balls into their bodies and still swipe a man's head clean off and then go fishing for the afternoon. Lots of fat, lots of muscle. And how's your aim, anyway?''

So it was that next morning, the scale still weighed opposite to Rack's intent, and so it went day after day until the harvest was over. Every day the bear and his servant ate their corn mush and corn bread and drank their corn likker and lay around in the shade, with onlookers gathering and lingering to see the marvel. The result was that witnesses were around all day and not far off at night. And it went on just the same when the buyers started showing up to haul away the corn.

Stories about the bear who had tamed a man brought more than just onlookers, too. More farmers than usual came to Rack Miller to sell their corn, so they could see the sight; and more buyers went out of their way to come to buy, so there was maybe half again as much business as usual. At the end of the whole harvest season, there was Rack Miller with a ledger book showing a huge loss. He wouldn't be paid enough by the buyers to come close to making good on what he owed the farmers. He was ruined.

He went through a few jugs of corn likker and took some long walks, but by late October he'd given up all hope. One time his despair led him to point a pistol at his head and fire, but the powder for some reason wouldn't ignite, and when Rack tried to hang himself he couldn't tie a knot that didn't slip. Since he couldn't even succeed at killing himself, he finally gave up even that project and took off in the dead of night, abandoning mill and ledger and all. Well, he didn't mean to abandon it—he meant to burn it. But the fires he started kept blowing out, so that was yet another project he failed at. In the end, he left with the clothes on his back and two geese tucked under his arms, and they honked so much he turned them loose before he was out of town.

When it was clear Rack wasn't just off on a holiday, the town's citizens and some of the more prominent farmers from round about met in Rack Miller's abandoned house and went over his ledger. What they learned there told them clear enough that Rack Miller was unlikely to return. They divided up the losses evenly among the farmers, and it turned out that nobody lost a thing. Oh, the farmers got paid less than Rack Miller's ledger showed, but they'd get a good deal more than they had in previous years, so it was still a good year for them. And when they got to inspecting the property, they found the ratchet mechanism in the scale and then the picture was crystal clear.

All in all, they decided, they were well rid of Rack Miller, and a few folks had suspicions that it was that Alvin Smith and his half-Black boy who'd turned the tables on this cheating miller. They even tried to find out where he might be, to offer him the mill in gratitude. Someone had heard tell he came from Vigor Church up in Wobbish, and a letter there did bring results—a letter in reply, from Alvin's father. "My boy thought you might make such an offer, and he asked me to give you a better suggestion. He says that since a man done such a bad job as miller, maybe you'd be better off with a bear, especially if the bear has him a manservant who can keep the books."

At first they laughed off the suggestion, but after a while they began to like it, and when they proposed it to Davy and the bear, they cottoned to it, too. The bear got him all the corn he wanted without ever lifting a finger, except to perform a little for folks at harvest time, and in the winter he could sleep in a warm dry place. The years he mated, the place was a little crowded with bearflesh, but the cubs were no trouble and the mama bears, though a little suspicious, were mostly tolerant, especially because Davy was still a match for any of *them*, and could grin them into docility when the need arose.

As for Davy, he kept true books, and fixed the scale so it didn't ratchet anymore, giving honest weight every time. As time went on, he was so well liked that folks talked about running him for mayor of Westville. He refused, of course, since he wasn't his own man. But he allowed as how, if they elected the bear, he'd be glad to serve as the bear's secretary and interpreter, and that's what they did. After a year or two of having a bear as mayor, they up and changed the name to Bearsville, and the town prospered. Years later, when Kenituck joined the United States of America, it's not hard to guess who got elected to Congress from that part of the state, which is how it happened that for seven terms of Congress a bear put its hand on the Bible right along with the other congressmen, and then proceeded to sleep through every session it attended, while its clerk, one Davy Crockett, cast all its votes for it and gave all its speeches, every one of which ended with the sentence "Or at least that's how it looks to one old grizzly bear."

THE RIFTWAR SAGA

〜⚬〜

Raymond E. Feist

THE RIFTWAR SAGA:

MAGICIAN (1982, REVISED EDITION 1992)
SILVERTHORN (1985)
A DARKNESS IN SETHANON (1986)

THE EMPIRE TRILOGY (WITH JANNY WURTS):

DAUGHTER OF THE EMPIRE (1989)
SERVANT OF THE EMPIRE (1990)
MISTRESS OF THE EMPIRE (1992)

STAND-ALONE RIFTWAR-RELATED BOOKS:

PRINCE OF THE BLOOD (1989)
THE KING'S BUCCANEER (1992)

THE SERPENTWAR SAGA:

SHADOW OF A DARK QUEEN (1994)
RISE OF A MERCHANT PRINCE (1995)
RAGE OF A DEMON KING (1997)
SHARDS OF A BROKEN CROWN (1998)

Raymond E. Feist's Riftwar fantasy series begins with the adventures of two boys, Pug and Tomas, each wishing to rise above his lowly station in life. Pug desires to become a magician, Tomas a great warrior. Each achieves his dream through outside agencies and his own natural abilities; Pug is kidnapped during the Riftwar, discovered to have magic abilities, and trained to greatness. Tomas stumbles upon a dying dragon who gives him a suit of armor imbued with an ancient magic, turning him into a warrior of legendary might.

As Pug and Tomas undergo their transformations and become more adept at controlling the powers that have been granted them, the scope of the novel expands to reveal more about the two worlds upon which the conflict known as the Riftwar takes place: Midkemia and Kelewan. Midkemia is a young world, vibrant and conflict-ridden, while Kelewan is ancient and tradition-bound, but no freer of conflict. The militaristic Tsurani, from Kelewan, have invaded the Kingdom of the Isles on Midkemia to expand their domain and seize metals common on Midkemia but rare at home. The only way open between these worlds is a magic Rift, and through that portal in space-time the invaders have established a foothold in the Kingdom. Gradually

Tomas learns that he has become invested with the power of a Valheru, one of the mystical creatures who are legends in Midkemia. The Dragon Lords were near-godlike beings who once warred with the gods themselves. The action in the first trilogy comes to a climax in *A Darkness at Sethanon,* with the resolution of the war between the Kingdom and the invading Tsurani, Tomas gaining control over the ancient magic that sought to conquer him, and Pug returning to the homeland of his youth.

The Empire Trilogy concerns itself with conflict back on the Tsurani home world, where for much of the first and second book we see ''the other side of the Riftwar.'' Lady Mara of the Acoma, a girl of seventeen in the first book, is thrust into a murderous game of politics and ritual, and only through her own genius and ability to improvise does she weather unrelenting attacks on all sides. Aided by a loyal group of followers, including a Kingdom slave named Kevin, whom she comes to love more than any other, Mara rises to dominate the Empire of Tsuranuanni, even facing down the mighty Great Ones, the magicians who are outside the law.

The latest series, the SerpentWar saga, is the story of Erik, the bastard son of a noble, and Roo, a street boy who is his best friend. The Kingdom again faces invaders, but this time from across the sea. The story of the two young men is set against the Kingdom's hurried preparation for and resistance against a huge army under the banner of the Emerald Queen, a woman who is another agent of dark forces seeking dominion over the world of Midkemia. More of the cosmic nature of the battle between good and evil is revealed and Pug and Tomas again have to take a hand in the struggle.

Feist sees Midkemia as an objective, virtual world, though a fictional one. He regards all the tales set in Midkemia as historical novels and stories of this fantastic realm. ''The Wood Boy'' is a tale from the early days of the Riftwar, when the Tsurani first were establishing their foothold in the Kingdom.

THE WOOD BOY

❦

A Tale from the Riftwar

RAYMOND E. FEIST

The Duke looked up.

Borric, Duke of Crydee and commander of the Armies of the West, acknowledged the captain at the door of his command tent. "Your Grace, if you have a minute and could come outside?"

Borric stood up, envying his old friend Brucal, who was now probably sitting before a warm fire somewhere in LaMut while he wrote long letters of complaint to the Prince of Krondor about supplies.

The war was leaving its second winter and a stable front had been established, with Borric's headquarters camp located ten miles behind the lines. The Duke was a seasoned campaigner, having fought against goblins and the Brotherhood of the Dark Path—the dark elves—since boyhood, and every bone in his body told him that this was going to be a long war.

The Duke donned his heavy cloak, and wrapped it around him. He exited his tent and a strange tableau greeted him.

In the distance, a group of figures could barely be seen as they approached the camp. Through the swirling snow Borric could see them slowly take shape. Grey figures against the dull white, surrounded by a haze of snowflakes, they approached at a steady rate. Finally, the figures resolved themselves into a patrol escorting someone.

The soldiers marched slowly, for the figure they surrounded was pulling a heavy sled, plodding along unfalteringly despite what appeared a considerable burden. As they came close, Borric could see that it was a peasant boy who labored to haul the sled to the camp. He moved with steady purpose, coming at last to stand before the commander of the King's Armies in the West.

Borric looked at the lad, who had obviously been through an ordeal. He was bareheaded, his blond hair encrusted with ice crystals. About his neck and face he wore a heavy jacket scarf wrapped several times around. He wore a heavy jacket and trousers, and thick sturdy boots. His simple wool coat was stained dark with blood.

The sled he had been pulling was laden with odd cargo. A large sack had been secured with ropes atop the sled, and over that two bodies had been lashed down. A dead man stared up at the sky with empty eyes, his lashes sparkling with frozen tears. He had been a fighter, from the look of him, and he wore leather armor. His scabbard hung empty at his side and his left glove was missing. Beside him lay a girl, under blankets, so that it appeared she was sleeping. She had been a pretty girl in life, but in death her features were almost porcelain, near perfection in their pale whiteness.

"Who are you, boy?"

The boy said, "I am the Wood Boy." His voice was faint and his eyes were vacant, as if he stared inward, though they were fixed on Borric.

"What did you say?" asked the Duke.

The boy seemed to gather his wits. "Sir, my name is Dirk. I am the servant of Lord Paul of White Hill. It's the estate on the other side of the Kakisaw Valley." He pointed to the west. "Three days' walk from here. I carry firewood."

Borric nodded. "I know the estate. I've visited Lord Paul many times over the years. That's thirty-five miles from here, and twenty behind enemy lines.'' Pointing to the sled, he asked, ''What is this?''

Weary, the boy said, ''It is my master's treasure. She is his daughter. The man is a murderer. He was once my friend.''

''You'd better come inside and tell me your story,'' said Borric. He motioned for two soldiers to take the ropes that the boy used as a harness to pull the sled out of the way, and indicated that another man should help the exhausted youth.

The Duke led the boy inside and let him know it was permissible to sit. He signaled for an orderly to get the boy a cup of hot tea and something to eat, and as the soldier hurried to obey, Borric said, ''Why don't you start at the beginning, Dirk?''

Spring brought the Tsurani. They had been reported in the Grey Tower Mountains the year before, bringing dire warnings of invasion from both the Kingdom rulers on the other side of the mountains and some of the more important merchants and nobles in the other Free Cities. But the tales that accompanied the warning, of fierce warriors appearing out of nowhere by some magic means, had been met with skepticism and disbelief. And the fighting seemed distant, up in the mountains between Borric of Crydee's soldiers, the dwarves, and the invaders.

Until the first warning by the Rangers of Natal —who had quickly ridden on to warn others— followed a day later by a column of short men in their brightly colored armor who appeared on the road approaching the estate at White Hill.

Lord Paul had ordered his bodyguards to stand ready, but to offer no resistance unless provoked. Dirk and the rest of the household stood behind the Lord of White Hill and his armed guards.

Dirk glanced back at his master and saw that he stood alone, his daughter still in the house. Dirk wondered what extra protection the master thought that afforded his young daughter.

Dirk found the master's pose admirable. The stories of Tsurani fierceness had trickled down from the early fighting, and the Free Cities would be wholly dependent upon the Kingdom for defense. Areas like White Hill and the other estates around Walinor were simply on their own. Yet Lord Paul stood motionless, without any sign of fear, in his formal robe, the scarlet one with the ermine collar. No hereditary title had been conferred on any citizen since the Empire of Great Kesh had abandoned its northern colonies a century before, yet those families with ancient titles used them with pride. Like other nobles in the Free Cities, he held in disdain other men's claims on title while treasuring his own.

As the invaders calmly marched into view, it was obvious that any resistance would have been quickly crushed. Paul had a personal bodyguard and a score of hired mercenaries who acted as wagon guards and protection against roving bandits. But they were a poor band of hired cutthroats next to the highly disciplined command that marched across the estate. The Tsurani wore bright orange and black armor, looking like lacquered hide or wood, nothing remotely like the metal armor worn by the officers of the Natal Defense Force.

Paul repeated the order that no resistance was to be mounted, and when the Tsurani commander presented himself, Paul offered something that resembled a formal salute. Then, with the aid of a man in a black robe, the leader of the invaders gave his demands. The property of White Hill, as well as the surrounding countryside, was now under Tsurani rule, specifically an entity named Minwanabi. Dirk wondered if that was a person or a place, like a Kingdom Duchy. But he was too frightened to imagine voicing the question.

The leader of this group of Tsurani—all short, tough-looking veteran soldiers—could be differentiated from his men only by a slightly more ornate helm, graced with what Dirk took to be some creature's hair. The black fall reached the officer's shoulders.

Dirk tried to guess what the role of the black-robed man might be; the officer seemed extremely polite and deferential to him as he translated the officer's words for him.

The officer was called Chapka, and his rank was Hit Leader or Strike Leader, Dirk wasn't sure which.

He shouted orders and the black robe said, "Only the noble of this house may bear arms, and his personal man." Dirk took that to mean a body-guard. That would be Hamish. "All others put weapons here."

The estate guards looked at Lord Paul, who nodded. They stepped forward and put their weapons in a pile, slowly, and when they were done they stepped back. "Any other weapons?" asked the man in black.

One of the guards looked at his companions, then came forward and took a small blade from his boot, throwing it in the pile. He stepped back into line.

The officer shouted an order. A dozen Tsurani soldiers ran forward, each searching the now un-armed guards. One Tsurani stood, holding up a knife he had found in a guard's boot, and the officer indicated that the man be brought forward. He spoke rapidly to the man in black, who said, "This man disobeyed. He hid a weapon. He will be punished."

Lord Paul slowly said, "What shall you do with him?"

"The sword is too honorable a death for a disobedient slave. He will be hanged."

The man turned pale. "It was just a small one; I forgot I had it!"

The man was struck hard from behind and collapsed. Dirk watched in dread fascination as two other Tsurani guards dragged the guard—a man Dirk hardly knew, named Jackson—to the entrance to the barn. A hoist hung over the small door to the hayloft—there was one at each end of the barn—from which a long rope dangled. The unconscious man had the rope tied around his neck and was hoisted quickly up. He never regained consciousness, though his body twitched twice before it went still.

Dirk had seen dead men before; the town of Walinor, where he grew up, had known a few raids by bandits and the Brotherhood of the Dark Path, and once he had stumbled across a drunk who had frozen to death in the gutter outside an inn. But this hanging made his stomach twist, and he knew it was as much from fear over his own safety as from any revulsion over Jackson's death.

The black-robed man said, "Any slave with weapon—we hang."

Then the officer shouted an order, and Tsurani warriors ran off in all directions, a half-dozen into the master's house, others into the outbuildings, and still others to the springhouse, the barn, and the root cellar. Efficient to a degree that astonished Dirk, the Tsurani returned in short order and started reporting. Dirk couldn't understand them, but from the rapidity of the exchanges, he was certain they were listing what they found for their officer.

Others returned from the barn and kitchen carrying dozens of commonplace items. The officer, with the aid of the black-robed man, began interrogating Lord Paul about the nature of various common household items. As the master of the estate explained the use of such common tools as a leather punch or iron skillet, the Tsurani officer indicated one of two piles, one on a large canvas tarp. When two of the same items were displayed, one instantly went into one pile, while the other might join it or be separated.

Old William, the gardener and groundskeeper, said, "Look at that," as two Tsurani soldiers picked up the tarp, securing the larger of the two piles, and carried it off.

"What is it?" whispered Dirk, barely loud enough for the old man to hear.

"They're queer for metal," softly said the old man with a knowing nod. "Look at their armor and weapons."

Dirk did so, and then it struck him. Nowhere on any Tsurani could a glint of sunlight on metal be seen. Their armor and weapons all appeared to be hide or wood cleverly fashioned and lacquered, but there were no buckles, blades, or fasteners of metal in evidence. From their cross-gartered sandals to the top of their large flared helmets, the Tsurani appeared devoid of any metal artifacts.

"What's it mean?" whispered Dirk.

"I don't know, but I'm sure we'll find out," said the old man.

The Tsurani continued their investigation of Lord Paul's household, until almost sundown, then they were ordered to gather their personal belongings and move them into the barn or kitchen, as the Tsurani would be occupying the servants' quarters. In a move that puzzled Dirk, the Tsurani officer stayed in the same building with his men, leaving Paul and his daughter alone in the big house.

It was but the first of many things that would puzzle Dirk over the coming year.

Alex lay curled up, his face a mask of pain while Hamish shouted, "Don't get up!"

The Tsurani soldier who had struck the young man in the stomach stood over him, his hand a scant inch from the hilt of his sword. Alex groaned and again Hamish shouted to the young man to remain still.

Dirk stood near the entrance to the barn while those servants nearby stood anxiously watching, expecting the worst at any moment. The Tsurani had revealed themselves as strict but fair masters in the two months since arriving at White Hill, but there was occasionally some breach of etiquette or honor that took the residents of White Hill by surprise, often with bloody consequences. An old farmer by the name of Samuel had gotten drunk on fermented corncob squeeze a month earlier and had struck out at a Tsurani who had ordered him back into his home. Samuel had been beaten senseless and hanged as his wife and children looked on in horror.

Alex continued to groan but did as he was bid by Hamish until the Tsurani soldier seemed satisfied that he wasn't going to move. The soldier said something in his alien language, spat in contempt upon the workman, turned, and walked away.

Hamish hesitated a moment; then he and Dirk hurried over to help Alex to his feet. "What happened?" asked Dirk.

"I don't know," said Alex. "I just looked at the man."

"It's how you looked at him," said Hamish. "You smirked at him. If you'd looked at me that way, I'd have done the same." The burly old soldier inspected Alex. "I had my fill of smirking boys in the army and knocked down a few in my time before I retired. Show these murderers some respect, lad, or they'll hang you just because they can and it's a slow day for amusements."

Rubbing his side, Alex said, "I won't do that again, you can bet."

"See that you don't," said Hamish. The old soldier motioned for Drogen, his senior guard, to come over. "Pass the word that the bastards seem touchy. Must have something to do with the war. Just make sure the lads know to keep polite and do whatever they're told."

Drogen nodded and ran off. Hamish turned to inspect Alex again, then said, "Get off with you. You'll live."

Dirk helped Alex for a few steps. Then the man's legs seemed to steady and Dirk let go of his arm. "They don't seem to take kindly to any sort of greeting," said Dirk.

"I think keeping your eyes down or some such is what they want."

Dirk said nothing. He was scared most of the

time when he was around the Tsurani and didn't look at them for that reason. That was probably a wise choice, he judged.

"Can you take the wood?" asked Alex.

"Sure," said Dirk before he realized that he was being asked to carry wood to the Tsurani quarters. Dirk picked up the fallen bundle and wrestled with it a moment before getting the unwieldy load under control. He moved to the door of the outbuilding and hesitated, then rolled the wood back on his chest and reached out to pull the latch rope.

The door opened slightly and Dirk pushed it open with his foot. He entered, blinking a moment to get his eyes used to the darkness inside.

A half-dozen Tsurani warriors sat on their beds, speaking in quiet conversation as they tended their arms and armor. Upon seeing the serving boy enter, they fell silent. Dirk went to the woodbox next to the fireplace, situated in the center of the rear wall, and deposited his load there.

The Tsurani watched him with impassive expressions. He quickly left the room. Closing the door behind him, he could hardly believe that just weeks before the bed in the farthest corner had been his own. He and the other workers had been turned out to the barn, except for the house staff, who now slept on the floor in Lord Paul's kitchen.

There was little need for wood save for cooking,

as the warm nights of summer made sleeping fires unnecessary. The Tsurani used their fires primarily for cooking their alien food, filling the area nearby with strange yet intriguing aromas.

Dirk paused a moment and glanced around, taking in the images of White Hill; familiar, yet cast in alien shadow by the invaders. Mikia and Torren, a young couple engaged the week before at the Midsummer's festival, were approaching the milking shed, hand in hand, and the invaders could be invisible for all the distraction they provided the young lovers.

From the kitchen, voices and the clatter of pots heralded the advent of the noon meal. Dirk realized he was hungry. Still, he needed to carry firewood to the other buildings before breaking to eat, and he decided the sooner started, the sooner done. As he turned to the woodshed, he caught a glimpse of a soldier in black and orange moving toward the barn. He idly wondered if the time would come when the invaders would be driven from White Hill. It seemed unlikely, for there was no news of the war, and the Tsurani were settling in at White Hill as if they were never leaving.

Reaching the woodshed, Dirk opened the door and saw Alex in back of the shed cutting more wood. The still-bruised man said, "You can carry, lad. I'll cut."

Dirk nodded and went in the shed, to get another armful of firewood. Dirk sighed. As youngest boy in service, the worst jobs fell to him, and this would just be another task added to his burden, one which would not free him from any other.

Before coming to White Hill, Dirk had been nothing, the youngest son of a stonecutter who had two sons already to apprentice. His father had cut the stone for Lord Paul's home, and had used that slight acquaintanceship to gain Dirk a position in Paul's household.

With that position was the promise that eventually he would have some sort of rank on the estate, perhaps a groundsman, a kennel master, or a herdsman. Or he might gain a farm to work, with a portion of his crops going to his landlord, even eventually earning the rank of Franklin, one who owned his own lands free of service to any lord. He had even dared to imagine meeting a girl and marrying, raising sons and daughter of his own. And perhaps, despite the Tsurani, he still might.

Reminding himself that he had much to be thankful for, he lifted the next load of wood destined for the fireplaces of the invaders.

Fall brought a quick change in the weather, with sunny but cool days and cold nights. Apples were harvested and the juice presses were busy. The

Tsurani found the juice a wonderful delicacy and commanded a large portion for themselves. A portion was put aside for fermenting, and the air around the kitchen was spicy with the smell of warm pies.

Dirk had gotten used to hauling wood to the Tsurani, and now was the one designated to keep all the woodboxes on the property filled, while Alex still did most of the chopping. Everyone began calling him ''Wood Boy,'' rather than his name.

Dirk also worked the woodpile, and the constant work was broadening his shoulders and putting muscle on him by the week. He could now lift as much as the older boys and some of the men.

He found that as the nights cooled his workload increased, for now he had to help plan for the coming winter. The sheep pens were repaired. The herd needed to be kept close, as starving predators would come down from the mountain to hunt. The cattle would be brought down from the higher meadows as well.

Fences needed repairing and the root cellar and springhouse needed stocking. The winters in the foothills of Yabon came quickly and the snow was often deep after the first fall, lasting until the thaw of spring.

Dirk worked hard and enjoyed those infrequent

moments he could steal to relax, joke with the older boys and young men, and talk to Litia, an old woman who had once been in charge of the poultry and lambs. She was kind to the awkward boy and told him things that helped him understand the world that seemed to be changing around him by the day.

Dirk now was faced with the realization that life's choices were down to a precious few. Before the Tsurani's arrival, he had stood a chance of learning to be a herdsman or farmer, and perhaps meeting a girl and starting a family on the edge of Lord Paul's estates, having land and a share of the harvest. Or he might save the tiny sum allotted him over and above his keep and someday attempt to start a trade of his own; he knew the rudiments of cutting stone and perhaps might pay a mason to apprentice him.

But now he feared that he was doomed to be a servant until death took him. There was no payment of wages above his keep; the Tsurani had taken all of Lord Paul's wealth—though it was rumored that he had two parts in three safely hidden from the Tsurani. Even if the rumor was true, he wasn't about to risk hanging to pay a lowly servant boy his back wages.

And there were no girls his own age on the estates, save Lord Paul's daughter.

The Midwinter's festival was supposed to be the time to meet the girls from town or the nearby estates, but the Tsurani had forbidden such travel for the Midsummer's festival, and Dirk doubted they would change their minds for the winter festival. Lord Paul's household had celebrated Banapis on Midsummer's Day by themselves, with little enthusiasm, because of the poor food and drink, and the isolation.

At least, thought Dirk, Midwinter's Day was likely to be a little livelier, as there was a good supply of fermenting applejack laid in. Then, remembering how morose his father could get when drinking, Dirk wondered if that was a good thing. Hamish had been known to drink himself into a dark and blind rage in the depths of winter.

Putting aside his own misery, he attacked the tasks the day put before him and was judged a hardworking if unremarkable boy by those of the household.

The festival was a pale shadow of its former self.

Traditionally the towns turned out, with those living on the neighboring estates coming in for the parties. A townsman would be selected to play the part of Old Man Winter, who would come into town on a sled pulled by wolves—usually a motley collection of dogs pressed into playing the part, often to comic results. He would pass out sweets to the children, and the adults would exchange small gifts and tokens. Then everyone would eat too much food and many would drink too much wine and ale.

And many young couples would be married.

This year the Tsurani had forbidden travel, and Dirk stood at the edge of a small crowd in the barnyard watching Mikia and Torren getting married under the watchful eyes of Lord Paul and his daughter. The Tsurani had let Dirk travel to the shrine of Dala and return with a priest of that order, so that the wedding could be conducted.

The couple looked happy despite the frigid surroundings, made slightly more bearable by the large bonfire Dirk and the others had built earlier in the day. It roared and warmed whichever side was facing it, but otherwise it was a cold and bitter day for a wedding, with low grey skies and a constant wind off the mountains.

The meal was the best that could be managed under the circumstances, and Dirk had his first encounter with too much to drink, consuming far too much applejack and discovering that his stomach would inform him of its limits before any of his friends would. The other boys stood around in amusement as Dirk stood against the wall behind the barn, sick beyond belief, his head swimming and his pulse pounding in his temples as his stomach tried to throw up drink no longer there.

He had somehow managed to find his way back to the loft in which he now slept. Because he was the youngest boy in the household, he got the worst pallet, next to the hay door, which meant a drafty, frigid night's rest. He passed out and risked freezing to death without the other boys' warmth nearby.

Late that night, he stirred as a shout from outside rang through the silent darkness. Dirk stirred as did the other boys, and Hemmy said, "What's that?"

Dirk pushed open the hay door. In the moonlight a drunken figure stood waving a sword with his right hand, while holding a jug of applejack with the left. He shouted words that the boys couldn't understand, but Hemmy said, "He's fighting some old battle, for sure."

Suddenly Alex said, "The Tsurani! If Hamish wakes them with all that shouting, they'll kill him. We've got to get him to shut up."

"You want to go and try to talk to him while he's waving that sword around," said Hemmy, "you go ahead. I'll take my chances up here. I've seen him drunk before. Puts him in a dangerous dark temper, it does."

"We've got to do something," said Dirk.

"What?" asked Hemmy.

"I don't know," admitted Dirk.

Then two Tsurani ran into view and stopped when they saw the drunken old soldier in the moonlight, his breath forming clouds of steam in the frigid night air.

"You stinkin' bastards!" shouted Hamish. "You come on and I'll show you how to use a sword."

The two Tsurani slowly drew weapons, and one spoke to the other. The second man nodded and stepped back, putting his sword away. He turned and ran off.

"They're going to get some help," whispered Dirk, afraid to be overheard by the Tsurani.

"Maybe they'll just make him put up his sword and go to bed," said Hemmy.

"Maybe," echoed Dirk.

Then a half-dozen Tsurani, led by the officer, came into view. The officer shouted at Hamish, who grinned like a grizzly wolf in the stark white moonlight. "Come and sing to me, you sons of dogs!" shouted the drunken old man.

The Tsurani officer seemed more irritated by the display than anything else, and said something briefly to the men. He turned and walked off without a glance back.

"Maybe they're going to let him alone," said Hemmy.

Suddenly an arrow sped through the darkness and struck old Hamish in the chest. He looked down in disbelief and sank to his knees. Then he fell off to the right, still holding his sword and jug of applejack.

"Gods!" whispered Dirk.

The Tsurani turned as one and walked away, leaving the dead bodyguard lying in the moonlight, a black figure against the white snow.

"What do we do?" whispered Dirk to the older boys.

"Nothing," said Alex. "Until the Tsurani tell us to get out tomorrow and bury him, we do nothing."

"But it's not right," said Dirk, fighting back tears of frustration and fear.

"Nothing is right these days," said Hemmy, reaching out to shut the hay doors.

Dirk lay in the loft, huddled against a cold far more bitter than winter's night.

Let me help you with that," said Drogen, as Dirk tried to close the kitchen door with a kick. The wind outside howled and this had been Dirk's fifth trip to the woodbox.

Dirk said, "Shut the door, please."

The new bodyguard to Lord Paul did as Dirk asked, and Dirk said, "Thanks. I've got to get this to the great hall." He hurried with the heavy bundle of wood and made his way through the big house. He entered the great hall, where Lord Paul ate dinner with his daughter Anika.

Dirk was very deliberate in arranging the new firewood, as it gave him a moment to watch Anika from beside the fireplace. She was a year younger than Dirk. Fifteen last Midsummer's day, she was perfection embodied to the young kitchen boy. She had delicate features, a small bow of a mouth, wide-set blue eyes, and hair of pale gold. Her skin held a faint touch of the sun in summer and was flawless pink in winter. Her figure was ripening, yet not voluptuous like the kitchen women, still possessing a grace when she moved that set Dirk's heart to beating.

Dirk knew she didn't even know his name, but he dreamed of somehow earning rank and fame someday, and winning her love. Her imaged filled his mind every waking moment of the day.

"Is something wrong, Wood Boy?" asked Lord Paul.

"No, sir!" said the boy, standing up and striking his head on the mantel. The girl covered her mouth as she laughed, and he blushed furiously. "I was just putting the wood away. I'm done, sir."

"Then get back to the kitchen, lad," said the Lord of the house.

Lord Paul was an Elector of the City. Before the

Tsurani had come, Lord Paul had voted on every important matter confronting Walinor and had once been the delegate from the city to the General Council of Electors for the Free Cities of Natal. He was by any measure one of the wealthiest men in the city. He had ships plying the Bitter Sea and farms and holdings throughout the west, as well as investments in both the Kingdom of the Isles and the Empire of Great Kesh.

And Dirk was now hopelessly in love with his daughter.

It didn't matter that she didn't know his name, or even notice he was there, he just couldn't stop thinking of her. For the last two weeks, since Hamish's death, he had found his mind turning constantly to thoughts of Anika. Her smile, how she moved, the tilt of her chin when she was listening to something her father was saying.

She wore only the finest clothing and her hair was always put up with combs of fine bone or shell from the Bitter Sea, or left down with ringlets that softly framed her face. She was always polite, even to the servants, and had the sweetest voice Dirk had ever heard.

Getting back to the kitchen, Jenna the old stout cook said, "Getting a peek at the girl, were we?"

Drogen laughed and Dirk blushed. His infatuation with Lord Paul's daughter was a well-known source of amusement in the kitchen. Dirk prayed Jenna said nothing to any of the other boys, for if it became obvious to the boys in the barn, Dirk's already miserable existence would become even blacker than it presently was.

"She's a pretty girl," said Drogen with a smile at Dirk. "Most men would look more than once."

Dirk liked Drogen. He had been just one of Lord Paul's men-at-arms until Hamish had been killed for disturbing the Tsuranis on Midwinter's Night. Since then he had become a fixture in the main house and Dirk had gotten several chances to talk to him. Unlike Hamish, who had been given to bouts of ill-humor, Drogen was a quiet fellow, saying little unless answering a direct question. Easygoing, he was reputed to be one of the best men with a sword in the Free Cities, and he had an open and friendly manner. He was handsome in a dark fashion, and Dirk had heard gossip that more than one of the servingwomen had snuck off with him on a thin pretext, and there were several tavern girls in the city who waited for his next visit. Dirk thought the man a nice enough fellow, though Jenna often had acid comments on Drogen's inability to think of much besides women.

Dirk stood and said, "I have to get more wood over to the Tsurani." He left the warm kitchen and, back out in the cold, wished he hadn't. He hurried to the woodpile.

Dirk picked up a large pile of wood and moved to the first of the three buildings. He pushed open the door and found the Tsurani as he always did. Quietly they rested between patrols or other duties which might take as much as half the garrison away for days, even weeks at a time. Occasionally they would return carrying their wounded. When resting they slept in their bunks, tended their odd, black-and-orange-colored armor, and talked quietly. Some played what appeared to be a gambling game of some sort involving sticks and rocks, and others played what looked to be chess.

Most were off on some mission for their master, leaving less than a dozen in residence at White Hill. They looked on impassively as he filled the wood-box. He left and serviced the other two woodboxes. When he was finished, he sighed audibly in relief. No matter how many times being the Wood Boy forced him to enter the buildings occupied by the Tsurani, having witnessed their capacity for ruth-less murder brought Dirk to the edge of blind panic when he encountered them alone. When he knew he had done with them for another night, he felt as if he was entering a safe place for some hours to come.

Done with his outside chores for the night, he

returned to the kitchen and ate his meager supper, a watery stew and coarse bread. The very best of the foodstuffs not taken by the invaders was served to Lord Paul and his daughter. He had overheard Anika complain about the food, only to hear her father reply that it wasn't too bad, all things considered. Dirk thought that by the standards he was used to it was a feast. Drogen and the other workers in the house got the pick of leftovers and there was never anything for a mere Wood Boy.

Dirk returned to the barn and ignored the moaning that came from under a blanket in the first stall. Mikia and Torren seemed unconcerned that their privacy was nonexistent. Still, Dirk reasoned, they were dairy people, a herdsman and a milkmaid, and he found farm people far more earthy and unconcerned with modesty than townspeople.

Litia sat in the corner of the next stall, her slight form shivering under a blanket as she sat on the dirt floor, huddled close to the warmth of a small fire. Dirk waved and she returned a toothless smile. He went over and said, "How are you?"

"Well enough," she said, and her voice was barely more than a whisper.

Dirk was concerned that the old woman might not last the winter, given the scant food and warmth, but others in the household seemed indifferent. You got old, then you died, they always said.

"What gossip?" asked the old woman. She lived for tidbits of news or rumors. Dirk always kept his ears open for something to enliven the old woman's evening.

"Nothing new, sorry to say," he replied.

With a wide, gummy grin, the old woman said, "And has the master's daughter favored you with a glance yet, my young buck?"

Dirk felt his face flush and he said, "I don't know what you mean, Litia."

"Yes you do," she chided him playfully. "It's all right, lad. She's the only girl your age here and it wouldn't be natural if you didn't feel a tug toward her. If those heathens who took our beds relent and let us visit with neighbors in the spring, the first young farm lass you meet will get your mind off my lord's wicked child."

"Wicked child?" said Dirk. "What do you mean?"

Litia said, "Nothing, sweet boy. She's a willful girl who always gets what she wants, is all. What you need is a good strong lass, a farm girl with broad hips who can bear you sons who will take care of you in your old age."

The bitterness in Litia's words was not lost on Dirk, even if he was young. He knew that her only son had died years before in a drowning accident and that she had no one left to care for her. Dirk said, "I'll try to get you another blanket from the house tomorrow."

"Don't get yourself into trouble on my account," said the woman, but her expression showed she appreciated the offer.

Dirk left her and climbed the ladder to the loft, where the young men slept. He was the youngest up there, for the boys younger than he stayed with their families. Alex, Hans, and Leonard were already resting. Hemmy and Petir would be up shortly. Dirk wished for another blanket himself, but knew that he would have to depend upon the ones allotted to him. At least one side of him would be warm at a time, as he would huddled next to Hemmy, the next older boy. He would turn a few times in the night to ward off the freezing air.

And spring was but two months away. Hemmy and Petir climbed up and took their places in the loft, and Dirk snuggled down as best he could in his blankets and went to sleep.

It was an odd sound, and Dirk couldn't quite make sense of it as he came awake in the dark. Then it registered: someone had cried out. It had been a muffled sound, but it had been a cry. Dirk listened for a moment, but the sound wasn't repeated. He tried to go back to sleep.

Just as he was drowsy again, he heard a creak

and the sound of someone moving in the barn. A dull thud and a strange gurgling noise made him lift himself up on his right elbow, listening in the dark. He strained to hear something, but he couldn't make out the sounds. Assuming it was Mikia and Torren again, he rolled over and tried to go back to sleep.

Again he was almost dozing when he realized something was wrong. As he turned over, he saw something moving rapidly toward him in the gloom, a large dark shape. He sat up, reflexively pulling away from what was coming toward him.

Two things happened at once. Someone slashed at him, a blade cutting into the fabric of his coat below his collarbone, and he struck the hay door with his back. He choked out an inarticulate cry, unable to speak for the terror which overwhelmed him. Then another body slammed into him with a strangled cry and he felt the door latch behind him give.

Never too sturdy, the latch parted as the weight of two bodies struck it, and with a muffled cry, Dirk fell out the hay door, down to the snow-covered ground below. He landed with a thud that drove the breath out of him.

Then the other body landed on him, and Dirk was knocked senseless.

He awoke as the sky was lightening. He was freezing and barely able to breathe. His left eye seemed glued shut and something on top of him held him firmly to the ground.

Dirk tried to move, and discovered that Hemmy lay atop him. "Hey, get off!" he said, but his voice was weak and strangled. A burning pain below his throat caused him to gasp when he moved.

His legs were numb from the cold, and he lay in a hole in the snow. He wiggled his bottom and managed to work his way upright and realized Hemmy was dead. The older boy's face was white, and his throat was cut. Terror galvanized Dirk and he lifted the corpse enough to get out from beneath him, forcing numb legs to do his bidding.

He pulled himself out of the snow and his muscles screamed at being forced to move. He climbed out of the hole and saw he was drenched in blood, Hemmy's blood.

"What happened?" he whispered.

As he staggered toward the barn he saw that the morning sun was still an hour from cresting the eastern horizon. His legs became wobbly and he leaned against the barn, looking up to see the rear hay door still opened. He paused a moment to get control over his frozen, stiff legs, walked around to the front, and looked at the large doors thrown open to the cold. He glanced down at the snow before the door and saw no unusual number of footprints. But off to the south side of the entrance, where snow remained unclear, he saw a single set of footprints and the parallel impression left by a sled's runners. Someone had pulled the large sled out of the barn. The depth of the runner tracks in the snow told him it was heavily loaded. The horses were long gone, having been eaten by the Tsurani the winter before, so whoever had moved the sled was pulling it.

Dirk went inside the barn and saw Mikia and Torren lying in each other's arms, their throats cut. Old Litia also lay dead in her own blood, her eyes open wide. Everywhere he looked, he saw death.

Who did this? Dirk wondered in panicked confusion. Had the Tsurani who occupied Lord Paul's estate gone mad and killed everyone? But if they had, there would have been footprints in abundance outside in the snow, and there were none. Most of them were gone on some mission or another, leaving only a few in the outbuildings this week. Then Dirk thoughts turned to the manor house. "Anika!" he said in a hoarse whisper.

He hurried through the predawn gloom to the kitchen and found the door open. He stared in mute horror at the carnage in the room. Everyone who slept in the kitchen was as dead as those in the barn.

He hurried up stairs and, without knocking, entered Anika's room. Her bed lay empty. He peered under it, afraid she might have crawled under it to die. Then he realized there was no blood in the room.

He got up and ran to her father's room, and pushed open the door. Lord Paul lay in a sea of blood, on his bed, Dirk didn't need to see if he lived. Beside the bed a secret door was opened, a door painted to look like a section of the wall. Dirk looked through the door into the small hiding place and realized that here was where his master had kept his wealth. The invaders had demanded every gold, silver, and copper coin held by those living in the occupied region, yet it was well documented that they had no concept of wealth on this planet. The servants had speculated that Lord Paul had turned over only one part in three of his wealth and the rest had remained hidden. Perhaps they had found he had hidden wealth and this was their way of punishing everyone. If the Tsurani had gone on a rampage—

"No," he said softly to himself. The Tsurani hanged those without honor. The blade was for honorable foes. Whoever did the killing had moved with stealth, as if afraid to raise an alarm and be overwhelmed, and had cautiously killed all the servants one at a time. The killer had been armed. . . .

Drogen!

Only Drogen and the Lord of the House, of all those who weren't Tsurani, were permitted arms. Dirk closed the secret door, too stunned to appreciate how clever it was. Once closed, it appeared indistinguishable from the wall.

He hurried down to the large dining hall and saw over the fireplace the two swords hung there, heirlooms of Lord Paul's family. He considered taking one down, then remembered that should the Tsurani find him with a sword in his possession, he would be hanged without any opportunity to explain.

He returned to the kitchen and took a large boning knife from the butcher's block next to the stove. That was something he had handled many times before, and the familiarity of the handle was reassuring to him.

He had to do something about finding Anika, but he didn't know what. Drogen must have taken her with the gold. He ran back to the barn to see if anyone else might have survived. Within minutes he knew that only he and Anika had survived.

And the Tsurani, of course.

Panic struck Dirk. He knew that if one of them

stuck his head outside one of the huts he would be hanged for carrying a kitchen knife, no matter what the reason.

He put the knife in his tunic, and climbed into the loft. He went to the canvas bag that served as his closet, holding his few belongings. He removed his only coat, and saw a long cut below the collar. Drogen had lashed out at him first, because he had awakened. He must have thought Dirk's throat cut. Then he had killed Hemmy, pushing him atop Dirk, causing them to fall through the hay door. Only the darkness and the fall had saved Dirk's life, he knew. Had he not fallen out of the barn, Drogen would certainly have insured the boy was dead.

Dirk put on his extra shirt for warmth, ignoring the sticky blood soaked into his undershirt and the shirt he already wore. Wearing the extra layers of clothing might be the difference between life and death. He considered pulling a tunic off one of the other boys, but he couldn't bring himself to touch the bodies of his dead friends.

He again donned his coat and took his only pair of gloves from the bag, along with a large woolen scarf Litia had knitted for him the year before. He put them on and checked the bag for his other belongings: there was nothing else there he could imagine would help him.

He hurried down the ladder. The only thing he

could think of doing was following the murderer. He was terrified of waking the Tsurani, and not certain they would care about the murder of people they obviously felt were inferior to themselves. They might blame Dirk and hang him, he feared.

Drogen. He had to find Drogen and rescue Anika and get the gold back for her. The boy knew that without gold the girl would be at the mercy of the town's people. She would be forced to depend on the generosity of relatives or friends. But he was terrified enough he couldn't move. He stood in the barn aisle, rooted with indecision.

After a time he heard a shout from across the compound. The Tsurani were up and one had seen something. A confusion of voices sounded from outside, and Dirk knew they would be in the barn in moments.

He hid himself in the darkest corner of the stall most removed from the door, and lay shivering in fear and cold as men came into the barn, speaking rapidly in their odd language. Two walked past where Dirk lay, once casting a quick glance in his direction. He must have simply assumed Dirk was another dead boy, for he said nothing to his companion, who climbed the ladder to the hayloft. After a moment, he shouted down, and the other responded. He heard the man return down the ladder and the two of them leave the barn. Dirk waited until it grew quiet again, then got out of the straw. He hurried to the door and peered out. From his vantage point he saw one Tsurani instructing others to search the area.

Uncertain of what to do next, Dirk waited. A Tsurani he knew to be of some rank came out and pointed to the tracks in the snow. There was some sort of debate, and the man who had sent the others searching seemed to be indicating that someone should follow the murderer.

Then the leader spoke in commanding tones and the other man bowed slightly and turned away. Dirk realized that no one was going to follow Drogen. He was going to get away with killing more than two dozen people and kidnapping Anika and taking all of Lord Paul's gold. The Tsurani soldier in charge seemed content to leave this matter to his own officer, when the bulk of the command returned from their mission.

Dirk knew that if anyone was to save Anika, it would have to be him. Dirk slipped out of the barn and around the side, and when he was certain no one was nearby, he went down the hill behind the barn and made his way into the woods. He hurried along through the birch and pines until he found the sled tracks. He turned to follow them.

*   *   *

Dirk slogged his way through the snow, his breath a white cloud before him. His feet were numb and he felt weak and hungry, but he was determined to overtake Drogen. The landscape was white and green—the boughs of pines and firs peering out from mantles of snow. A stand of bare trees stood a short distance away, and Dirk knew he had left the boundary of Lord Paul's estate.

The murderer was making good time, despite having to pull the heavy sled. He knew that he gained on Drogen each time he had to pull the sled up a hill, but each time he went down the next slope, Drogen probably gained some of that time back.

Dirk stopped to rest a moment. His best chance of finding the murderer, he knew, was to catch him at night. Dirk glanced around. He had no idea how much time had passed; a good part of the day, he realized, but he couldn't tell from the grey sky where the sun was and when darkness would arrive.

A rabbit poked its head above a nearby ridge and sniffed. Dirk wished he had some sort of weapon, or the time to rig a snare, for a rabbit cooked over an open fire would be welcome, but he knew such wishes would go ungranted.

He continued on.

* * *

It began to snow as darkness came, and it came quickly. Dirk's plan of following through the night vanished along with the sled tracks. Dirk tried to follow the tracks, but there was no light. It was the blackest night he could remember, and he was terrified.

He found a small clump of trees overhung by a large pine bower thick with snow that acted like a roof, and he crawled in for the meager shelter it provided. He built up a low snow wall around him, having been taught as a boy that such a wall would shelter him from the wind. He dozed but didn't sleep.

A soft sound woke him. He heard it again. He poked his head out from under the pine bower and saw that snow had fallen from a branch in a large clump.

He crawled out and looked for tracks. There were places where the snow had fallen lightly, and he could barely see the tracks, but they were there, and they pointed the way.

Dirk began again to hunt down the murderer.

At sundown he saw the light of the fire, high on a ridge to the east. Drogen was making his way toward the city of Natal. It was free of the Tsurani invaders. Once there, Drogen could make his way to Ylith and from there anywhere in the world, the Kingdom, Kesh, or the Island Empire of Queg. How Drogen was going to cross the frontier, Dirk didn't know, but he assumed the man had a plan. Maybe he just counted on the Tsurani holding tight to their campfires and not having too many men in the field in the dead of winter. From what he had heard, there had been almost no fighting between them and the Free Cities and Kingdom forces since the first heavy snow of winter.

Dirk slogged his way toward the fire.

He finally reached a place from where he could get a glimpse of the site.. Slowly approaching as quietly as he could, Dirk saw a single man resting on the sled, warming his hands on the fire. Drogen must have thought himself free of pursuit, for he had taken no pains to hide his whereabouts. At his feet, Anika lay in a bundle of furs. Dirk had aired them out every fall after fetching them out of storage, so he knew the girl was well protected from the cold. She appeared to be asleep—probably exhausted from terror, Dirk thought.

Dirk stopped, again rooted by fear. He had no idea how to proceed. He made up and discarded a dozen plans to attack the murderer. He couldn't imagine how to attack a trained warrior, one who was paid to fight.

Dirk stood freezing on his feet, watching the fire grow dimmer. Drogen ate, and still Dirk remained motionless. Cold, exposure, hunger, and fear were on the verge of reducing him to tears.

Then Drogen threw more wood on the fire and wrapped a blanket around himself. He lay down on the ground between the sled and Anika, who moved, but didn't awake. He was going to sleep!

Dirk knew that he could only rescue Anika and regain Lord Paul's gold by sneaking up on Drogen and killing him as he slept. Dirk had no compunctions about the act; Drogen had killed everyone Dirk had known since leaving his family to work at the master's estate, in their sleep, and he deserved no more than they got. Dirk just feared he wouldn't be up to the task, or would inadvertently wake up the killer.

Dirk moved his legs, trying to regain circulation in the freezing night, and eventually he judged it safe to approach the camp. Stiff legs and an inability to catch his breath drove Dirk to a heart-pounding frenzy. He found his hands shaking so badly he could barely manage to get the heavy knife out from within his jacket.

The familiar handle was suddenly an alien thing that resisted fitting comfortably in his palm. He crept forward and tried not to let panic overwhelm him.

He stopped on the other side of the sled, uncertain which way to approach. He decided that he'd approach Drogen's head.

Dirk held the knife high, and crept around the sled, slowly, moving as carefully as he could so as not to make noise. When he was just a few feet away, Drogen moved, shifting the blanket around his shoulders. He snuggled down behind Anika, who didn't move.

Fear overwhelmed Dirk. He knew if he didn't move now, he would never move. He struck down hard with the knife and felt the point dig into the murderer's shoulder.

Drogen shouted in pain and convulsed, almost pulling the knife out of Dirk's hand. Dirk yanked it back, and struck out again as Drogen tried to rise. The point again dug deep into his shoulder, and he howled in pain.

Anika awoke with a scream and kicked off the furs, then leaped to her feet, spinning around and trying to understand what was happening. Dirk pulled the blade out and was ready for a third strike, but Drogen charged, driving his shoulder into Dirk, knocking him aside.

The boy rolled on the ground and found Drogen sitting atop Dirk's chest, his hand poised to deliver a blow. "You!" he said as he saw the boy's face in the dim light of the dying fire. Drogen hesitated.

Dirk lashed out with his knife and struck Drogen in the face, cutting deeply. Drogen reared back, his hand to his cheek as he cried out in pain. Dirk acted without thought. He pushed hard with his knife, driving it deep into Drogen, just under his rib cage.

Drogen loomed above Dirk in the dim light, his eyes wide in silent astonishment. His left hand dropped from where it had momentarily touched his cheek. With his right hand he grabbed Dirk's tunic, as if he were going to pull him upright to ask him something. Then he slowly toppled backward. He didn't release his grip on Dirk's coat and he pulled the boy upright, then forward.

Dirk's legs were pinned under Drogen, and he was forced to bend forward.

Dirk frantically pried the dying man's fingers from his coat. He fell back and the pain in his side was a searing agony. He saw the blade of the knife protruding from his coat and his head swam. Using his elbows, he pulled himself back and got his legs free of Drogen's weight. Dimly he was aware of a sobbing voice saying, "No."

Dirk was in a fog as he reached down and pulled out the knife from Drogen's body. He turned as a girl's voice again said, "No!"

"You killed him!" screamed Anika as she rushed toward Dirk. The disoriented boy stood uncertain of what was occurring. He tried to focus his eyes as his head swam from pain. "I—" he began, but the girl seemed to fly at him.

"You killed him!" she screamed again as she fell upon him. He stepped back, his heel striking Drogen's body and he fell, the girl suddenly atop him. She landed heavily upon Dirk, her eyes wide in shock. She pushed herself up from atop Dirk and looked down between them.

Dirk followed her gaze and saw that the knife was still in his hand. Anika had impaled herself upon the blade. Confusion beset her features and she gazed at his face and at last said, softly, "The Wood Boy?"

She fell atop Dirk. He moved her aside, but held her in his arms, and he sank to the snow, holding her. She looked up at the sky, eyes glassy, and he gently closed them.

Then Dirk felt a hot stabbing pain in his side and bile rose in his throat as he realized somehow he had been cut. He touched the wound and hot pain shot through his body, and his eyes seemed unwilling to focus. He knew that he couldn't move with the blade there, and reached up to grip the handle again. Mustering all the resolve he could, he pulled the knife from his side, and screamed at the agony of it. After a moment, the pain subsided and was replaced by a throbbing torment, but one that didn't make him feel as if he was going to die.

He slowly stood, and turned to confront the girl.

Then he passed out.

Borric said, "She helped him kill her father and the rest?"

"I don't think so, sir." Sadly Dirk said, "I think Drogen tricked her, convinced her to elope with him to gain the secret of where her father's gold was. She was an innocent girl and he was a rake known to have wooed many women. If he killed everyone without awakening her, then bundled her up in those furs and carried her straight to the sled, she wouldn't have seen. Once away from the Free Cities, she might never have known." He looked as if he was about to cry, but held his tone steady as he said, "She fell upon me in a fright, and without knowing what had occurred at home. Else she wouldn't have been so frantic over Drogen's death, I'm certain. Her death was an accident, but it was all my fault."

"There was no fault in you, lad. It was, as you say, an accident." After a moment, Borric nodded. "Yes, it's better to think of it that way. Lad, why did you come here?"

"I didn't know what else to do. I thought if Drogen planned on coming this way, I would, too. I knew the Tsurani would take my master's gold and hang me as likely as not . . . it was all I could think of.''

"You did well,'' said Borric softly.

Dirk put the cup down and said, ''That was good. Thank you, sir.'' He moved and winced.

"You're hurt?''

"I bound the wounds as best I could, sir.''

Borric called for an orderly and instructed him to take the boy to the healers' tent and have the wound treated.

After Dirk had left, the captain said, ''That was quite a story, Your Grace.''

Borric agreed. ''The boy has special courage.''

"Did the girl know?'' asked the Captain.

"Of course she knew,'' said Borric. ''I knew Paul of White Hill; I've done enough business with him through my agent in Bordon, Talbot Kilrane. I've been to his home, and he's been to Crydee.

"And I knew the daughter.'' Borric sighed, as if what he thought tired him. ''She's the same age as my Carline. And they're as different as two children could be. Anika was born scheming.'' Borric sighed. ''I have no doubt she planned this, though we'll never know if she anticipated all the murders; she may have only suggested to the bodyguard they steal the gold and flee. With her father behind Tsurani lines and all that gold in her possession . . . she could have cut quite a social figure for herself back in Krondor or even in Rillanon. She easily could have disposed of the bodyguard—he clearly couldn't admit to anyone his part in this, could he? And if word of the killings reached us, we would assume the Tsurani murdered the household on some pretext.'' Borric was silent. Then he said, ''In my bones I know the girl was the one behind all this . . . but we'll never know, for certain, will we?''

''No, Your Grace,'' agreed the captain. ''What of the bodies?''

''Bury them. We have no means to return the girl to her family in Walinor.''

The captain said, ''I'll detail men to the digging. It'll take a while to dig through the frozen ground.'' He then asked, ''And the gold?''

Borric said, ''It's confiscated. The Tsurani would have taken it anyway, and we've an army to feed. Send it under guard to Brucal in LaMut.'' He paused a moment, then said, ''Send the boy, too. I'll pen a note to Brucal asking the boy be found some service there at headquarters. He's a resourceful lad and as he said, he has nowhere else to go.''

''Very well, Your Grace.''

As the captain turned to go, Borric said, ''And Captain.''

''Yes, Your Grace?''

"Keep what I said to yourself. The boy doesn't need to know."

"As you wish, Your Grace," said the captain as he departed.

Borric sat forward and tried to return his attention to the business at hand, but he found his mind returning to the boy's story. He tried to imagine what Dirk had felt, alone, armed only with the kitchen knife, and afraid. He had been a trained warrior for most of his life, but he remembered what it was to be uncertain. He recognized the boy's act for what it had been, an unusual and rare act of heroism. The image of a lovestruck, frightened boy trudging through the snow at night to confront a murderer and rescue a damsel lingered with the Duke, and he decided it was best that the boy be left with that one shred of illusion about the girl. He had earned that much, at least.

Short Novels By Bestselling Masters

In Three Spectacular Volumes

"Microcosmic glimpses of broadly imagined worlds and their larger-than-life characters distinguish this hefty volume of heavyweight fantasy.... There's enough color, vitality, and bravura displays of mythmaking in this rich sampler to sate faithful fans and nurture new readers on the stuff of legends still being created." —*Publishers Weekly* (starred review)

Legends 2

Terry Goodkind tells of the origin of the Border between the lands in the world of *The Sword of Truth,* in "Debt of Bones."

George R. R. Martin sets his piece a generation before his epic, *A Song of Ice and Fire,* in the adventure of "The Hedge Knight."

Anne McCaffrey, the poet of *Pern,* returns once again to her world of romance and adventure in "Runner of Pern."

Legends 3

Robert Jordan relates crucial events in the years leading up to *The Wheel of Time*™ in "New Spring."

Ursula K. Le Guin adds a sequel to her famous books of *Earthsea,* portraying a woman who wants to learn magic, in "Dragonfly."

Tad Williams tells a dark and enthralling story of a haunted castle in the age before *Memory, Sorrow, and Thorn,* in "The Burning Man."

Terry Pratchett relates an amusing incident in *Discworld,* of a magical contest and the witch Granny Weatherwax, in "The Sea and Little Fishes."